# all of the
# above

# all of the **above**

**JAMES DAWSON**

First published in Great Britain in 2015 by Hot Key Books
Northburgh House, 10 Northburgh Street, London EC1V 0AT



A CIP catalogue record for this book is available from the British Library.

ISBN: 978-1-4714-0467-2

6

This book is typeset in 10.5 Berling LT Std using Atomik ePublisher

Printed and bound by Clays Ltd, St Ives Plc

www.hotkeybooks.com

Hot Key Books is part of the Bonnier Publishing Group
www.bonnierpublishing.com

## Also By James Dawson

*Under My Skin*
*Say Her Name*
*Cruel Summer*
*Hollow Pike*

*This Book is Gay*
*Being a Boy*

*For Kerry*

In art, as in love, instinct is enough.

Anatole France, *The Garden of Epicurus*

# AUTUMN

# Chapter One

## New

When I was little, a year seemed like the longest thing in the world. Do you know what I mean? Winters, in my head, were snowier than they actually were, while summers were all paddling pools and bubblegum ice pops. And then, as I got older, time almost ground to a halt – staring out of windows; one Netflix episode rolling right into the next; waiting for my friends in America to come online. The last summer before we moved, I can hardly remember going outside at all.

But then it changed. This year, the fabric of time itself changed, I swear. Bear with me. Although records show there were indeed 365.24 days, each made of twenty-four hours, I fail to believe they were the same minutes I used to wish away. The metronome switched up a gear, the world turned faster – so much so that these days I find myself desperately clinging to milliseconds as they slip through my fingers like water. If I'm honest, this year was a club remix – it was when the beat kicked in.

A lot can happen in a year.

* * *

I'd only been in Brompton-on-Sea for the last week of the holidays and I was already able to distinguish the townies from the tourists. The bulldog faces of the locals testified to the shelf life of ice cream, candyfloss and crazy golf. Truth be told, Brompton was a little rough around the edges. Mum called it 'faded seaside glamour', I called it 'shitty'.

First day at Brompton Cliffs Academy, too old to be a new girl. Schools are schools, right? The new one was a photocopy of the old one – and like a facsimile, it was more tatty and cheaper-looking too – peeling Stonewall posters, broken lockers. To make things worse, my brand-new cherry-red Docs were already scraping away my heels. At their current rate, by the end of the day, bone would be exposed.

I might as well have been strutting nude down the corridor – that's how openly people were gawping at me. It occurred to me that a New Girl at a relatively small sixth form must be pretty big news. As I joined the drizzle-damp procession of pupils filing through the student entrance, I wore my Unimpressed Face. I always think Unimpressed Face is a good default. Better than Needy Face, Try-hard Face or Victim Face. I was getting the full-body scan: *Who is she? Is she new? Is she pretty-and-by-that-I-mean-competition?* I wondered how long it would last for. I didn't like the spotlight one little bit, I felt . . . lumpy.

I'd been told, via a letter from the head of sixth form, to report to 'The Little Hall' for assembly at nine. I'd arrived late on purpose to avoid awkward mingling in a sea of strangers. Like I didn't feel exposed enough already. I was pretty sure

I'd make friends sooner or later, I just wished they were waiting for me on arrival like an airport driver with a name card. I'd pre-emptively wasted some time at the newsagents en route, buying a super-sad-looking cheese sandwich (one half orange cheese, one half yellow – why? How?) and some crisps, anticipating further social horror at lunchtime. Oh it was fine. I could feel the corner of a book poking into my back through my bag. As I recall I was on my annual reread of *Azkaban*. You're never truly by yourself when you have a book in your bag.

The directions Mr Wolff, the Head of Sixth Form, had provided were easy to follow: the Little Hall was located past a plastic-plant-paradise of a reception area and was signposted clearly enough. It also didn't take a genius to figure out that all the pupils out of uniform, the sixth-formers, were obviously heading in one direction like a train of ants. Or lemmings.

A boy with extreme Needy Face held the door open for me and I slotted myself into the hall. It was set up like the drama studio at my old school – there was a rostrum with a lighting rig and a few rows of patched-with-gaffer-tape padded benches to sit on. There was a sour smell like something had been left under a seat all summer to rot – or perhaps spilled milk. Most of the rows were pretty full, which was a good thing – now I didn't have to make any decisions about where to sit, I just had to find any available space. As ever, the back rows had filled first, so I plumped for a space near the wall at the furthest end of the front row where I'd be tucked away.

I don't think it's arrogant to suggest that every pair of eyes was on me as I took my seat. *This too shall pass*, I told myself.

One of my online friends, Beth, had a foolproof plan for fitting in and making friends:

1. Ask thoughtful, interesting questions.
2. Laugh at other people's jokes.
3. When they least expect it, say something FILTHY.

It really did seem to work, but I also didn't want to be the one to make the first move – again, Needy. I'm going to be honest now: socially speaking I'm a middly person. Although I did my two-year braces sentence to sort my snaggleteeth, I've never been one of the truly unfortunate cases – the ones who stand out like beacons however hard they try – you know the ones I mean. Some days I look at those guys and my heart just breaks because I feel so impotent. Like school roulette isn't hard enough as it is! I wonder what messed-up messitude they must have done in a past life. I console myself knowing they're the Mark Zuckerbergs of tomorrow and we'll all be working for them in ten years.

On that first day, looking back, I was as boring as organic gluten-free porridge with no sugar. If I wanted, I could be totally invisible at Brompton Cliffs. I had been a wallpaper chameleon at my old school and hadn't ruled that option out here. I could sail through my last two years of school without anyone knowing I was even there.

Luckily, I didn't have to make the first move. I'd only been in my corner for about a minute – putting my phone on silent and stowing my headphones – when I felt a tap on my shoulder. I turned round to see the biggest pair of eyes I'd ever seen; it was like a bush baby Pokémon staring down at me from the row behind.

'Hello,' said the girl. 'You must be Victoria Grand, the new girl.'

'I prefer Toria . . . but yeah, hi.'

'We've been expecting you! Oh! Did that make me sound like a Bond villain? Sorry. I'm Daisy Weekes.' She smiled sweetly with dainty little teeth. She was a living, breathing porcelain doll, right down to her golden ringlets.

'Wow,' I said. 'News travels fast.'

'Oh,' Daisy said. 'No. I was sent to find you. I'm supposed to show you around. I'm your tour guide! Or your *Toria* guide!'

I could not have felt more like a tool. Arrogant much? 'Oh, sorry, that's embarrassing.'

Daisy giggled. 'No! It's true, you are headline news. Being a new girl *is* a pretty big deal, although not as big a deal as the fact that the canteen is now serving cinnamon swirls. But every guy in here is probably sizing you up right now. You're fresh meat. Be careful not to slip in the drool.'

*Laugh at other people's jokes.* I laughed way too enthusiastically, practically throwing my head back like a whinnying horse. Luckily Daisy didn't seem to notice, but even so I reeled it in a little.

'I like your coat,' Daisy said, stroking one of the epaulettes of my US Army fatigues coat with a chipped purple nail. I was going through a vintage phase.

'Thanks. I like yours too.' Daisy was wearing a vast black fur. I could only pray it was fake. It had to be, right? Her child-like body was swaddled in it, her silk-fine blonde curls bunched up around the collar. This was as close as I was going to get to meeting Luna Lovegood.

'You can come sit next to me if you like,' she offered, and I could have cried with relief. 'Unless you don't want to.'

'No, that'd be great, thanks. Better than being a total loner.' At my old school, I'd only had two friends – but at least I'd never been alone. In school, like on the Serengeti, jackals pick off strays first.

Daisy smiled and made room on her bench. 'True, but you're really pretty so I didn't know if you'd feel more at home on the back row.'

I assure you I am *not* really pretty – my forehead is more of a fivehead – but I turned to see what she meant. On the back row were our Plastics. Every school has its own popular group, I got that, but they're always slightly different. At my old school the popular girls were a lot tougher – hard pramfaces with over-plucked eyebrows and foundation like butterscotch cake icing. These girls were more polished – metres and metres of expertly highlighted hair tousled to resemble luxe birds' nests. One of the leaders must have declared floral prints were on-trend because the back row resembled the pot-pourri my mum put in the bathroom.

It was time to deploy my 'something filthy'. 'Oh I'm not one of *those* girls,' I said with a smile. 'I haven't got time for all the hair and handjobs.'

Daisy giggled and it was like tinkling flower bells. 'You've totally sussed them out! They always smell so nice though.'

I wasn't sure what to say to that but laughed politely because of social skills. Some newcomers filed into the row and sat next to Daisy. The first was a milky-pale chunky girl hiding behind greasy hair-curtains, the second was a guy who looked like a walking teddy bear.

'Hi Dais,' said the guy. 'Is this the hotly anticipated Victoria Grand?'

'Everyone calls me Toria,' I said. Feeling braver, I offered my hand and he looked terrified of it. Was that too formal? Had I just committed social suicide? Was I doomed to be known as Handshake Girl until the end of time? Thankfully he took it and gave it a very limp shake. Limp handshakes are the *worst*.

'This is Beasley and Freya,' Daisy explained.

'Hey,' Beasley said, blushing and wiping his hand on his trousers. 'How's it going?'

Freya couldn't even look me in the eye, only muttering a greeting under her breath before taking out a battered paperback and starting to read. 'I'm good, thanks,' I said. I tried to think of something funny or complimentary to say, but I was at a loss.

'How are you finding Brompton-on-Sea?' Beasley plonked his thick behind onto the bench. His T-shirt was a little too tight so he kinda looked like he had boobs.

I winced. 'Honest answer or polite answer?'

'Oh god, honest answer. I was born here – hating this dump is in my genetic make-up.' He was a tiny bit camp and I wondered if he was gay. However, I had figured out a long time ago that, as with asking women with big bellies if they're pregnant, asking a guy if he's gay when you've only just met is a no-no.

'In that case,' I said, 'it's pretty tragic. What's with all the fish and chip shops?'

'It's the one thing we're famous for. Brompton fish and chips are the best in the country. Fact.'

'My old town was famous for curry.'

'I hate curry!' Daisy stuck her tongue out.

Beasley sighed. 'The nearest Indian is twenty miles outside town and it keeps getting shut down by hygiene inspectors. This is kinda racist, and it probably isn't even true, but I heard they were serving stray cat.'

I laughed (this time a little uncomfortably) and assured him that that urban legend did the rounds in every town. I considered telling them I was part Indian before one of them said something actually racist, but decided against it. White people don't have to announce their ethnicity, so I don't see why I should have to explain that my mum Shamed The Family by marrying my (very much not Punjabi) dad. I'm assured that it was pretty scandalous back in the day, but that particular dust settled when my granddad died shortly after I was born.

Looking around, I clocked the ethnic mix of the school wasn't a mix at all. There were, like, three Asians and one mixed guy. I was at White People High. Not surprising; Brompton-on-Sea isn't exactly a cultural melting pot. Because of my first name (my middle name is Esha) and paleness, a lot of people don't know I'm mixed unless I tell them, which means I've probably had all sorts of white-girl privileges, but also meant that back home, or rather at my old home, people used to say shockingly racist stuff about brown people in earshot, not knowing they were slagging off half my family.

Mr Wolff, who had the smile, silver hair and jawline of a retired catalogue model, came on stage and we fell quiet.

The inauguration to the sixth form was pretty much as I'd expected. What was somewhat reassuring was that sixth-form life was new for everyone, not just me, even if everyone else did have their friends all pinned down. There was a lot of chat about responsibility and how if we acted like adults, we'd be treated like adults. I phased out after the first few minutes, to be honest, and started hungrily daydreaming about the yellow/orange cheese sandwich.

I'd been paired with Daisy, it transpired, because we were taking exactly the same options: English Lit., English Lang., French and Art. I so wish I could be one of those hard-core girls who does Physics, Maths and . . . Space Robotics or something, but that's not my skill set, sorry to be yet another cliché. I like creating stuff, and I used to write poems for a while. Before I got a computer, I used to make little books and magazines out of scrap paper; once I did get a computer, I started my blog and taught myself Photoshop. I'm quite proud of that.

After assembly, Daisy and I headed to French. My *avoir*s and *êtres* were more than a little rusty, but it quickly became clear that Daisy was really, really good at French. We'd both got A-stars last year (I know, thank you kindly) but I suspected her A-star was better than mine and if she'd been able to achieve A-star-star she would have. She was generous though – helping me along when I got stuck.

I noticed that her notebook was covered in tiny illustrations. Like a little comic strip. 'They're cool,' I said. 'What are they?'

'Oh, that's Geoff the Cross-Dressing Squirrel.'

'What?!' I felt the interrobang was necessary.

Daisy smiled and slid her book over. 'Oh, it's just this little soap opera I do for Beasley. It's about Geoff and all his squirrel friends.' She pointed to one little squirrel with googly eyes. He wore a boob tube and hooker boots.

'This is Geoff? Oh, he's fancy.'

'I know!' She pointed to another squirrel, this one with hair falling over one eye. 'That is Evil Celine, his arch nemesis.'

'Well, the clue's in the name!' It was quite complex. Evil Celine had stolen a baby from Geoff and his strapping boyfriend, Rhett, and had replaced it with an evil one. Compelling stuff. The doodles were hilarious and I knew at once I wanted Daisy to be a Proper Friend.

The first part of the morning was tolerable. It sort of felt good to have some order back in my life. Does that make me sound autistic? Since we'd moved, I'd been free-falling – too much time on my hands – and there was something reassuring about having my options narrowed and my time neatly divided by a clock and a bell. At break Daisy explained how the school worked. The sixth form was autonomous from the rest of the school. We had our own wing – a modern annex that looked a bit like a Travelodge – and a special line at the canteen. We also had a common room and this was new to us all.

'I guess we should check it out,' Daisy said. 'Although most of the people in our year are a bit rubbish, I'm afraid.'

'Most people are.'

Daisy shook her head, curls bouncing. 'No! I think there's always diamonds if you dig deep enough.'

We entered the common room and I got a sense of what Daisy meant. For one thing, it reeked of pickled-onion-flavour Monster Munch. Not good. There were airport-style padded chairs in rows, a few beanbags and a vending machine, but it was mostly like a large classroom with all the desks taken out. A ping-pong table and two computers, which had almost definitely been retired from use elsewhere in the school, were shoved down at the far end.

Also, Loud Boys. Why is it that popular guys are always noisy chimp-like creatures? It must be an evolutionary thing, but there was a lot of high-fiving and back slapping and just *noise*. Literally making whooping noises at one another like something from *National Geographic*. Perhaps there had been a local sale on checked shirts and preppy beige trousers, but in Brompton Cliffs common room it was practically a male uniform. Forget *Stepford Wives*, this was *Hollister Sons*. Summer-holiday tans and boy-band hair finished the look. Once more I got the distinct impression I was being evaluated for sexual purposes.

They'd be sorely disappointed – they had nothing that interested me and I was hardly their type. I'm afraid this isn't a story where the plain girl falls for the jock guy and they learn to overcome their differences through dance.

Like any sixth-form common room, it was broadly divided up into social groups. These things are clichés because they are true. The horsey popular boys in their checked shirts gathered around the table tennis set. Some dick threw a ping-pong ball at one of the Pot-Pourri Princesses: 'Oi, Grace, fire this out of yer minge.' Charming. Grace, to her credit, told him where he could shove it.

The princesses were sat together (apparently dipping carrot sticks in hummus was another thing they did) as were the music crowd. Having a Thing is so important at school. It pigeonholes you, and people like people in pigeonholes. That's always been my downfall; I crash between stools – I'm Thingless.

'Oh look,' said Daisy. 'There's Freya.'

Once again, Freya was hiding behind a book, in this case something with a witch on the front. We headed over to where she was squashed into the corner. She was with a couple – the guy was dressed in braces, a cravat and tweed trousers, while the girl was a punky East Asian in a baby-doll dress with pink tights. Daisy threw herself into their laps. I considered Daisy's fur coat and torn purple fishnets. The penny dropped: these were the AltKidz.

'OMG! How are you?' Daisy gushed. They stood and wrapped her in broad hugs, squealing excitedly. They mustn't have seen each other in a couple of weeks. 'Alex and Alice, this is Toria, the new girl. She's super nice. Can we keep her?'

'Greeting and salutations!' Alex bowed in greeting. 'An honour, dear Toria, welcome to our fine seminary.'

'Hi, nice to meet you.' Was this guy for real?

'Hey,' said Alice, idly playing with her hair. There was a pink heart gemstone in the corner of her left eye. 'I like your coat.'

I was so pleased I wore that coat. 'Thanks. You look . . . awesome.' Her candy/pastel-goth look had clearly taken some work and I respected that.

'Thanks.' Alice seemed a little bored with me already, her face sulky.

'Alice and Alex?' I asked. 'That's cute.'

'I know, isn't it ghastly? I assure you it was entirely coincidental.' Alex sat back down and pulled Alice onto his knee. Alice was instantly happier.

'Hey, Freya.' I sat down next to her. 'What are you reading?'

'A book,' came the muffled reply as she shied further away from me. I decided not to push it; she was obviously cripplingly shy.

'So, Toria – divine name by the way – what brings you to this enclave? I can't possibly imagine you opted to come here.' Alex ran a hand through his wild reddish hair, no doubt styled that way to add to his mad professor vibe.

'She's in witness protection,' Daisy said, sipping on a Diet Coke.

I smiled. 'Not true. I actually murdered my last school. All of it. Full-on high-school massacre. I served my time and they've given me a new identity.' Daisy and Alex laughed but Alice rolled her eyes. Oh god, what had I said to piss her off? Was she a high-school massacre survivor or something? 'Nah – my dad has taken a lecturing job at the university. We had to move. Sorry – boring.'

'That sucks,' Alice said.

'What? My story?'

'No. Like having to move and stuff. Sucks.' She spoke as if moving her mouth was exhausting to her.

'Yeah. I suppose so – but I'd have had to move in a couple of years for uni anyway.'

'Glass half-full!' Daisy said. 'If life gives you lemons . . .'

'Ask for tequila and salt,' I said, smiling. The others laughed along and I wondered if this might be OK. I might be able to get through this.

I became aware of one of the Hollister Sons sidling up to Freya, the way a tiger prowls through undergrowth towards its prey. He was holding his phone steady, evidently filming her as she read. 'Boil,' he said in a sing-song voice. 'Boil, say something for the camera . . .'

Freya pretended not to hear him. I latched on to the joke. Freya doesn't speak much – let's get her to say something. This school really was a clone of my last one. I wasn't sure what to do. I couldn't help but notice selective hearing had also befallen Alex and Alice – they pretended to hear only each other cooing into their respective ears.

Daisy sighed. 'Donovan, leave her alone.'

He pretended not to hear her, crawling even closer along the bench, shoving the camera in her face and infiltrating her personal space. Not cool.

'Boil . . . can you speak? Are you a mute?'

I was about to say something when a bag swung down like some *deus ex machina* in a Greek tragedy. The canvas rucksack crashed into the side of Donovan's head and he rolled off the bench onto the floor, dropping his phone in the process. Everyone laughed – both his horsey friends and my adopted crowd.

The bag belonged to a girl who stood alongside Beasley. She had pink hair and a nose ring and she was the coolest thing I had ever seen.

## Chapter Two

# Her

I think it's important to make a disclaimer here. Polly Wolff, the girl who attacked Donovan, has the foulest mouth of any person I have ever met or am likely to meet in the future. She could make sailors and convicts blush and fluster. There's not a lot I can do about this except try to edit as I retell my tale. If you don't find swearing big or clever, I imagine Polly Wolff would tell you to **** right off anyway, so you would be unlikely to be friends.

Back to the common room. 'Go **** yourself, Donovan,' said the girl with pink hair.

'God, chill out.' Donovan picked himself up, rubbing his head. 'Psycho.'

'That's right, tell people I'm a psycho so you feel better when a girl kicks the living **** out of you. Now **** off.'

Donovan skulked away and the new girl and Beasley joined us in our corner. Beasley turned to Freya. 'You OK, Freya?'

She pretended she'd missed the whole kerfuffle, lost in her book. She nodded for a moment before returning to the land of fiction. I sat awkwardly, waiting for an introduction.

Daisy greeted the pink-haired girl with a hug. 'This is the new girl, Toria. Toria, this is my best friend, Polly.'

'Hey,' I said. Polly was effortlessly cool: tall and willowy enough to be a model, wearing a baggy black jumper, the collar hanging off one angular shoulder. The pink hair was messy, pulled into a knot on the top of her head. It looked regal, like she was wearing a crown.

'Hey there, Toria Grand. All I've heard about today is this new girl all the boys want to ****.'

*Say something filthy*. We must have been to the same school of making a first impression. 'Oh god, really? Daisy said I'd be fresh meat.' I couldn't think of anything filthy of my own, and I didn't want it to turn into a competition.

I was as wary of her as I was impressed. She had green-blue ocean eyes and they were definitely sizing me up. She didn't trust me. Maybe she was right not to. I don't know.

'Don't sweat it,' Polly said, sitting down opposite me and tucking one long leg under the other. 'You're new genetic material and the rest of us are inbred. Your unspoiled DNA sings to us.'

I laughed. 'Well, at least I'm making a contribution. Although I think I'll leave reproduction off the agenda until, you know, I know where the toilets are.'

More laughter. I hated myself for being Needella Needyson again but I really wanted them to like me. I don't know why. It was my first day, I was probably feeling extra vulnerable or something. NEEDY FACE.

Beasley added quietly, 'I heard that Nathan Blue thinks you're hot. That's, like, a big deal.'

'Which one is he?'

Daisy subtly pointed out one of the checked-shirted masses. 'The tall one. If we had a prom, he'd be prom king.'

I could barely keep the disgust off my face. He looked like a slightly melted Ken doll. 'Oh god no.'

'Hmm, don't rule it out.' Polly smirked. 'He's got a massive ****.'

I felt myself blush. I'm not great at sex chat. I knew I was meant to gather my sassy gal pals and discuss blow jobs at length at sleepovers but I had never had sex and, regardless of what friends had told me back home, I thought it *was* a big deal.

'That's gross!' Daisy said, saving me the trouble.

'If his penis is anything like his face, I'm not interested.' I figured that was a safe bet.

'I speak from experience,' Polly said frostily and I wanted to die at once. I wouldn't have put them together in a million years.

'Oh sorry . . . I –'

'Toria, I'm ******* with you! I'm kidding!'

I exhaled, social/potentially actual suicide avoided.

Polly addressed the whole group. 'Now. The real question is: would it be tacky to blow off the rest of the first day and go shopping or is that actually quite cool?'

I won't lie. The first couple of weeks weren't easy. I couldn't decide whether I was imposing on Polly's group or not. Without question it was 'Polly's group'. She and Daisy and Beasley had been best friends since Year 6; Alex had lived next door to Polly his entire life, and Alex and Alice had been inseparable since Polly had set them up two years ago.

She couldn't help it. When Polly walked into a room or down

a corridor people stared at her, and it wasn't just the pink hair. They were scared of her. Rightly so. During my first two weeks at Brompton Cliffs, I saw her twist a guy's balls, almost snap someone's thumb off and lead a guy down a hallway by his hair. Trust me, they all had it coming – they'd been having a go at Polly herself or one of her friends. She served as a protector for the whole group – a Robin Hood figure standing up for her personal band of Merry Men (and women). Eagle-eyed readers among you will have noticed that Polly is Mr Wolff's daughter. Not that that made her life any easier; after every ball twist or truancy she was almost publicly flogged so the whole school could see she wasn't getting preferential treatment.

I'm aware I've bombarded you with a whole heap of people, but each and every one of them is important to what's happened this year. Allow me to help out with a visual representation of how sixth-form life is here at Brompton Cliffs, which I carefully observed over the first couple of weeks. It works something like this. (Bear in mind, like I said, I am not a mathsy person):

**Figure 1. The Social Dynamic of the Group**

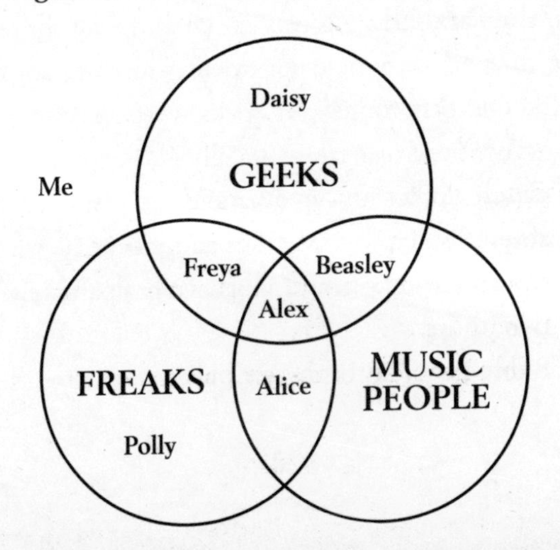

I didn't quite belong. I sat with them at lunchtime and break time, but I couldn't work out if Daisy had forced the others to tolerate my presence. I couldn't even decide if Daisy really liked me or not – she was so relentlessly sunny with everyone she came into contact with. I was starting to feel like that bit of loo roll that gets stuck to your heel – I was just being dragged around with them.

While the routine of school was comforting, evenings and weekends stayed much as they ever had been: online. I would get home, where Mum would be waiting to descend on me like a vulture. 'How was your day? What were lessons like? Did you make any new friends? Have you got any homework?'

Daily bombardment.

I guess the problem was that, while Dad had started work at the end of August, Mum hadn't even started looking for a new job yet. Back home, she'd worked at the university library, but there were no positions here. She had that caged-animal stir-crazy look in her eye that only someone who'd endured too much *Jeremy Kyle* and *Loose Women* got.

Once I'd fended her off, she'd go and watch *Pointless* with a glass of rioja and I'd go to my room and stay there until it was time for bed, only pausing to eat. Here are some of the things I liked to do online:

1. Catch up on my favourite vlogs. I subscribe to about eighty, so that takes some time.
2. Commenting on said vlogs. Can also take up to two hours.
3. Reblog cool stuff on Tumblr.

4. Google stuff off Tumblr that I think I should get into.
5. Sneer at popular people on Facebook. I'd have ditched Facebook years ago if it weren't for the fact it's holding half my photos hostage.
6. Download American TV. It's not my fault they don't show it over here faster.
7. Make my own gifs. I'm getting pretty good at this.
8. Check my fandoms. I belong to several fandoms, but by far my favourite is manga and anime: *Angel Beats!*, *Puella Magi Madoka Magica*, some yaoi stuff, *Neon Genesis Evangelion* and, of course, *Sailor Moon*.

Don't feel bad for me, I came alive online. I reckon I was way funnier and cooler there than I was in real life. By that point, I'd established that Beasley and Alice also liked anime, but Alice was still being decidedly chilly. I didn't know what her problem was.

My mum and dad were renting a house not far from school while they sussed out the property market in the area. It was OK, I guess. It was on one of those toy-town housing developments full of identical dream homes. Lots of conservatories, built-in barbecues and BMWs – not a lot of soul.

We lived next door to one of the Pot-Pourri girls. Within the first week I saw her leaving for school at the same time as me and recognised her from the common room. On the second Monday, we left at the exact same time and sort of walked next to each other. It was really awkward. Fortunately, she broke the ice.

'Hi, I'm Summer. You're Toria, right?'

'Yeah. New girl.'

'How's it going?' She had an aspartame voice. Her cloud of blonde hair was backcombed and her eyelashes were spidery with mascara.

'Not too bad, thanks.' We must have looked so weird walking together. I was in my army coat, flat black hair parted dead in the centre and she looked like a slightly neglected Barbie doll.

'Cool. We think you're really cool.' I could guess who WE was. 'Love your shoes.' She pointed at my leopard-print Converse.

'Thank you.' I knew I should return the compliment but it would have been a lie. Thankfully we got talking about teachers – who was cool and who was evil – so that passed the fifteen-minute walk.

A couple of nights later, we ended up walking home together too. Summer invited me inside her house because her brother had a load of French A-level stuff that her mum said I could have since she wasn't taking it.

It was so weird. Her room was a shrine to some boy band I'd never heard of. They'd only been around since the spring but Summer insisted the fandom was a 'family'. Every spare inch of wall was covered with posters and cut-outs. If it was anyone else's room but a teenage girl's, you'd legitimately think you were in some psycho's murder room. It was truly chilling; the eyes followed you wherever you moved. I made an excuse after five minutes and left, knowing that Summer Perkins and her friends were *not* my people. That was a watershed moment.

If I was ever going to be one of the cool, pretty hair girls, it would have been then.

I took the road less travelled.

Weekends were the worst. My online friends all seemed to have their weekends planned out months in advance – either visiting family or attending cons in places I couldn't afford to get to. My new friends at school, if that's what they were, hadn't invited me to anything and there was no way I was going to invite myself along. So I was stuck at home.

I remember one Saturday morning Mum came to wake me up with a cup of tea. She plonked it on my bedside table and peeked under the duvet. 'Victoria? Are you getting up?' Mum is the ONLY person left on earth who calls me Victoria.

'No. Let me sleep until Monday morning.'

She pulled the duvet back. 'Up! It's not healthy laying in bed all day. You should be outside! Getting fresh air! Meeting nice boys!' I tutted in dismay. 'Why don't you text some people from school?'

That really stung. No one ever texted me. I rolled back over. 'Go away. I have chronic fatigue syndrome.' I pulled the duvet back over my head. What was the point in getting up? There was nothing to get up for.

I invented projects for myself to pass the time. One weekend I unpacked my box of *Sailor Moon* books and spread them out across my bedroom floor. I lined them up in neat rows, in the correct order, and took pictures of my collection for Tumblr. I dipped in and out of them, reminding myself of my favourite bits.

I decided to sketch some of my favourite images, so this involved unpacking my box of art supplies. I painstakingly copied the poses, taking diversions onto the internet to look at cosplay ideas. When I came to colouring I found many of my felt tips had dried up so I started a new project, trying each one to see if it still worked. Somehow, whole days decayed in this manner.

One long Sunday afternoon, Mum had caught the train to meet my Auntie Minna in London while my dad was watching Formula One. An endless angry wasp buzz came from the lounge, and rain fell like pins onto the conservatory roof. This was a new nadir of boredom. Unpacking the very last box from the move, I found my old poetry book in and among some old sketchbooks.

I know. Yes, I had a poetry book. It sounds pretty lame, but for a while poetry was like 'my thing'. When I was fourteen I entered a national competition and, while I didn't win, I was a finalist in my age group, had my poem published and won fifty quid in book tokens.

I wrote about Mum. I don't know if she ever knew it was about her. I don't honestly know if she ever read it. At the time we really weren't getting on, even worse than now. That's what I don't get about her. In her time, she was meant to be like this major rebel who spurned Vishnu to run off and marry a white guy, but when I dip-dyed the ends of my hair she acted like I was selling drugs to kids or something. You'd think she'd cut me some slack. Anyway, here is the poem (don't laugh):

**She and I**

**by Victoria Grand – Year 9 – Ilkley Grammar School**

She says home, I say go.
I say wish, she says bone.
She says friends, I say best.
I say please, she says test.
She says fun, I say pain.
I say stop, she says again.
She says work, I say drone.
I say listen, she says phone.
She says smile, I say teeth.
I say woman, she says bleed.
She says eat, I say starve.
I say whole, she says half.
She says words, I say noise.
I say girls, she says toys.
She says saying, I say said.
I said she said, she saw red.
Stop pain, teeth bleed
Half-woman, starve again
Listen! Fun! Test friends
Phone home, words work
Toy bone, smile please
Best wishes, whole drone
Go. Eat girl's noise.

The poem that won was written by some private-school kid pretending to be the Unknown Soldier. I never really stood a chance did I? I used to write my poems in a vintage notebook I'd rescued from my grandma's attic: sepia-tinged pages bound in skin-soft brown suede. It smelled musty, like libraries and cleverness. I inhaled a lungful. Rereading it, it wasn't *quite* as cringe as I'd remembered.

The next weekend, which somehow scraped into the crap underneath the bottom of the barrel to be even MORE boring, I was called on to accompany Mum and Dad into town 'to help'. I think, in truth, they felt sorry for me so were trying to keep me occupied, although they didn't say so.

The high street was a pretty sad affair. A lot of shops had shut altogether to be filled with temporary tourist tat shops that would no doubt be clearing off now the summer season was over. Thankfully there was a comic shop with a pretty good selection, although the guys behind the counter stared at me like I was a shoplifter, or worse, a lost girl looking for the make-up counter.

While Mum went into the traditional butcher's (Worst. Hindu. Ever), I waited outside because I didn't like the smell of raw meat. My Spidey Sense tingled. I heard them before I saw them: Summer and the other Pot-Pourri girls tottering down the high street, their hot-pant legs the colour of briny frankfurters. God, I really hoped they didn't see me out shopping with Mum. I turned my comic-store bag around so they couldn't see the logo.

The Pot-Pourris advertised their presence with whooping, laughing and shrieking. They swung held hands, spreading out to take up as much space as possible. They were hard to ignore and I suspected that was the intention. Their colourful petals had already attracted a couple of guys I recognised from school.

One of them gave Becca Ferguson a piggyback.

It would be pretty easy to hate them, but they weren't doing any harm. They looked to be having a really good time. I didn't want to be with them but I did wonder when *my* life was going to begin and what I'd do if it didn't.

The answer came about three weeks into the first half-term. I'm skipping to the good bit, I promise. It was a weirdly sunny day for late September and so, instead of going into the common room, most pupils congregated outside, enjoying a final outing for the shorts and flip-flops. This made life harder because no one had told me where 'the gang' was going to be. That felt a lot like I wasn't invited – Daisy and Beasley both had my mobile number – but I nevertheless set off in search of my new acquaintances, aimlessly wandering the outdoor areas like a Bedouin. Moreover, I *still* hadn't successfully broken in my new Docs. I'd basically bound my feet with plasters, but they were still rubbing.

It didn't take long to find Freya, who was sat alone on the grass verge next to the football pitch, you guessed it, reading. A group of uniformed Year 9s at various lay-bys on the puberty highway were giving her a hard time.

'I'm telling you man . . . she's deaf or something,' said one cockroach.

'Boil!' Freya's surname was Doyle. 'Show us your tits.'

They howled with laughter. The first spoke again. 'Boil, I'll give you ten quid if you show us your tits.'

Behind her book and behind her hair, Freya blushed. I'd had enough. I wasn't scared of spotty stoat-faced Year 9s. I strode up to Freya's side and yanked up my T-shirt to reveal my bra. Today, a purple one with tiny pink dots.

'Happy now?'

'Oh my god!' The little boys didn't know what to do. One laughed, one blushed, another walked briskly away, caught in the act.

I carried on. 'You said you wanted to see some tits! Here you go. Something to wank over, you little tosspots.'

'Freak!' the littlest, spottiest, yet noisiest one said before pelting in the other direction.

'Nice!' I turned to see Polly ambling down the slope. 'And nice tits too.'

I chuckled (I do have nice boobs – they make up for the total lack of arse) but I was still fuming. 'Dicks.'

'That was inspired, by the way. I'd have punched them, but yours was funnier.'

'Thanks.' She joined me alongside Freya and we sat on the grassy embankment.

'There isn't an initiation, by the way, but if there was you'd have just passed it,' Polly told me. 'We've been talking about you a lot. We couldn't decide if you thought we were freaks and if you'd run off and join the Pretty Girl Gang at the first opportunity.' Today she was wearing a torn-up T-shirt with a Kewpie doll on the front.

'God, no way. I spent an evening at Summer Perkins's house. That was enough.'

'Is her hair a wig? I heard her hair was a wig and that she's secretly bald.'

I laughed. 'No. I think it's attached.'

'What? A **** Brompton rumour that wasn't true? I guess that means I'm not a hermaphrodite then. Shame.'

This was the first time I'd had a one-on-one conversation with Polly. It felt good. I was a little in awe of her, but determined not to show it. 'If you've been talking about me,' I said, feeling brave, 'does Alice, like, properly hate me? She's been giving me the stink-eye since I arrived.'

Polly unwrapped a bagel from her satchel. 'No, that's just Alice. She's only happy when she's depressed.'

'Oh, I see.'

'She's a drama addict, not to mention self-styled Manic Pixie Dream Girl. Her and Alex are very . . . melodramatic. She thinks that Alex fancies you, but she'll come around.' Polly smiled. 'I'll make her, because I want you in my friend bag.'

'"Friend bag"?'

'Where you put the keepers.'

I smiled, despite not wanting to seem too eager. 'Good. I very much want to be in the friend bag.'

Polly's eyes blazed – a little manic almost. 'Good! What are you doing tonight?'

'Homework.'

'I'll pretend I didn't hear that because tonight is going to be the night of your ******* life.'

'Oh yeah? Why's that?'

'Tonight, ************, you're coming with us to play crazy golf.'

# Chapter Three

# Him

It probably sounds like I'm gushing about Polly, and I am. There is nothing better than New Friend Feeling™: when you realise there's someone you totally get and totally gets you. It's way better than finding someone you fancy, because New Friend Feeling™ is more honest without all the sex stuff and hormones getting in the way and convincing you that good arms are actually a shining personality.

Polly's not some wish-fulfilment fantasy I invented; I really did think she was wonderful. For those first few weeks, she could do no wrong. I knew it wouldn't last, and it didn't.

But more on that later.

When Polly first invited me to play crazy golf, I assumed she was joking. I'd seen the shabby 'Fantasyland' on the seafront a couple of times when I'd ventured into town during the holidays, but it had been overrun by little kids and tourists. Like everything in Brompton, it was 'faded'.

Still, Polly assured me it was 'theirs' after dark. While I'd been up in my room on my laptop, that's where everyone else had been, apparently. Of course I agreed to go. For someone so aggressive, Polly was oddly magnetic – people stuck to her like paperclips.

After school I went home for tea, or as southern people called it 'dinner'. Dad was working late, as usual, so it was just Mum and me and a third plate wrapped in sweaty cling film. Since we'd moved to Brompton, I'd noticed Mum's designated 'uncorking time' had steadily crept back from six to four. Now I think about it, there was no way of knowing if the goblet-sized glass of red wine Mum had when I got home was her first of the day. I suppose I wasn't meant to notice. They seem to think I'm still upstairs playing with my Barbies.

Grumble. I almost can't be bothered to get on to my parents – it feels too much like I should be lying back on a leather couch. I'm also aware that one day they might read this and I don't want to feel like I'm chucking them under the bus. They did MAKE me. I suppose I should be a little bit respectful. OK, a lot respectful.

You know that moment where you realise The Awful Truth about your parents? I'd had that about two years earlier. Up until I was about fourteen, my dad was goofy and funny, and my mum was beautiful but strict. Now all I saw was a mean woman and an ineffectual man. Harsh, I know, but it works both ways. My dad always said I'd been a 'happy accident' but I, of course, now knew that translated as: I was a mistake.

Pre-me, my parents had this hip life. Young cool music journalist and cute indie librarian. Predating the hipster movement by about ten years, they met at a Pulp gig in Manchester and fell madly in love. So in love I guess they didn't trouble themselves with silly things like contraception. Sometimes Mum looks at me and I swear I can see her *blaming* me for stealing the last sixteen years from her.

These days, my dad has a great job but no common sense, so my mum is in charge of money. Although I'm pretty pale-skinned, I look loads more like Mum than Dad – all cheekbones and raven hair – which means as I age I'm only going to look more severe, like bloody Maleficent. Something to look forward to. Personality wise, I'm more like Dad, affable and chill. At least, I hope I am.

'How was school?' Mum asked, now on her second glass of wine (that I knew of).

'Fine.'

Standard answer. We always ate at the dining table with the TV off. It's a house rule.

'Fine. All I ever get is fine. It's OK to not be fine, Vicky.'

'Please don't call me Vicky. I hate it more than olives and prejudice.'

She held up her fork to silence me. 'Oh dear god, don't overreact. I'm not having this stroppiness, I'm just not, so put a lid on it right now, please.'

'Mum! I only said . . .' There was no point. She was spoiling for a fight and I wasn't going to give her one. 'Whatever, sorry,' I said, sounding exactly like the stroppy teen I'd just been warned about.

'Have you made any new friends yet?' she asked in the way you'd ask a four-year-old on their first day of nursery.

I can't put my finger on when I stopped liking my parents. You don't stop *loving* them, but I didn't like them any more.

I used to think my mum was this beautiful Princess Jasmine figure. There's a photo in the hall from years ago – my mum and dad in super-fancy clothes at an awards thing. Mum's wearing this amazing peacock-blue sari and I used to want to *be* her. When I grew up I'd wear that sari and dance and drink champagne and be just like her. But Aladdin wasn't what I wanted any more. I was working on being anything *but* her.

'Maybe.' I poked a slug-like mushroom off my chicken chasseur. 'I'm going to meet some people from school tonight.'

'Oh, OK.' I could see she wanted to ask if it was at a crack den in a way that wouldn't stifle me. I'll give her this, she's at least *read* the Good Parenting books.

'Don't worry. We're only playing crazy golf.'

Relief, followed by disbelief. '*You're* going to play *crazy golf*?'

'Yep. I know.'

I arrived late to make sure I wasn't the first to get there. I hate that. Brompton Front glittered like a miniature Vegas with arcade lights. As I walked past the machines were busy with kids I recognised from lower down the school. They huddled around claw-grab games while a pair of hard-as-nails-looking girls were so good at *Dance Dance Revolution* they could do it backwards without facing the screen.

There was a bijou funfair on the pier but, out of season, it had shut at six thirty. With the lights all off it was straight out of *Scooby-Doo* – I could make out the silhouette of the ghost-train skull and the roller coaster was like a ribcage. The crazy-golf course was underneath the pier, but set back from the beach. Down there it smelled of sea – that smell the sea has . . . sea-y? How else would you like me to describe it? Luckily, it was masked by the scent of freshly made fish and chips, vinegar, doughnuts and candyfloss. Heaven.

The tide shivered over the shore but there was tinny music coming from the crazy-golf sound system. It wasn't the Eurodance of the arcades, it wasn't even English – it was K-pop. They were playing Korean music in Brompton? Maybe this really was Polly's space after all.

The wooden sign over the entrance featured a NOT MICKEY MOUSE welcoming kids in. Basically a poorly painted imitation Mickey Mouse with a much creepier smile – his tongue poked out of the edge of his mouth like he'd had a stroke. His manic leer seemed to say 'Roll up! Roll up to the circus of nightmares!' The sign *actually* read 'Fantasyland – Fun for All the Family!'

I saw the others already waiting on the other side of the archway near the ticket booth. They were sprawled over the children's play area like a *Vice* magazine spread, drinking cheap fizzy dessert wine straight from the bottle.

Polly stood on a swing straddling Daisy. Alice, as ever, sat on Alex's knee on the roundabout. Tonight he was dressed like Sherlock Holmes (and not the foxy Cumberbatch version). Beasley teetered in the centre of the see-saw, waving his golf club like a majorette. Were they waiting for me? That was sweet.

'Hey!' I said. 'Sorry I'm late.'

'No worries,' said Polly. 'Wine?'

I actually hate wine, I think it both looks and smells like cat wee, but I accepted the lukewarm bottle so I didn't look loserly. 'Thanks.'

'We were in the middle of a heated debate,' Beasley explained. 'If you had to have sex with someone from *Sesame Street* who would it be and why?'

'Oh my god!' I exploded.

'I said Elmo,' said Daisy, climbing off the swing to hug me. 'And now everyone says I'm a paedo. Tell them I'm not, Toria.'

'That is so wrong!' I laughed. 'You can't have sex with them, they're . . . Muppets!'

'Cookie Monster is quite sexy, don't you think?' Polly grinned.

'No, I don't!'

'Come on, you have to pick . . . or, like, your mum dies.' Beasley dropped his club on his foot.

'I'll opt for my mum dying. The Muppets are more important. Which would you pick, Beasley?'

'It was my question, so I don't have to answer. When I lived in America I went to Sesame Street. I got to meet Big Bird.'

I would later learn that was a lie. Sometimes Beasley lies.

'Cop out.' I perched next to Alice and Alex. 'So what's this all about?' I said, waving an arm at the golf course. 'Do you actually play crazy golf?'

'Well, of course,' said Alex, continuing to chew, or indeed *masticate*, a dictionary. 'It's the most sublime pastime in all the kingdom. We take it very seriously.'

'We don't,' Alice droned, more interested in filing her nails.

'We jolly well do. It's a fight to the death.'

Polly swung out and delivered a gentle kick in Alex's face, which he ducked. 'We don't keep score but we do play.'

'We're just waiting for Nico and Zoë to arrive and then we'll get going,' Daisy said with an adorable kitten-like yawn.

Beasley explained. 'Nico and Zoë go to the other sixth-form college in Brompton. They couldn't get into Brompton Cliffs because they live too far away.'

'Oh, I see.'

Polly sprang off the swing, bumping Daisy into the woodchips. '**** it, let's get going. We need to teach Toria what to do anyway. Let's get you a club. You got money?'

She led me to the kiosk. There was one hatch for clubs and admission and another for ice creams and stuff. Tonight both were operated by one guy: a stoned-looking rodentman with greasy hair. He reminded me of the drunk teacup mouse from *Alice in Wonderland*. 'Oh look, a new one,' he said, deadpan.

'Ignore this ****,' said Polly. 'This is Jamie and he is what happens if you fail your exams.'

He glared at her with dewy pink-rimmed eyes. 'Thanks, Polly. Love you too.'

'That's why we come here. Jamie makes us all work harder.' Clearly used to Polly's shit, he handed me a club and a score card as I slipped him the money. 'You won't need the score card,' Polly reminded me.

'There is only one rule,' Alex explained as we pushed through a turnstile to the first hole. The course was set in a synthetic tropical garden with lanterns strung between imported palm trees. 'You can't move on to the next hole until you pot your ball and you can't steer it in with your toe, Polly Wolff.'

'I'll do what the **** I want.'

'No cheating, Pol.' Daisy gave her the most serious glare such a pixie could manage.

'OK, I won't. Unless I get really ******* bored.'

With a vaudevillian flourish, Alex welcomed me to the first hole. 'Welcome, dear lady, to Brompton's finest crazy-golf establishment.'

'God, why don't you just whip it out for her?' Alice muttered, not nearly quietly enough.

Let me talk you through the golf course. It's important. Not to the story, but to me.

Hole 1: Hole 1 was a straight putt through a giant fibreglass skeleton's mouth. It was purely decorative, Alex explained – it's dramatic and foreboding, but it was actually a clear shot to the hole. Beasley swore that once upon a time the jaws used to open and close mechanically, but literally everyone else thought he'd dreamt that.

Hole 2: this was where it got exciting. On Hole 2, you hit your ball down a slope to the lower level. Polly told me that this one was pure luck – no amount of skill could compensate for the gravity and acceleration of the ball as it rolled downhill. Your only hope was if you bounced back off the guard at the bottom and rebounded into the hole. 'Just smack it and hope for the best,' Polly told me. 'Coincidentally, my life mantra.'

By Hole 3 – a water feature with a hump bridge – it was clear that, while it was true no one was keeping score, everyone except Daisy *was* competitive. In fact, never had crazy golf been so hard core. In particular, Beasley, Polly and Alex seemed in it TO THE DEATH. Polly had a love/hate relationship with her ball – if it went the right way she'd kiss it, if it didn't go in it would get called a ******* little ****. Even Alice lightened up – when she potted her ball she performed a fairly convincing pole dance around her club.

If we had been keeping score, I'd have been doing pretty well – I totally fluked the third hole and got a hole-in-one.

Hole 4 was Daisy's favourite – the 'Disapproving Seal'. It was a straight line barricaded by a painted stone seal. Time and weather had worn its face, and Daisy was right – its expression could only be described as 'disapproving'. I felt judged by this statue. I judged him right back. There was no way you could get a hole-in-one on this one unless you got lucky.

Hole 5 was a hard chicane, and then there was Hole 6.

Oh, Hole 6.

Hole 6 is where I met *him*.

That creaky little windmill would become a memorial for our meeting. *He* is Nico Mancini. If his name sounds like he's out of a romance novel, it's because HE SHOULD BE IN A ROMANCE NOVEL. He loudly announced his arrival with a cry:

'I can't believe you started without us. You are all dead to me.'

I turned round to see who was calling. I actually saw Zoë first – a strikingly beautiful black girl with silver glitter framing her eyes. Her ears were so pierced they seemed weighed down by metal.

Nico was behind her. However I describe him he'll sound hideous, so rest assured he was *beautiful*. Seriously, if Nico had been born five hundred years ago he'd have been a muse to artists and sculptors and poets. He had thick curly hair falling over his forehead and heavy straight-line eyebrows. They were what I noticed first about a second before I noticed his smile and accompanying dimples. And then he noticed me.

'Oh, hi. You must be the new girl.'

'Yeah. I'm Toria.'

'I know. Pols has been telling us all about you.'

Zoë introduced herself with a broad hug (she also asked where I got my coat, so she passed). I couldn't think of a single thing to say. I couldn't take my eyes off him and, although he greeted the others, he kept looking back at me.

Let's talk about Instalove. A lot of my online friends have book blogs and, by and large, Instalove is one of the worst tropes of young adult fiction. I mean, it's crap, right? Two people – be they undead or not – meet and know within *seconds* that they're gonna get married and be together until Happy Ever After.

Until that moment by the windmill, I was one such haterade drinker, but that was because I'd never felt Instalove. Turned out it was very real. It's not *love*: love I think, like a pretty weed, needs time to put down roots. Instalove is a separate thing. Within the first two minutes of meeting Nico, I'd unlocked a fictional photo album in my mind – all the dates we'd have: the pier, the park; all the kisses; all the arguments and in-jokes. Does anyone else do that or is it just me? I couldn't stop it; it was an avalanche of fantasies and now I was buried.

Instalove, Instalust, call it what you want. I just *wanted* him.

It was decided that Zoë and Nico could pick up the game from where we were. Nico seriously affected my A game; all of a sudden I was square-shaped and tongue-tied. Trying to play crazy golf sexily is no small feat, let me tell you. Worse still, the windmill was pretty tough – there was only a narrow pipe going through the middle and you had to avoid the creaking, rotating sails. Could I get my ball through that hole? No, no I could not. Luckily Nico and Beasley were having similar difficulty, either that or they wanted to linger with me while the others moved on to Hole 7.

'So where did you move from?' Nico asked. He stood like Jesus; his club across the back of his shoulders and his hands dangling over that.

'Up north,' I replied, suddenly wary of my cloddish accent. 'My dad got a job at the university.'

'Sucks. You miss your mates?'

'Not as much as I thought I would.'

This was true. My old friends would never have done this. Chloe and Katie from back home were very into doing work on school nights (nail-biting high achievers – you know the type. Being perfect looks exhausting, I'm very glad I'm not), and doing things with their families on a weekend.

'Woo-hoo! Your turn,' Beasley said, finally getting his ball through the tunnel.

I positioned myself in front of my ball and managed to tap it into the side of the windmill, in the process blocking Nico's next move.

'Nice one! Thanks for that!' he said.

'Sorry, I snookered you. Or golfed you . . . Is that a thing?'

'It can be.' I wondered if I could trick him into showing me what to do, like in the movies where the guy stands behind the useless girl and shows her how to make the swing. 'So Pols says you're pretty cool.'

'And she's hard to impress,' Beasley chipped in from the other side of the windmill. 'I don't know what you did to win her over. We tried to introduce someone new into the group last year, and she killed her and wore her skin to school.'

I smiled with a self-impressed glow in my stomach. 'Did she really say that?'

'You're in her friend bag. She doesn't mess about with that.' Somehow Nico used his ball to knock me through the tunnel.

'Wow! Good shot! Yeah, she mentioned the friend bag.' The fact that Polly, the COOLEST GIRL IN THE WORLD, had been talking about me with Nico, THE HOTTEST GUY IN THE WORLD, made me so freaking happy. A hugely optimistic part of my brain wondered if she was trying to set us up.

The game gave us plenty to talk about, and before we knew it we'd sailed past Hole 7 and caught up with the others at Hole 8.

Hole 8: was amazing. By far the most impressive hole on the course – a pirate ship, skull and crossbones billowing in the sea breeze.

We took the stairs up to the 'top deck' of the ship where the others were waiting for us.

'This one is a capricious tyrant,' Alex told me. '*Regard.*' On the top deck of the ship there were three holes. 'Two of them lead to the target, but one takes you back to the entrance.' I looked behind me and saw there was a funnel at the foot of the stairs we'd just climbed.

'Well, which hole is it?'

'We're not telling you that!' Polly grinned. 'That's cheating.'

'It's all very metaphorical,' Alex went on. 'Like how we're

all shooting blind, unsure whether we're really going forwards or backwards.'

'How deep of you,' I said, setting up my shot. 'It's not a metaphor. It's multiple choice. This has a two-in-three chance of success. I reckon real life isn't so stacked in your favour.'

'In real life,' Polly added, 'they'd all take you back to the beginning. The way to get ahead is to do this.' She picked up her ball and tossed it over the side of the pirate ship. It landed on the level below and rolled towards the hole. It stopped short of getting her a hole-in-one.

'That's cheating!' Daisy exclaimed.

'That's the point,' Nico said. 'Cheaters usually win.'

'That's the way to *win*,' I agreed, 'but it's more fun to *play*.' I tapped my ball and it rolled into the left-hand-side hole. There was a sharp intake of breath and I heard the ball plop out of the hole underneath the steps and back to the beginning. 'I lived, I learned, I won't do it again. See – it is like real life after all.' I swung my club over my shoulder and headed back to the start.

Hole 9: Hole 9 was an anti-climax to be honest, like they'd spent all their time, money and imagination on the pirate ship. This one was a straight line but with lots of bumps along the way. Theoretically you could get straight down the middle, but it was pretty tricky. Tricky but boring. The worst.

'Hole Ten looks like a ****,' announced Polly and it really did.

Hole 10 was supposed to be the Loch Ness Monster emerging from the water but, like the seal, the paint was worn and chipped, and rather than a prehistoric beast, it looked like a partially submerged member. You had to steer your ball through the humps. Nico set about giving the head of the beast a handjob with both arms wrapped round it.

'I really think I've mastered the technique,' he bragged.

'Oh, he's loving it,' Beasley laughed. 'You can see it in his eye.' The poor thing, appropriately, only had one eye.

'You've certainly had enough practice,' Zoë said and everyone called BURN.

'What's up, Zoë? Scared of the schlong?' Nico put on a voice, apparently like how he thought a penis would sound. To Nico, a penis would sound Swedish. Or kinda deaf.

'Oh, Zoë, don't hate me, I don't want to hurt you. I want to be your friend . . .'

'Sorry, dickmonster. Just not my bag.' Zoë turned to me. 'Yes, I am a lesbian.'

I shrugged, unsure if I was meant to be horrified or impressed. My old school had an LGBT committee and was in the local papers when two Year 13 guys proposed to each other in the canteen, so this wasn't especially exotic. I realised though, that for Brompton, it probably was.

'Oh OK. Cool.'

I sensed I was being tested again and evidently I passed because the game carried on.

Hole 11 was the hardest yet and the only one where you had to putt uphill.

Poor Beasley, who I increasingly sensed was the butt of many a joke, stood behind the hole, in charge of fishing the balls that overshot out of the bushes and palms.

I simply couldn't get my ball up. Even if I could get it up onto the flat, the ball rebounded off the backstop and rolled back down.

'OK,' I said to Nico once my arms were dead weights. 'This one *is* starting to feel like a metaphor.'

He laughed. 'You want me to go catch it up at the top?'

'I don't wanna cheat.' I hit my ball up to the top again, where a Converse-clad foot pinned it down.

'Oh we all do it,' Polly called down from the top of the ramp. 'We don't keep score, remember?'

I smiled, unconsciously covering my mouth with a hand. I forgot I didn't have teeth like tusks any more. Nico took my other hand and we ran up the slope in tandem.

Hole 12: the final hole. What had once been a grand volcano finale, with a working fire on top, was now a damp squib. As Beasley explained, the working flame was against health and safety regulations and so it had been permanently turned off. It was still quite tricky: you had to get the ball up a little ramp, through the volcano and out the other side.

And then it was over. My ball plinked into the hole in three moves and the course was done. I didn't feel as triumphant as I might have; I didn't want the night to end. Somehow two and a half hours had vanished in a matter of seconds. See what I mean about time changing? My face hurt, actually ached, from laughing.

This lot were so good. The way they held hands, and groomed each other, and took the piss . . . They were speaking a foreign language I so badly wanted to learn. I suddenly felt a terrible pressure to be funnier, cleverer and more like them, but I only felt like an outlier as they slowed to translate for my benefit.

Game over, we gathered by the kiosk and handed in the

clubs and balls. Daisy had lost her ball at Hole 11, so we had to fish a rogue one out of the bushes before we could return.

'That was fun,' I said, trying to wedge myself into conversations that were going on without me. 'I was sceptical, I'm not gonna lie. Who knew crazy golf could be so good?'

'Are you tripping?' Nico said. 'When wasn't it amazing? You're not one of those hipsters who pretend everything's awful are you?'

I answered that with a question: 'If I was a true hipster, wouldn't I think this was ironic retro fun?'

'You have a point,' Polly interjected. 'We like that no one else ever comes here. Some nights we don't even play, we just sit on the pirate ship or swings and shoot the ****. None of our ***** parents let us all go to each other's houses. It was either here or the graveyard . . .'

'And that's where the Goths go.' Beasley finished her sentence, reaching over her to hand his club to Jamie.

'****!' Polly suddenly announced. 'I was meant to be home, like, half an hour ago. Basically, my parents are ******* psychotic. I'm actually running. Toria . . . you're a dude. See you outside school tomorrow at eight thirty.' And with that she was gone, her pink ponytail swinging behind her.

'They really are really nuts,' Daisy said. 'If you think her dad's bad, wait till you meet her mum. She is so scary.'

'It's true,' Beasley added. 'Imagine if Satan and Cruella de Vil had a baby of pure evil.'

'Wow. I thought my mum was bad.'

'Hey,' Nico said, unchaining his bike from the rack. 'Are you doing anything Friday night?'

I pretended to think about it for a second. I was clearly doing nothing. 'I don't think so.'

'Awesome. Come to our gig? It'll be *awful*, we've barely rehearsed, but everyone's coming.'

I was 'everyone'. I had a genuine inspirational teen-movie moment and my eyes glazed over. I wondered if this was what belonging felt like. Maybe this was an unexpected upside to moving; I might get to reinvent myself as someone who got invited to stuff. Yeah *I know* that sounds mushy but it really did feel special. Oh, who cared: if Nico was going, I was there.

# Chapter Four

# Dandelions

The next morning I walked to school with bumper zip-a-dee-doo-dah in my step. I practically twirled through the park like a Disney princess in song. My head was full of the fake Nico memories I was determined we would one day share. Maybe we'd come to this park and hold mitten-clad hands. Maybe we'd have a picnic and he'd feed me strawberries dipped in melted chocolate on a rustic tartan throw. Perhaps we'd roll in the autumn leaves and I'd cackle when he rolled in dog turd.

I knew this was borderline mentally ill, but my mind was galloping *way* ahead of itself. He probably didn't even fancy me. If I were a lesbian, I don't think I'd fancy me. I'm not really my type.

This much was certain: I'd never been as convinced of a crush. I had dated a guy at my old school. It didn't end well. He was called Nick 'Smithy' Smith. I vaguely knew him because we went to the same primary school, and he asked me out in the run-up to the Year 11 ball. His best friend was dating my friend Chloe, so they set us up. He was cute – really cute – but had nothing to say for himself. He was very into hockey. I was not into hockey. I am still not into hockey.

We dated for a while. By 'dated', I mean we made out at the few parties I was invited to. I lost my finger virginity to him. After a while it was pretty clear I was doing it because everyone else was doing it, not because I was madly in love. Call me corny ('Hey, Corny!') but I kind of wanted my penis first time to be with someone I properly cared about, not just someone who shared my urgency to cast off virginity like a cursed shawl made out of leprosy. I'm not some creepy abstinence cult member, I just wanted it to be good. So many of my firsts were crap, I felt I should try to ensure one was done the right way.

A word on 'slut shaming': if you think me fooling around one time at Chloe's End-of-Term Barbeque in some way affects me, my 'character' or my story, I want you to sit down with a calendar and see if you can pinpoint the exact moment you were brainwashed by the patriarchy into thinking women aren't allowed to have sexual feelings.

We do. Well, I do.

When I dumped Nick it got ugly. He told his friends I was frigid, I retaliated and said he had 'farmer fingers'. I regret that (although he does live on a farm). I learned the hard way that these things do tend to get messy. Why is it that however hard you try to avoid drama it always pops up like dandelions? One more reason to be grateful for the new start in Brompton.

I met Polly outside the sixth-form entrance as promised. When I arrived, she was reading Edgar Allan Poe and drinking coffee (or tea, I guess) from a slick chrome flask.

'Ooh I love Poe!' I said, really, really hoping to wow her with my knowledge of American literature. 'Which one are you reading?' I hoped it was one of the three I had bothered to read.

'"Tell-Tale Heart".'

Oh thank god for that. I hadn't read it, but it was in that episode of *The Simpsons*.

'Love that one. The heart still beating under the floorboards. Creepy.'

'It's hilarious,' Polly told me. 'He kills the old dude for giving him side-eye! Harsh or what?' Today she was wearing a smart shirt, buttoned all the way to the top, with men's slacks. Effortless and cool as ever. I always felt like I was dressed like a kid around Polly. I wondered if it was time to bin the leopard-print Cons. 'Do you want some coffee? It's my mum's and it's ******* rocket fuel.'

'Sure, why not?' Because I'd be jittery all morning is why not, but I didn't want to seem rude. Polly slid the chrome beaker across the bench. 'Thanks,' I said. Dear god, the coffee *was* strong. I fought to stop my eye twitching. 'I had so much fun last night. Like, the most fun in ages.'

'Fantasyland is the nuts. And I saw you getting along with Mr Mancini . . .'

My face baked. 'Oh god. Was it that obvious?'

'There was an element of hair tossing and eye fluttering.' She re-enacted said movements.

I cringed. 'I didn't even realise I was doing it.'

'Our Nico is a very handsome young man. You've got eyes. I wouldn't feel too bad about it – you wouldn't be the first girl to find him on Facebook and **** herself off.' Despite her smile I sensed Polly was disappointed, like that she'd maybe thought I was special but falling for the obvious hunk was crushingly predictable.

I couldn't help myself. It was like picking a cornflake scab. 'Does he . . . have a girlfriend?'

'How do you know he doesn't have a boyfriend?'

No way – I'd have picked up on something. 'Well . . . does he have either?'

'Nope. He's a free agent. For now.'

I couldn't keep the joy off my face. Polly rolled her eyes.

'Has he said anything about me?'

'No.' Polly must have sensed my impending woe because she added, 'Although I haven't spoken to him since last night. He did stick by your side all through the ******* game of golf, so I'd take that to be a good sign.'

'And he invited me to the gig on Friday.'

Polly smiled. 'Look at you all smitten! There is smit all over your face. C'mon, ****, let's get to assembly and save seats for the others.'

My single-minded obsession infiltrated periods one and two, and then I had a free with Daisy, so she had to bear the brunt of my incessant Nico chatter. Sixth-formers had a study room off the main library, which a lot of students couldn't be bothered to walk to, so it was a better, quieter, alternative to the common room.

'Do you think I should add him on Facebook or something?' I asked Daisy. I'd spoken of little else since Literature finished. I was aware that this probably wasn't doing a lot to endear me to my new friends, but it also made me feel like part of them as it were – I wasn't just New Girl any more.

'Yeah, why not? He's on Facebook all the time.' Daisy whipped out her French homework with a sigh. We had to translate a whole chapter before next lesson. The study room was in the old part of the school so it was more Hogwarts-like – high leaded windows, red wine carpets and soaring bookcases. It smelled of proper library: well-thumbed pages and index cards. On this side of the wall sixth-formers were allowed to talk, as long as we did so quietly. 'Nico is super friendly. You should be his friend.'

'But I want to snog his face!'

'You should still be his friend. He's a good egg.' Daisy smiled. It was toasty warm in the library, but Daisy wore a chunky-knit sweater and a peacock-print scarf.

I hadn't really thought of that. I didn't want to make a mess and, from what little I understood of dating, you should never poop where you eat. But I really did want to snog him a lot.

Daisy yawned and I hoped I wasn't boring her. She looked tired, like she hadn't slept. There were dark circles around her saucer eyes. With sun pouring through the window and hitting her face, she glowed, a fine layer of tiny white hairs showing on her cheeks.

One last Nico thought before I got on with my French. 'I think Polly was pissed off when I said I fancied him.'

There was a twinkle in Daisy's eye. 'I wondered if she was OK with it. She said she was.'

'What's that supposed to mean?'

'Nico and Polly went out with each other for about five minutes last year after we first met him.'

The bubble burst, taking my heart out in the process.

'Oh.' Big, sad pause. 'She never said.'

It was over then. No wonder Polly hadn't seemed impressed; I was moving in on her ex-boyfriend. There are golden rules of friendship. However much I wanted to snog Nico, I had met Polly first, I liked her and wanted her to be my friend. I was sure there were plenty more guys as divine as Nico in Brompton. I knew there weren't, but I needed to anaesthetise myself with a white lie.

I must have looked like an emoji sad face because Daisy jumped right in. 'Oh no, nothing like that. It wasn't serious at all. Nico has been out with *plenty* of girls since Polly, and she really doesn't care.'

I didn't care for her use of the word 'plenty', but I let it slide. 'I don't know, Daisy. You can't go out with your friend's exes.'

'He's not like a proper ex. It was more like an experiment. They were just playing around.'

See? Drama sprouts up through the cracks. 'Do you think I should talk to Polly about it?'

'No. Polly doesn't talk about feelings.'

'What?'

'She really doesn't. She thinks it's a waste of time.'

I laughed, because I imagined that was a hundred per cent true, but I also felt stupid. For a moment I'd truly believed it could be easy. It's never easy.

'What about you?' I asked. 'Who are you into?' It occurred to me that Daisy hadn't once mentioned a guy – or a girl – in that way. 'Who's on the Daisy Weekes crush list?'

Daisy looked me dead in the eye and said, 'No one. I am asexual.'

'What?' She said it in the same way I say, 'I'm a Capricorn.' She held my gaze. 'Are you for real?' I'm not a Tumblr virgin, I know all about asexuality, but I couldn't work out if she was kidding or not.

Daisy being Daisy, she simply smiled. 'Yes. I don't want to have sex with anyone just now, thank you very much.'

And that was that.

Later that night, I added Nico on Facebook and waited. I chatted to Marianna, my friend in California, for a while, but he still hadn't accepted the request by the time we'd done. What if he thought I was a super-needy cyber stalker? Once you send a Facebook friend request, you can't undo it – what if he'd seen the request? He'd also see me remove it – oh, it's a house of cards.

My poetry book was sat on my desk where I'd abandoned it the week before. Lifting the mug of cold tea off it, I took the book to my bed and sat where I could see Facebook. Then I did something I hadn't done in YEARS: I picked up a pen and started writing.

I wrote about the Pot-Pourri girls. Well, not just them. I wrote about those *type* of girls – the ones who want to be famous for nothing. You know the ones I mean.

**Dolly**

Bisque china bulb head
Two-way mirror eyes
So you can see inside.
Tip-back blink action
And tiny tears
To get her way.
Stewardess smile, bottle-hole O.
One hand closed for grip
The other open for goodbyes.
A cotton thread away from broken
Polyester flesh
No pendulum organs
Meat spoils.
Sugar and spice, free from vice
Or voice.
Sold her tongue for coin teeth.
Child-pageant hair drilled into her skull
Holes hidden with roses and white ribbons
For surrender.
Faux coy, real naked
Dress her in calligraphy
And exclamation marks.
Decorative, and tea-party ready
She waits with cup and saucer.

Somehow two hours passed. How? My eyes were tired and my right hand claw-like from pen-grip. It felt good though.

Really good. I'd forgotten how much fun words could be when teachers weren't telling you which ones to put where. I blinked, looked up and saw I had a notification:

*Nico Mancini accepted your friend request.*
*Write on Nico's Timeline.*

* * *

Friday came around pretty quickly. This is going to sound deranged, but I was actually enjoying school. Daisy was in all my lessons, but I also had a few with Polly or Beasley. I had one free a week with Alice and (thank god) we liked a lot of the same manga stuff so we had *something* to talk about. I think now she'd heard about my crush on Nico she believed I wasn't trying to steal Alex out of her nest.

Beasley was just adorable. It turned out he lived a few streets away from me so we could walk to and from school together. He had to be Brompton's leading authority on horror films. By the time we'd walked together a few times, what I hadn't learned about Hollywood Hexes – film sets where people died – wasn't worth knowing. *The Crow, Poltergeist, The Exorcist* . . . I'd never seen any of them, but Beasley was obsessed and made me promise we'd have a film night soon.

The only thing was his propensity to, shall we say, 'stretch the truth'. I did not believe, for example, that his father had once had sex with Kylie, or that he'd spent some of his childhood living in Disneyland. I guessed he was only telling such tall tales because he wanted people to like him, and I wanted to like him so I let them slide.

It was official. I had friends. Go, me. The only downside of hanging out with Polly and the gang was that the Hollister Sons sniggered at me every time I entered a room. I had no idea what I'd done, but from what I could gather they either thought I was a lesbian or a gypsy or both. To be honest, either of those things would at least serve as a USP. I had nothing. If you're not an emo, a Goth, a jock, a princess, a freak or clever enough to be a geek, what are you meant to call yourself? Don't you dare say 'normal'.

Thankfully, as I'd thought of little else, the night of the gig came around swiftly and Polly invited us to hers to get ready. She assured us that the getting-ready part would be ten times better than the gig. I'd resigned myself to the fact that, despite the bubbles in my tummy, Nico and I would just be friends. This was better – less messy. Easier.

Polly, it turned out, lived in a mansion. A full-on Addams Family mansion. There was even a little turret room and it overlooked the sea. It made sense: if her mum was Satan, why wouldn't she live in a haunted house? Thankfully I walked there with Beasley, otherwise I'd have never dared ring the bell. You couldn't even *get* to the front door unless you rang the bell at the gates. I fully expected there to be a slavering hellhound guarding the perimeter.

'Her mum is a head teacher too,' Beasley explained as we entered through the creaking gates. 'Polly is the by-product of too-excellent parenting: clearly defined boundaries and numerous reward systems. She was bound to go nuts. It's the equivalent of those dog people who only buy the really clinical dried-food pellets.'

'Polly's not nuts.'

'You have met Polly, right? She's crayfish, but I love her. We all go a little crazy sometimes – that's from *Psycho*. And *Scream*.'

Polly met us at the door, her endless legs in denim cut-offs. 'Hey *****, come on up.'

It was clear that Polly didn't want Beasley or I spending any more time than necessary in the main part of the house, which was decorated like (and as quiet as) a museum. Her parents must be into antiques; there were old things sat on top of old things inside of old things everywhere. My mum wouldn't stand for it; she'd call them 'dust collectors'.

I followed Polly and Beasley to what could only be the turret room – up one flight of stairs and then another shorter flight. 'I live in the tower,' Polly said. 'I'm ******* Rapunzel. When is some ****** gonna rescue me? I've been waiting seventeen ******* years.'

Polly's room was awesome cool though. It wasn't what I'd been expecting at *all*. I'd been expecting something dark and chaotic, but there were no posters, trinkets or photos – everything was pale, calm and zen. There was an intricately woven wrought iron bed on a shaggy rug, fairy-lights coiled around the bars, filling the room with an almost enchanted glow. Other than the whitewashed walls and floors the only colours were the spines of her hundreds and hundreds of books – one whole wall was dominated by sleek modular bookshelves.

But none of those things really mattered. Up in the hexagonal tower, windows curved across one whole side of the room and, with the shutters open and even though it was night, I could see out over the sea for miles and miles as far as the lighthouse on the cliffs. The ocean rippled like black satin and I could hear the sad clanging of the buoys.

'Your room is so cool,' I breathed.

'Thanks.' Polly dived onto the bed on which Daisy was already sat. Beasley grabbed her computer chair – itself cool – leaving me with a furry beanbag. It's very hard to be elegant on a beanbag.

'Seriously, this could be in an Ikea catalogue.'

Polly laughed. 'How ******* dare you!'

'That was a compliment!'

We listened to music for a while. Polly's taste was pick 'n' mix: K-pop, Bowie, Kate Bush, Siouxsie and the Banshees, but also Girls Aloud, One Direction and Kanye. I started to wonder how much thought and energy Polly put into being so eclectic. It looked effortless, but I was starting to suspect a carefully cultivated randomness. I'm pretty tidy, but I'd never seen a bedroom so neat – and that included my parents'.

'God, I suppose we should get ready.' Polly dragged herself off the bed. 'What time are Judas Cradle playing?'

'About ten,' Beasley said.

'Oh, that's ages,' I said.

'Can we do you a makeover?' Daisy squealed, fluttering around me like a butterfly on Red Bull. 'Please?'

'On me?' I said, horrified. 'Why? Do I look like crap?'

'No! I just like playing with hair and stuff! Please please please? It'll be fun, I promise.'

I looked to Polly, who shrugged. 'You should let her. She does amazing make-up.'

'It's true,' Beasley added. 'She made me up as "Born This Way" Lady Gaga two Halloweens ago. It was uncanny. I tweeted Gaga a picture and she totally said she loved it.'

I didn't want to say, but I suspected the last part was a lie and there is no amount of make-up in all of MAC that would have made pudgy Beasley look like Gaga. Instead I resigned myself to this terrible fate. 'OK, but don't make me look like a drag queen.'

I want to stress that this was not the type of 'makeover scene' where they pulled out my ponytail and took off my glasses, but I did look good afterwards. Polly did *something* with my ever-lank hair, making it look voluminous while Daisy saw to my face. I had never had a proper 'smoky eye', thinking it was something my mum would do for a grown-up work party, but I have to hand it to Daisy, I looked amazingly femme fatale. While they got me ready, Beasley DJed and took photos. I obliged – pouting and posing with duck face like a glamour model whose rent is due in the morning.

I wish there was a simple way to describe the *lightness* of those early days before the trouble started. When I think of them now, the memories are fuzzy and delicate, like we were chubby little cherubs hanging out on powder-pink clouds or something.

By the time the 'makeover' was done, we were running late. After we'd hurried down the hill to The Mash Tun, Nico's band had already started playing. Damn. On the way in, we were stamped with big red NO BOOZE ink on our hands because we didn't have fake IDs. That sucked.

The Mash Tun was a total dive. Every town has a scummy music venue. It smelled of beer, vomit, BO and wee. It was about half-full, with most people there around our age. I guessed most were from the uni – the same one Dad worked at – although they had bands play at the Union too.

'My god, this place is gross.'

Daisy pulled a toilet roll and some hand sanitiser from a giant handbag almost as big as she was. 'Not our first time.'

'Ah I see. I wondered why you were dragging that thing around.' I had to stoop to shout in her ear.

Polly was already pushing her way through the crowd, not that anyone seemed to mind. Most people were loitering, pints in hands, with only a handful of hard-core listeners crowding at the front of the stage.

Here was the big surprise of the night. Judas Cradle were actually very good. Nico stood slightly back, keeping time on the bass. He wore a tight NIN T-shirt with the sleeves rolled up to reveal hard little arms. I wanted to lick one. I know! I understand these thoughts were not entirely right. Maybe *I'm* not entirely right. On his left forearm was an intricate tattoo of a black cartwheel thing. I wondered what it signified.

Zoë played the keyboard and synth – the current song had a dirty, angry bee buzz throbbing underneath it – it was a lot more electro than I'd been expecting. Every town has a Next Big Thing garage band and usually they want to be a) Radiohead, b) The Velvet Underground, or c) The Sex Pistols. Judas Cradle were none of the above and a lot more polished than any I'd seen back home. They were good.

For one thing, you could actually hear what the singer was singing (I always think the vocals should be highest in the mix at gigs – otherwise how do you know what the lyrics are about? Surely songs are just poems with music?). The lead singer was the most beautiful boy I'd ever seen. Not beautiful like Nico, beautiful like an androgynous alien from the planet Bowie. Bleached white-blond hair, glass-fine features and more eyeliner than me, Polly and Daisy combined. You couldn't take your eyes off him – well, for at least a minute, and then mine strayed back to Nico.

'He's called Etienne,' Polly screamed in my ear, nodding at the singer. 'I have been in love with him for two years. He doesn't even know I exist.'

'That sucks!'

'Why doesn't he love me?' Polly whined before snapping out of it. '**** it. He says he's saving himself for marriage anyway.'

'For reals? He doesn't look entirely human.'

'He gets that a lot.'

Most of the set was grimy, sleazy electro-y stuff. There was one standout ballad – it was called 'Papercuts' and Etienne went from wild-eyed (allegedly celibate) sex kitten to heartbroken fragile waif. '*A favourite book, all I want to touch, but you leave me with cuts, these sweet papercuts*.' The song reminded me of snow, of winter. It was my favourite.

They finished the set on their most popular number, 'Gasoline Caroline', before heading off to cheers and screams. There were a few Judas Cradle groupies packed around the stage like horny sardines, and I felt irrationally jealous of them. GET AWAY FROM MY NICO.

(I will look into therapy.)

After what felt like an eternity of hanging around, Nico and Zoë came to find us in the crowd. Most of the audience had left as soon as the set finished, but a few (including the groupies) hung around. I was thrilled to see that Etienne seemed to be the big draw, not Nico. Were they visually impaired?

'Hey!' he said, still sweaty – the black T-shirt had damp patches that I wanted to sniff. (Again, I know.) 'Thanks for sticking around. How was it?'

Everyone showered him with compliments, even Polly. 'Honestly, your best gig, dude. The synth is sick.'

'I know, right? Best thing we ever bought; we should have done it years ago.'

'I suggested that,' Beasley said proudly.

'Yes, my friend, you did. Why are you drinking Coke? God! Losers!' Nico left his bass behind the bar and convinced the bar girl to get us all cider. They had a band rider apparently and most of the band were over eighteen anyway. I hadn't realised Nico was a year older than us. Immediately I started to panic about him going away to university and abandoning me, before I forced myself to get a grip.

We all gladly accepted the cider. There's only so much Coke you can drink before you can feel the diabetes actually happening within. Nico handed me a pint.

'Hey, Toria. I can't believe you came.' He seemed genuinely surprised.

PLAY IT COOL, I told myself. 'Of course I came!' WAY TO PLAY IT COOL, COOLIO. 'You know . . . everyone was coming . . . and it sounded fun.'

'Well, cheers.' He plinked his plastic pint glass against mine. Is it a glass at all, if it's plastic? Something for you to dwell on later. 'What did you think? Be honest.'

'OK, honestly –' I sipped my drink – 'I thought you guys were excellent. I mean that. I'm not just . . . blowing smoke up your arse or whatever that saying is.'

'Really?' His face lit up.

'Really. I'm not gonna lie, I wasn't expecting much . . . some of my old friends were in bands and they . . . really sucked. Sucked so bad! But I really loved that. "Papercuts" was my favourite.'

His smiled broadened to show his dimples. Not being able to touch him was *killing* me. 'No way! I wrote that one.'

'Seriously?' I thought about telling him I wrote poems, but stopped myself at the last second in case he thought it was lame.

'Yeah.' He steered me away from the group. 'Don't ever, EVER tell her I told you this, but it's about Polly.'

My heart kerplunked. I wanted to ask him why he was toying with my very soul, but instead I said, 'Oh . . . OK.' What did that mean? Was he still in love with her?

'I don't think she pays enough attention to realise, to be honest.' I don't know if he could see my big sad pug eyes but he changed the subject abruptly. 'You look awesome tonight, by the way. Does that sound mega cheesy? Like, "Hullo, pretty lady, be my carer," or something?'

'Do I? Thank you . . . it was, erm, Daisy . . . She did my make-up.'

'You look hot!' he shouted at exactly the same time as the song ended. His words echoed round the room like it was a canyon. 'Oh god! That's so embarrassing!'

Polly smirked. 'Slick, Mancini. Real slick.'

I caught her eye. She didn't seem angry, but I felt awful at once.

'Well, it's true,' Nico said. Zoë appeared and tugged on Nico's sleeve – they had some band stuff to sort out or an amp to shift or something. 'Urgh, I better go help. Don't go anywhere, OK?'

'OK.' That made me feel a little better, but I was still baffled. 'Oh, one thing. Before you go, what does Judas Cradle mean?' I tried to be flirtatious, I really did. It probably came off as psychotic, making weird eyes like the snake in *The Jungle Book*.

'Oh, it's a medieval torture device. Prisoners got sat on a big wooden pyramid and then they weighed their legs down so it went all the way up their ass.' He scurried off to help Zoë.

I really wished I hadn't asked.

I got home that night to find Mum passed out on the sofa. Some old Christopher Lee horror film was playing on the telly, but she was face-down-in-a-cushion asleep, an empty bottle of wine and a half-finished tub of Twiglets spilled over the carpet. 'Dad?' I shouted but didn't expect a reply. She didn't get this wasted when he was home.

All the fun I'd had that evening gurgled down the plughole, replaced by a painful knot in my gut. I angrily kicked off my shoes, intending to wake her. I thought I'd better put her to bed and hide the evidence. I don't know why I do this every time, but I'd rather cover for her than listen to a fight. My dad is useless at stuff like this. He either sulks or does his head-in-the-sand ostrich impression, less use than the proverbial chocolate teapot.

I went to the sofa and crouched at her side. 'Mum . . . Mum, wake up.' I shook her shoulder.

She snorted out of her nostrils and came to. There was an equal amount of eyeliner smeared on her face and the cushion. 'What time is it? You're home early.'

'I'm not. It's late. After midnight.'

'Where's Dad?'

'I dunno.' I suspected he'd been out for dinner after work with some other lecturers and it had turned into a mammoth session. Dad does his drinking out in public where everyone can see it. Mum, like a lot of women, I suspect, kept her drinking behind closed doors. 'Come on, let's get you to bed.'

I went to help her up but she brushed me aside. 'Get off! I'm fine! I'm not a bloody invalid.' She staggered across the lounge, unsteady on her feet. I braced myself to catch her. 'Did you have fun tonight, Vicky?' She walked like the carpet was sprung, bouncing slightly on every footstep.

'Yeah, it was fine,' I said, humouring her. What else could I do?

'Good! You should have fun . . . you're young. You should be out! Making friends and meeting boys!' She stopped at the foot of the stairs, her eyes glassy. 'You're a good girl, aren't you? Nice girl! Not like your old mum. No, no . . . you don't want to be like me. I'm an embarrassment . . .'

I'd been to this pity party before. It wouldn't be spoken of in the morning. 'Mum. Go up to bed. I'll get you some water.'

By the time I placed the pint of water on her bedside table, she was already unconscious.

# Chapter Five

## Papercuts

After the night of the gig, I was on the inside of the outside. I'd never belonged to anything before – I even eschewed the Brownies because they make you wear poo-coloured garments – and it felt *strong*. It suddenly made sense why people join clubs and societies and cliques. It was nice to feel like a part of something. The side-effect of this was that most of the school now thought I was a freak. The sixth-formers were pretty used to Polly's temper, Beasley's mannerisms or Alex's outfits, but the lower school – particularly gobby Year 9s – had now taken to screaming DYKES when Polly and I walked down the corridors together.

'It doesn't matter,' Polly told me one day in the library study room. She was surreptitiously eating a Müller Crunch Corner under the desk when the librarian wasn't looking. 'This is why we're going to revise the **** out of these end-of-term tests. *We're* the ones who are getting the **** out of Brompton. They can call us geeks and freaks or dykes and faggots, but in two years we'll be in London or wherever and they'll be pregnant, dead or working on the pier. It's school karma.'

'I hope so,' I told her. 'My first two essays were Cs. That'll be me frying the doughnuts at this rate.' The time obsessing over Nico (more about him in a second) and time spent on the crazy-golf course was cutting into my study time. Mum, perhaps to punish me for finding her so drunk, had thrown an eppy about my first two essays. For the first time ever, I'd been grounded to study.

Over the library table, Polly took my hand and drew a smiley face on my thumbnail with a Sharpie. 'Toria, we are not going to let you ******* fail. We leave no one behind.'

'Thank you.' I could feel myself blushing. So this was what having proper friends felt like. Back home, my old friends had made everything a competition – trying to outdo each other, failing to realise you get nothing for finishing first.

'We got your back. Daisy has French and I've got English. You'll be fine.'

Meanwhile, as we crept towards half-term, Nico *was* interested. I could tell:

1. He texted constantly – sending pics from rehearsals or telling me how dull his lessons were.
2. He liked everything I put on Facebook.
3. On 12 October he asked me to send him a selfie – all above shoulder height, I stress. The last thing anyone needs to see is me squidging my boobs together with my arms like something off *Nuts* magazine.

4. He always came to Fantasyland if he knew I was going to be there.

I decided, shortly before half-term, that I would have to have a chat with Polly. She didn't seem overly concerned about me and Nico texting, but I was becoming attached to both of them and didn't want to make an epic mess just when things were going well. I finally plucked up the courage one evening at the golf course. Some of the others were playing. Alex had invented a hybrid of golf and croquet that he and Alice and Nico were trying out. I sat on the swings with Polly and Freya, who was, of course, reading.

'Can I talk to you about something?' I said, my voice strangled and feeble.

'You can.'

'Look, I know you used to date Nico . . .'

Polly guffawed. 'Bless you, child. I'd hardly call it dating.'

'OK, well . . . whatever. I like him, but I don't want to do anything if that'd piss you off.'

'It's not me you should worry about.'

'What?'

She leaned in conspiratorially. 'You didn't hear this from me, but Beasley has a major crush on you.'

My eyes almost fell out of my head. 'What? Beasley Beasley? I thought he was . . .'

'Gay? Well, duh. The boy plays the ******* flute. It's pretty much a single entendre.'

'Then how can he have a crush on me?'

Polly smiled. 'Poor Beas. I know he's gay, you know he's

gay, Freya knows he's gay.' Freya nodded with a wry smile, not looking up from her book. 'The only person who doesn't know Beasley's gay is Beasley. Or if he does, he's fighting it.'

'God, why?'

Polly shrugged. 'Beasley really wants to be normal.'

'Being gay is normal,' I said defiantly.

With an inquisitive tilt of her head, Polly scrutinised me. 'You're way too cool for this ******* town, Grand.'

'Well, duh,' I agreed with a grin. 'Oh god, I don't wanna upset Beasley. I love Beasley. But not like that. Do you think I should talk to him?'

Polly shook her head. 'Nah, he'll get over it. He's probably more concerned about you stealing Nico from him to be honest. I give you my blessing, by the way, if that's what you're after. Nico is . . . a dude.'

She didn't seem too certain, but I took her blessing gratefully. I'd worry about Beasley later.

It was getting cold and I was starting to wish I'd worn a jumper. Polly changed the subject. 'Hey, are you coming to Zoë's Halloween party during the hols?'

'Yeah, she mentioned it in passing. Was that an invite?'

'Of course it was. Zoë's dad is the vicar . . .'

'What?!'

'I know! He's mega chilled out though. He's letting her use their house while they're on holiday. It's gonna be epic.'

'OK, cool. What should I dress up as? I hate fancy dress.' I think it pretty much always looks naff and what are mixed-race girls meant to go as? I've oscillated between Pocahontas and Princess Jasmine pretty much my whole life.

'I think a few of us are going to do a *Beetlejuice* thing this year.'

'What's *Beetlejuice*?'

Polly looked at me with a mix of disgust, pity and horror before she stood up and screamed across the golf course. 'STOP EVERYTHING. TORIA HASN'T HEARD OF *BEETLEJUICE*.'

One night later I was sat in Polly's bedroom with the title sequence of *Beetlejuice* rolling on her laptop. 'So you know who Tim Burton is, right?'

'Of course. I love *Corpse Bride*.'

'Well, this is his early ****, when he was *really* ******* twisted. I can't believe you've never seen this!'

'It came out like ten years before we were born! How have you even heard of this? Are you secretly thirty?'

Polly laughed. We were in our pyjamas – hers Hello Kitty, mine bunny rabbits. This was a proper sleepover. I popped a kernel of slightly frazzled microwave popcorn into my mouth. Sweet, obviously – Polly and I were on the same page when it came to popcorn. Salty popcorn is the foodstuff of the Antichrist. 'No. But my sister is.'

'I didn't know you had a sister.'

'Well, half-sister, from my mum's first marriage.'

'Ah, OK.'

Obviously I loved the film. It was nuts. Apparently Beasley wanted to go as Beetlejuice while Alex and Alice were going to go as the dead bride and groom. When we got to the scene where the dead couple go into the afterlife, Polly paused it on the receptionist – a green-skinned beauty in a pageant sash and crown.

'I'm going as her. Look how ******* fierce she is. I'm going to dye my hair red.'

'Yeah, she's cool. Are you going to paint yourself green?'

'Yeah.' Polly took a breath. She went to press play but hesitated. 'And it's sort of an in-joke.'

I was confused. 'Is it?'

'Yeah.' Polly held her wrists up.

'What am I looking at? I don't get it.'

Polly took my hand and ran my fingers over her alabaster skin. I could feel shiny ridges, silky scar tissue in neat, minute parallel lines. They were so delicate I'd never noticed them before, but now I could feel them, I could see the skin glisten, almost like pearl. 'I cut myself. Just like she did.' She nodded towards the green receptionist.

My stomach clenched like a fist. This is going to make me sound like a baby or an idiot or both, but I'd never understood self-harm and it scared me. I think probably it scares a lot of people who've never been there. Like, I could never get past the *hurting* part, or the fact that the scars would remain forever. There's also that fear that I'm not quite deep enough to get it, so I usually keep quiet on the issue.

I forced myself to speak. I remembered Daisy telling me that Polly never talked about real things. Well, here she was, letting me feel her scars. 'Oh, OK . . . I get it.'

'Do you?'

Busted. 'Not really.' Tears were stinging my eyes and I didn't know what to say. 'I . . . do . . . is it something you still do?'

'God no! It was years ago, when I was, like, fourteen.'

That calmed me down. Her jovial tone made it clear this wasn't a cry for help.

'I figured you'd probably seen.'

'I hadn't. You were pretty neat, I see . . . kind of like your room!'

Polly laughed. 'Ha! Yeah. It was pretty OCD cutting.'

There was a long pause. Polly went to press play again, but I stopped her. 'Do you want to talk about it?'

'Not really. It's all a bit Camp Tika-Boo Hoo, isn't it?'

I searched her eyes. She was trying to gloss over it, but under the paint there were cracks in those walls. 'Polly! Tell me about it. To be honest, I don't get how you could do that to yourself. So . . . help me understand.'

Polly rolled her eyes but caved in. 'Uh. Intervention. I was young and I thought it was cool.' My eyes must have widened in shock. 'What, you want me to lie? I thought I was the saddest sad person and the angriest angry person in the whole world and that cutting myself would be a good way to deal with that. Surprise, surprise, it wasn't.'

'Why did you stop?'

'I'm not gonna lie. It's kind of addictive, but I started masturbating instead. Much healthier form of release!'

We both laughed. 'But seriously?' I said.

'Because I didn't want to be a ******* cliché. I could see what I was turning into. *That* teenage girl. I refuse to be a ******* statistic. Ever. So I stopped. It was hard and I still sometimes look at pencil sharpeners funny, but I just stopped.'

'No one helped you?'

'Everyone pretended not to notice. I hid it pretty well.'

My eyes stung again, but in a different way. 'Wow. You're tough. Like seriously tough.'

I thought for a second she might cry too, but it passed in a second and her lip curled. 'You are such a mushy ******. Shut the **** up!' She pressed play. 'Watch the film!'

The film finished and I brushed my teeth. It felt like I'd punched through a dam tonight: Polly Wolff was strong but she wasn't invincible. It made me like her even more. I guess I'd had her on a pedestal and that's not especially healthy. It was nice to have a human friend.

When I got back to her room, Polly was on all fours rummaging around in her cupboard.

'Hey, I can't find the foot pump for the blow-up bed. I hope you're full of puff.'

I did not fancy blowing up a mattress manually. 'That's OK, why don't I come in with you?' Polly had a stupidly big bed – we'd practically be sleeping in different postcodes.

'Is that OK? It'll take ten ******* years to blow up otherwise.'

I agreed and we climbed into Polly's vast bed together. It was freezing cold. Bed: pleasurable. Getting in and out of bed: un-pleasurable.

'God, it's freezing!' Polly shrieked.

'Snuggle!' I commanded and we squished our bodies together – my chest pressed to her back. Polly was gloriously warm, like a gangly hot-water bottle. 'That's better.'

'We should totally be filming this for Nico,' Polly suggested and we both cracked up.

**The Poem**

I tried to write a poem
But it got awaa
a
a
a
a
a
aay from me.
Tried to catch it in my hands like a firefly
and found it burned.
Canary in his cage, refusing to sing
Because he's an allegory.
You can't force it, little girl
Said the bird to the girl.
Leave the window wide
And trust it'll blow back.
I said 'you can't chew trust'
He said 'you chew enough doubt.'
Can't punch the wind
Or get time in a headlock.
Can't unglue your feet from the earth
When you keenly feel gravity's thumb.
Someone said it was a war,
That I required tanks and steamrollers.
What I needed was a ladder

And binoculars.
Turned off Google Maps
Let the poem find me.

## Chapter Six

# Moonlight

My Halloween costume was pretty easy. It was decided that I was going to go as Lydia Deetz, the Winona Ryder character from *Beetlejuice*. I wore a black-and-grey kilt, an old school shirt and a black cardigan. The only thing I had to really endure was a scratchy black Cleopatra wig.

As a group we looked pretty cool. Beasley's Beetlejuice costume and make-up were perfect and Polly was almost unrecognisable as Miss Argentina. She wore a swimming costume and heels, making her well over six feet tall. She really did look like a supermodel, albeit a green-skinned one.

I love Halloween, I always have. My mum describes me as a morbid child – way more interested in vampires, ghosts and witches than fairies and princesses. But Halloween is great for two reasons. First of all, it's an excuse to carve pumpkins and watch horror films (both of which we did at Beasley's house earlier that week – *Halloween* and *Evil Dead*) and, secondly, it's the earliest date at which you're officially allowed to be excited about Christmas.

Mrs Wolff drove us to the Old Vicarage where Zoë lived. Polly's mum lived up to her hype. She looked like an especially sour-faced newsreader, with big dyed hair the same colour as her golden skin, like a human Labrador. 'I mean it, Polly,' she said as she pulled up outside the vicarage. 'I'll be back here at twelve on the dot and I don't want you to be in a state. Is that understood? I'm not having a repeat of last Halloween.' My mum was many things, but she'd never dressed me down like that in front of my mates.

'Yes, Mum,' Polly droned robotically.

The Old Vicarage was right at the top of the hill, overlooking the bay. It was tumbledown in a *Secret Garden* kind of way, with willow trees and pampas grass spilling over the garden railings. It would be enchanting enough, but Zoë had draped lanterns from tree to tree and hung 'corpses' from branches. Two leering pumpkins greeted us at the gate like sentries.

'This is so cool!' I said.

'Halloween is Zoë's thing,' Beasley explained.

'Doesn't her dad think we're all doomed to Hades for all this pagan witchcraft voodoo evil?'

'Bob – yeah, we call her dad Bob – is the sweetest guy in the world,' Polly said as we followed the ramshackle path towards the front door. 'When Zoë was twelve, he sat her down and asked if she was gay and that whatever she said, both he and Jesus still loved her.'

'Wow.' I felt instantly bad for being judgy. There was a severed arm hanging out of the letterbox, but the door was ajar so we pushed our way in. I could hear laughing and music – the party was already underway.

Everybody was in the lounge, kitchen or back garden, from what I could tell. I saw that Zoë had got some of those red plastic cups off the internet so it felt like a proper American house party – nice touch. The crowd looked pretty chilled – I recognised a few people from the Judas Cradle gig and some Music People from school. Others I didn't know and I guessed they were from the sixth-form college. These were Good People though, I could tell. No Mean Girls or jocks drinking beer through a funnel.

A game of spin-the-bottle was already happening in the lounge – I saw Etienne and some of his fans getting involved. 'This time with tongues,' someone screamed gleefully. We passed them and headed into the kitchen where we found Daisy with Alice and Alex. Daisy had gone her own way and come as Jake from *Adventure Time*. Just when I thought she couldn't be more adorable.

We got some drinks and headed into the garden. I'm not gonna lie – I don't like being drunk – more specifically, I have a irrational fear of vomiting. I know, I know, it's insane, but it's a thing so I'll have to live with it. After three drinks I usually bow out quietly and switch to Diet Coke. My mum is hardly good advertising for heavy drinking either, is she? Zoë, as Catwoman, was smoking outside with her arm round a gorgeous girl dressed as a skeleton in a figure-hugging catsuit. 'Hey hey hey, you made it. You got drinks, yeah?' Zoë's eyes were puffy and squinty. I could tell at once she was high.

Zoë and Polly chatted as Skeleton Girl took the joint and took a long toke. I knew what was coming next. 'You want some?' the girl said.

'No thanks, I'm fine,' I said, worried I was sounding like a Tea Party member. I might as well have clutched my pearls. Look, I know she wasn't offering me crystal meth, but at some point when I was little that whole DRUGS ARE BAD message had installed itself so deeply that now I couldn't shake it.

'Have some,' Zoë insisted, being polite, not peer pressure-y. 'It's good shit, man.'

I shook my head and gave Polly a subtle glance. Sparing me any further embarrassment, Polly took the spliff instead. 'I'll take that, thanks.' She took a drag and passed it back to Zoë. I could have hugged her.

'Hey!' Beasley stuck his head out of the kitchen door. 'Come play spin-the-bottle!'

'**** off,' Polly said instantly.

'Oh OK,' I said, wanting to be away from the pot before I became a heroin addict. That's just how my brain works. I figured spin-the-bottle was the lesser of two evils. I set off towards the kitchen and Polly reluctantly followed.

Etienne had grown bored and was now setting up a playlist on Zoë's laptop. We gathered in the lounge. I was thrilled to see Nico was in the group.

'Oh hey,' he said. 'I didn't recognise you in your wig! *Beetlejuice*, right?'

'Correct! And you're . . .?'

'A mime. Terrifying.' He pulled out a beret and stuck it on his head. The rest of his stripy ensemble now made sense.

'That *is* scary. I'll keep my eyes peeled for invisible boxes and suitcases. Are you playing?'

'Are you?'

I nodded. 'Yeah, might as well. I've never played spin-the-bottle; I feel like I'm missing a piece of the puberty jigsaw.' Nico laughed and I was pleased at my wit – check me out making little jokes! Guys like funny girls, right? Wait, is that right or do they just see them as mates? Damn, it was harder than I thought.

We formed a circle on the living-room floor. Alice forbade Alex from playing and Daisy just wanted to watch, so it was me, Polly, Nico, Beasley and a few other people I didn't recognise. There was only one other fit guy, so it was more like Russian roulette than I'd have cared for.

First spin: some girl with braces called Ella spun first and got Beasley. There was screaming and cheering as they leaned in and very briefly kissed. It was the kind of kiss you gave a cousin.

'Ooh racy. I'm moist,' Polly said with an arched brow.

Second spin: Beasley got Nico. I caught Polly's eye and she could barely conceal her amusement.

'I'm game if you are,' Nico said with a grin.

'Oh he's game,' Polly muttered under her breath next to me.

'Oh whatever,' Beasley said, blushing. 'One, two, three . . .' They leaned into the centre of the circle and their lips brushed together. Ridiculous, but I was jealous.

Third spin: Nico got Polly. 'Just like old times,' he said.

'Only this time I'm sober!' Polly leaned in and they kissed. Their kiss was the longest yet and I couldn't look.

Polly spun the bottle and it whirled round the circle. I knew, just KNEW, it would land on me and it did. Nico and Beasley had set the bar for sexual fluidity and now if I refused I'd look uptight or, worse, homophobic. Oh, sod it. Polly was obviously the hottest girl at the party; there were worse options in the circle. Rather Polly than the sweaty mosher guy sat opposite her. I turned to her and we kissed. Her lips were cashmere soft. It was nice.

'If you'll excuse me . . . I need to be by myself . . .' Nico said with a sly grin.

'Pervert!' Polly said.

'Girls don't get it on for guys to wank over,' Zoë said from her perch on the sofa.

The game went on for a while. The rules changed and before we knew it, we were swapping costumes and spitting vodka into each other's mouths. It was stupid fun, but it was fun.

The game drifted apart. There's only so much screaming at kissing you can do, and someone got out a Twister mat instead. As the circle broke up, Nico took my hand and we weaved towards the stairs. I stalled in the hallway, suddenly more sober than I'd ever been in my whole life. I'd seen enough TV to know what happens if you are led upstairs by a hot guy. My heart hop-skip-jumped. I wasn't ready, both in terms of having not worried about this moment enough for it to be satisfying and also in that I hadn't trimmed my pubes. Rookie mistake.

'Where are we going?' I asked, sounding like a scared little girl.

Nico looked confused for a second. 'Oh! Oh no! This isn't like a date-rape thing; I just wanted to show you something. Shit, I realise that is exactly what I'd say if I was going to date-rape you, but I actually mean it.'

I smiled and let him lead me on. 'I'll trust you on this occasion.'

His grey Pugs not Drugs T-shirt was stuck to the base of his back, a little dark circle of sweat. Why did that make my skin flush? 'Come on. This'll blow your mind.'

We went past the first-floor landing and into the attic, which was up another flight of stairs. The room was musty and cobweb strewn, full of boxes and old furniture covered with dust sheets so they looked like crap ghosts. The room had a cool, silvery sheen and it took me a second to figure out why. There was a gangway cleared through the junk to a huge arched window. Pearly moonlight flooded the attic and it was ethereal somehow. 'Come take a look,' Nico urged, leading the way. He unlatched the window and threw it open. To my horror he ducked down and climbed outside.

'Nico! Are you freaking insane?'

'Don't jump! It's not worth it!' he said in his most melodramatic voice. 'It's fine – there's a ledge.'

Which was stronger? My dislike of heights or my lady-boner for Nico? Turns out hormones can override paralysing fear – just. I gripped the window ledge and tentatively poked my head outside. Nico was right, there was a sturdy balustrade running all the way around the roof – we couldn't fall unless we climbed over it.

'Oh wow,' I said, breath officially taken.

'I know, right?'

The attic window looked out over all of Brompton-on-Sea. The moon rippled on the sea like cream in black coffee, with boats drifting along the horizon. Far below, cars buzzed along the coast road like fireflies. It was a toy town or model village and, up here, we were like the gods of Olympus. I pinched a cargo ship between my thumb and forefinger. 'That's amazing.'

'It looks nicer from up here, doesn't it? You can't see how crap it is. You can't see the needles on the beach or the boarded-up shops.'

'I suppose everything looks nice from a distance.' We leaned back against the roof tiles, looking up at the sky and out over the town. I don't recall at what point I'd gripped Nico's hand for support, but I had. 'It's beautiful. I can see my house. It looks like a doll's house.'

'Look how *tiny* it is,' Nico said. 'Down there it feels pretty big, but the whole town is from here to here.' He held his hands up, a metre apart, sandwiching the whole town within. 'God, I can't wait to leave,' he sighed.

It made me sad. I didn't want Nico to leave. I wanted us to stay on this roof forever. A gust of wind blew my wig askew and I clung harder to his hand. 'I don't know,' I said, my voice frail. 'If I hadn't come here, I'd have never met you . . . guys.'

Nico looked right at me, into me, and my legs may as well have been hollow elastic tubes, that's how wobbly I felt. 'Yeah,' he said, 'well, you're a complication.'

I was pretty sure that wasn't a compliment. 'Sorry?'

'Ha! No, you're an excellent spanner in the works. It would have been so easy to set fire to this town and walk away in slow motion with the heat on my back, but then this amazing girl washes up like a bottle on the beach and I don't know . . .'

I gulped hard, and it felt like there was a stone in my throat. 'Are you saying I'm an amazing girl?'

'No, I'm talking about some other girl! Of course I mean you!'

'Good!' My heart inflated like a balloon, fit to burst. I forced myself to reply and not just gurn like the village idiot. 'Well, strictly speaking, my dad drove us here down the M1; I didn't wash up on the beach.' I smiled and he smiled right back.

'You know what I meant, pedant! I'm glad you came, Tor. I'd sort of given up on this town and then you arrived.'

There was a pause like the pause at the peak of a roller coaster.

He moved his face closer to mine and I could feel his warm breath on my cheek. He licked his lips. He didn't say a word, but he was searching for permission to kiss me, I could tell. I did so by moving a fraction closer, and he took his chance.

The roller coaster plummeted and we fell into the kiss.

At first he was inquisitive: light brushes against my lips. As I responded he got braver, his tongue searching for mine. I forgot the cool wind as his arms absorbed me, bodies pressed together. We were coiled together like a pair of horny snakes and it was brilliant. Our hands scouted out bold new territories, exploring arms and waists, fingers tracing my spine or slipping under the rim of my wig. Instinctively, I ran my hand over his hard chest and continued on to his equally taut stomach. I wondered if I was supposed to reach for his crotch, but he surfaced for air, so I didn't have to worry about it for long. 'God, I've wanted to do that since I first saw you,' Nico said, pulling back an inch.

I wasn't sure whether to be cool or be honest. 'Same.' I settled on honest. This time I initiated the kiss, drunk on the taste of him. He tasted like beer and spearmint gum.

I have no idea how long we were up there, and I would have stayed forever if my fingers and face hadn't started to go numb.

'We should go inside . . .' I said. I didn't want to stop but I was still aware I wasn't quite . . . ready. This wasn't how I wanted to lose my penis virginity: half frozen and on display to passing aeroplanes. I needed time . . . time to process things. It would have been so, so easy, but something inside me was hitting the brakes.

'Yeah, I'm fricking freezing,' Nico agreed without a trace of disappointment.

As I went to clamber back in through the window I saw Beetlejuice, or rather Beasley, watching us from the front garden. How long had he been watching for? Oh crap.

'Oh balls,' I said.

'What?'

'Nothing. I might need to go have a quick word with Beasley. I would very much like to do more kissing though, please.' Damn, that was Queen of Needy.

'Tor, we can kiss as much as you like. I just wasn't sure if you had me in the Friend Zone or not. I'm your Tesco Express for kisses – 24/7.'

Oh helium heart! That was exactly what I needed to hear. At the very back of my mind there had been a niggling worry that it might have been a one-off party snog. Apparently not.

The party was even busier when we got downstairs – a load of pierced, tattooed types had arrived, and it was a little more raucous than before. I made a beeline for Beasley who was trying to pour himself a Malibu and Coke, alone in the kitchen. I say *trying* because he was so blinky-wobble drunk, he was struggling to line the bottle up with the cup.

'Hey, Beas, let me get that for you.'

'There's Toria! We lost you!'

Maybe he hadn't seen us, but I wasn't buying it. I poured him a very weak drink – he'd already had enough – and led him to the sticky kitchen table.

'Are you OK, Beas? You seem a little wasted. Like ex-Disney Channel girl wasted.' I sat opposite him.

'I'm FINE!' he said in a high-pitched voice. 'Maybe the problem is, you're not drunk ENOUGH. Do a shot! Do a shot! Do a shot!'

'I'm OK, thanks. Look, I know you saw me and Nico on the roof and I know you might . . . have a problem with that.'

He swayed and blinked for a moment. 'And this, *this* my friend, is why you never tell Polly Wolff *anything*. You know she's such a bitch . . . I never told *anyone* when she thought she was pregnant. Oops!' He clamped a hand over his mouth. 'She wasn't by the way. Don't tell her I said that, she'll kick my ass.'

'I won't. But can we talk about it? Beasley, I love you but not like that. You're totally one of my best friends though. Isn't that better?'

'NO,' he moaned. He rested his heavy head on the table. He looked up at me like a sad beagle. 'It's not fair. I never get anyone.'

I took his hand across the table as there was a loud crash from the lounge, followed by Zoë screaming at some of her guests to be more careful. 'You don't have to answer this question, but you should. Is it really me you're after or is it Nico?'

His eyes narrowed like he was about to get angry but instead he slumped more over the table. He closed his eyes and a tear pooled in the corner by his nose. 'Of course it's Nico. It was always Nico.' His voice quivered.

'It's OK, it's OK. You don't need to say anything else.'

He nodded, eyes screwed shut to hold back the flood. 'Please don't tell anyone.'

'I won't. I really, truly promise.' I stroked his arm. 'But you know Nico isn't . . .?'

Beasley shrugged. I was about to talk further when there was a cry from upstairs. Shouting . . . arguing.

'Just ******* call a ******* ambulance!' It was Polly.

Beasley sat up straight and rubbed his eyes. 'Is that Polly? What's going on?' he said, sniffing. We stood together and followed the voices. People were leaking out of the lounge to see what the fuss was. I pushed past them and hurried up the stairs, pulse skittering in my neck.

Zoë, Nico and Alice were crowding around the bathroom door.

'What's going on?' I asked. You know when you can actually feel the colour draining out of your face? Well, that. I knew, from a primal, instinctual place, something was *seriously* wrong. My first fear was that Polly had cut herself again – perhaps too deeply this time.

I was wrong. I pressed myself up against Nico to see into the bathroom. Polly was crouched over Daisy who was splayed over the tiles.

She looked dead.

# Chapter Seven

# Blind

'What happened?' I gasped.

'She fainted or passed out or something,' Nico mumbled, also pale-faced.

'Please!' Polly's face was wet with tears. 'Just call an ambulance.'

'We can't! My dad will kill me!' Zoë was crying too.

This wasn't the time to stand around sobbing or to worry about Zoë's dad. I had got my phone out of my pocket and started to dial when Daisy stirred. It was so well-timed I wondered for a moment if she was faking in a strange bid for attention.

I dismissed the idea though. Daisy looked genuinely awful – her lips were chalk-white and her skin was sallow. She clung to Polly's arm, trying to drag herself up. I held off from dialling the third nine.

'Was she drunk?' I asked Nico, who only shrugged.

'Daisy?' Polly asked. 'Daisy, can you hear me?'

'Yeah, yeah. I'm fine. Please don't fuss. I felt light-headed.' Daisy sat up with our help, her eyes unfocused. 'I'm fine.'

'Are you sure? Should we call an ambulance?' Polly asked, wiping her tears.

'No. Don't be silly. I'll be OK. Can I please have some water?'

Zoë went to grab a glass. I crouched next to Polly on the bathroom floor. 'Daisy, have you taken something?' See? This is why drugs are bad.

'No, god no.' She tried to stand but she was unsteady on her feet. It was like watching Bambi learn to walk all over again.

'Maybe you should sit down,' I suggested and guided her to the rim of the bathtub.

'Polly, I want to go home,' she said, her mouth turning down at the edges, her voice wobbling.

'OK. Shall I call your mum?'

Daisy nodded and rested her head on my shoulder. I looked to Polly for some sort of explanation, but I didn't get one – she was already calling Daisy's parents.

And I didn't get an explanation for some time. Daisy's fainting spell signalled the end of both the party and my snogging for the evening. Halloween was on the Thursday and I didn't see anyone again until the Saturday night when we met up at the crazy-golf course. Daisy was absent.

'Have you heard from Daisy? Is she OK?' I asked as we got clubs and balls.

'Yeah, she's fine,' Polly said, not looking me in the eye.

'Well, was she drunk, or what?'

'Yeah, and I think she's coming down with something. She's not coming out tonight.'

I knew when I was being fobbed off, but I let it go because Nico arrived. Follow-up is always awkward. We *had* texted, pretty much constantly, since Halloween – apparently we were equally needy and addicted to mutual reassurance: *I had such a good time/You're a great kisser/When can we do it again?* I guess it's how you let someone know you like them. Better than being left hanging I supposed.

Still, seeing him again was tricky. 'Hey,' I said.

'Hey.' He took the initiative and kissed me lightly on the lips. Just like that, the awkward was banished. This was INSANE. How often does the guy you like like you back? This was too good to be true. Or maybe it wasn't. Perhaps soap operas and teen novels teach us that falling for someone has to be a big three-act melodrama, when actually it's like falling off a log.

So this is where the story should end, right? The girl got the guy. Wrong. If only it were that simple.

I threw a quick glance to Beasley who was hugely interested in his toes.

We played golf, but we couldn't keep our hands to ourselves. It felt naughty somehow. We couldn't stop, however much we didn't want to rub it in people's faces. One thing was for sure: although a huge (sensible) part of my head told me this could damage my fledgling friendships, there was no way I could stop it. We were Jack and Jill, tumbling downhill, gathering momentum as we went. By that stage, Nico and I felt inevitable, and I liked it.

He walked me home even though he lived on the other side of Brompton. We held hands. This wasn't like with Smithy, I wasn't *experimenting* or *playing* at Boyfriends & Girlfriends the way kids do on the playground. This felt real, at least to me it did. The potential was as real as his fingers knotted with mine. It was as exciting as it was scary. The future seemed closer than it ever had before: an approaching tornado made out of mortgages, Saturdays in Waitrose and Highland minibreaks.

I had concerns, of course I did. I think concerns are only natural. It was a lot of change – I'd never had a proper boyfriend before. I was also terrified about the fact he was leaving in a year, but you can't talk about things like that too early because they make you look like a psycho or a stalker. I told myself to enjoy the walk and stop worrying about a future that might not happen.

When we got to mine, we positioned ourselves behind a sturdy oak tree – so we couldn't be seen from the windows – and kissed for what felt like hours until my back was bruised from the gnarly tree trunk and my lips were swollen. Snogging: nature's own collagen filler. Hands down, kissing Nico was my new favourite thing ever. I was resolved. This close wasn't close enough. I wanted Nico to be My First.

'But I want to wait a while first,' I told Polly on the first day back. My fears about her ripping my face off with jealousy were totally unfounded. Quite the opposite in fact. She seemed happy and keen to know all the gory details. We were in the study room, hiding behind textbooks to disguise the conversation.

'Why?' Polly asked. 'You like him? Go for it.' Her bright red Halloween hair had faded to an orangey colour – not her best look.

'I dunno, I guess I want it to be special. You know, like, mean something.'

Polly rolled her eyes. 'Nothing means anything.'

I laughed. 'Oh that's deep.'

'No it's not. It's anti-deep.' She nibbled on a pear. 'You're overthinking it. If you like him, you should have sex with him. Why all the drama? It's like New Year's Eve.'

'What?'

'The more you build up to it, the more of a let-down it is. For realsies.'

I didn't want to admit that she probably had a point. 'Also . . . I'm nervous. There, I said it!'

'Well, of course you are,' she said. Then she added, 'But don't be. Nico is one of the good ones.' There it was again, for a split second and gone again: a spectre of sadness at the back of her eyes. Sometimes I wondered if I'd only truly met Polly twice – once when she told me about her cutting and once when she was freaking out about Daisy.

Speaking of Daisy, she rapidly became notable by her absence. OK, I got that she was sick, but when she hadn't returned to school by the Thursday after the hols I was worried. What was weirder still, no one wanted to talk about her. It was as if she'd been erased from existence. When I brought her up, the subject was rapidly changed. When Mr Gregory took the register, he no longer called her name – he obviously had the inside story. All I got from Polly, Nico and the others was 'she's sick'. I sent text after text to Daisy herself and got no response.

On the Friday, I decided I wasn't going to wait any longer. 'I'm going to go round to Daisy's tonight, I think.' Everyone looked at me as though I'd announced I was about to birth a squid. 'You know, I might take her some chocolate and magazines or something.'

We were in the common room. Freya lowered her book for a second. 'You don't take chocolate to an anorexic person,' she muttered before vanishing behind the book once more.

My jaw fell. Polly threw a venomous look in Freya's direction. Beasley and Alex grimaced. 'Oh brilliant.' This was the first time I'd been properly angry since I'd arrived at Brompton Cliffs. 'Thanks for keeping me in the loop.' I did something I wouldn't normally do. I picked up my bag and swished out of the common room like I was effing Beyoncé or something.

I had nowhere to go but I was just so mad. I ended up leaving campus to get a hot chocolate, although the £2.75 price tag did little to calm me down. This proved that my lovely 'insider' feeling was an illusion. I'd been left out in the cold, not worthy of such key information. I went to my next lesson and had to hold back tears the whole time. After about half an hour of petulant anger I became angry with myself – more than angry, livid. My own pathetic social status concerns had eclipsed the actual issue – Daisy was anorexic.

Of course, it all made perfect sense. She was *clearly* ill. She was . . . frail. I'd sort of thought when I met her, *gosh she's really skinny I wonder if she's anorexic,* and then forgotten it. I loved Daisy and didn't want to think bad thoughts about her. Or maybe I didn't want to think of her as a sick person. But sick she was.

* * *

Polly came round that night. Judas Cradle were playing a gig in Paignton so I was having a Friday night to myself with some films. It was actually nice to spend some time catching up on my YouTube channels. When Mum called up saying, 'Vicky, you have a friend here,' I was shocked. I didn't even know Polly knew where I lived.

Mum fussed over her. Isn't it so annoying how your parents are so much nicer to other people's children? Thankfully Mother didn't appear too drunk at this stage, although her lips and teeth had blueish traces of red wine on them. This was why I didn't bring friends home more often. I remember once, back home, I brought Smithy back to mine and she actually flirted with him. I could have stuck my head in the oven.

She sent us upstairs with Doritos and dips and a bottle of Sprite. I abandoned the food next to my laptop. 'Cool room.' Polly nodded at my posters and manga figurines.

'Not as cool as yours.' My room felt like a kid's room.

'Look.' Polly perched on my bed, which I *really* wished I'd made. 'I'm sorry about today, but you didn't need to throw a ******* ****-fit.'

'I know,' I conceded, 'but I was upset. Why didn't you tell me about Daisy? I felt like such an idiot. Can you imagine if I'd actually rocked up on her doorstep with a load of food?'

Polly half smiled. 'That would have been . . . unfortunate.'

'Well? Why didn't you tell me?'

'Because it's none of your business.'

I nearly burst into tears at that – partly because I felt excluded and partly because I hated myself for being so self-involved.

'I'm sorry but it isn't. Daisy hates people knowing; she's so embarrassed about it and she's trying so hard to get better.'

My eyes glazed over and I pinched my nose. Crying is so unhelpful. 'I wouldn't have minded . . . I love Daisy.'

Polly smiled. 'And she loves you. That's why she specifically didn't want you to know. She didn't want you to think of her as The Anorexic Girl. Everyone else does.'

'So *everyone* else knows? Great.'

'OK, you need to chill the **** out. This isn't about you, Tor. She's been sick since she was nine. She's been in and out of hospital. We all thought she was getting better – we hoped she wouldn't ever have to go back again – she's been out for about eighteen months. I thought it was a bit like me and my cutting . . . I sort of hoped she'd grown out of it.'

I took a breath. This really wasn't about me. Polly was right, I was being a dick. 'She's in hospital?'

'Yeah. Her body mass has dropped too low again so they're monitoring her food.'

'Oh god. Poor Daisy.'

Polly said nothing for a moment. 'We really thought last time would be the last time.'

She looked like she might cry. I was seeing Real Polly again. I went to sit beside her on the bed. 'Hey, it's OK. I'm sorry I gave you a hard time. I'm sure she'll be OK. I guess she's in the right place.'

Polly's blue eyes burned through her smudged kohl. 'It's so ******* hard, you know? You just want her to ******* eat. Have you ever had an anorexic friend?'

'No,' I admitted.

'Every day is this . . . battle. Her versus food. Even when she's eating it's a battle. I wish I could take the pain for her, you know? I think I could handle it.'

'Give her some credit. You said it started when she was nine? She's made it seven years.'

Polly nodded. 'Seven years of questioning every single thing she puts in her mouth. It's not like it is on Tumblr; it's not all arty black-and-white pictures of ribcages and ******* thigh gaps. I've watched her literally sweat over a handful of raisins. You know she's never had a period?'

Oh god. I struggled to find words. 'Well . . . maybe *we* can take some of the pain. Just by being there for her. Like you said, we can't make her eat. We *shouldn't* make her eat, she has doctors to do that. I suppose we have to give her reasons to eat. We need to be her reason to eat.'

Polly lay down on my lap, resting her head on my thigh. I stroked her ketchup-coloured hair off her face. 'You're pretty ******* wise, Grand.'

'Hardly.'

'We're going to the mental-health unit tomorrow if you want to come.'

'Do you want me to come?'

'Yeah, I really do.'

Alcohol hand gel and disinfectant. Hospital smell. No flowers allowed; they were a contamination risk. Obviously no grapes or chocolate. The adolescent mental-health unit was trying so hard to be cheery it was depressing. Walls painted the colour of sunshine, but it was so sterile. The ward was in disguise – framed pictures, throws and band posters – but there was no mistaking that smell. Daisy was in hospital. The heating whacked up, she wore just a T-shirt and I saw for the first time how frail she was, little more than elbows and knuckles.

'This is my collage.' Daisy showed us a sheet of A2 card with dozens of women cut out of magazines. 'On one side I have to glue women who look realistic and on the other side I have to glue women that look too thin.'

I was with Polly and Beasley in an activity room. It had the feel of a primary-school classroom. Daisy's mum was here too, but was presently off talking to the doctor. To my surprise she was very overweight and I couldn't stop a mean voice in my head from blaming her somehow, like it was her fault for overfeeding Daisy or something. I knew it didn't work like that. I suppose I needed to send my anger somewhere and screaming into my pillow hadn't helped.

'It's great,' Beasley said, examining her work.

'I've done it before,' Daisy admitted sadly. 'I know how to cheat. You have to make sure you put more on the too-skinny side so they think you have appropriate body perception.' She spoke so matter-of-factly. Polly had explained to me that, when it came to food, you couldn't trust a word that came out of Daisy's mouth. She knew every trick in the book to avoid eating. Seven years of 'accidentally' putting too much salt on food so it couldn't be eaten; seven years of carrying an empty McDonald's bag around so people thought she'd already had lunch; seven years of lunchtime clubs and crushed ice.

'Well, cheat,' Polly whispered. 'Just get out of here.'

'I will. I'm *gaining.*' The last word was spat out. Daisy looked as if she might cry. 'Although I got in trouble for trying to put stuff in my pockets at the weigh-in.'

I reached over the table and took her hand. It was freezing cold and as small as a child's. 'Do you want us to bring anything?' I said.

'You're very kind, but no thank you. I'm not planning on being here long.'

'Dais, what's going on?' Beasley said, his eyes glistening. 'You've been doing so well.'

Cornered, Daisy's face changed. She looked hard, vicious and ugly. It was like our Daisy was possessed, inhabited by a dark and tormented demon. 'I am trying, Beasley! God!'

'We know, we know,' Polly said soothingly. 'What he means is: why didn't you say something to us? We could have helped.'

'It's not that easy, Polly. I . . . I guess I was getting stressed out. Sixth form is harder than before. I don't know.' She shrugged. 'I just didn't want food any more. It was easier if I didn't eat.'

Polly had explained that usually anorexia is about feeling lost and helpless. In a world where everything was so out of control – even her own body – food was something that Daisy *could* control. I'd tried so hard, but I still couldn't get my head around it. If I don't eat every couple of hours I get a) hungry and b) evil. I honestly had no idea how broken Daisy must be to be able to ignore that hunger. So I'd looked it up. Daisy was every bit as hungry as I was; she just chose to fight it. That battle Polly had talked about.

'What's it like here?' I asked quietly.

'Oh it's basically Disneyland. What do you think?' she snapped before cooling. 'I'm sorry. I'm so sorry, Toria. I hate it here so much. There's one other anorexic girl and then a load of horrible boys. I hate them.' One of the 'horrible boys', an exhausted-looking guy with angry cigarette burns all over his arms glared at us from the other side of the activity room. 'They *force* me to eat. They sit next to me and make sure I swallow. All they care about is my weight so they can shove me back into the real world. "Quick, feed her up!" I feel like a Christmas turkey.'

'You know why they do it, and that's what your therapy's for.' When she wanted to be, Polly could be almost maternal. 'You just tell me if you're having the thoughts, OK?'

'I know. I know.' Daisy explained how her therapists had taught her to recognise the onset of thoughts about food – how to anticipate changes and recognise triggers before she relapsed.

For the rest of the visit, we chatted about school and gossip and the Daisy I knew returned. She lit up as I told her about Nico. I tried to play it down a little for Beasley's benefit, but I think even he saw the effect it was having on Daisy. 'I have got to get out of here,' Daisy concluded. 'I'm missing too much fun. I miss the golf course. I can't believe you're going without me!'

'You are getting out of here,' Polly said with steely-eyed determination. 'And you're not coming back. Ever.'

I was angry after that visit. So angry. Blisteringly angry. I got out my poetry book and wrote, as squally rain pummelled my window.

**The Alphabet Diet**

A is for Atkins and absent periods
B is for Best Bikini Body Bones!
C is for cotton-wool balls soaked in orange juice
D is for double chins and bingo wings
E is egg-white omelettes
F is fingers for dessert
G is for glycaemic index and garden salad
H is for hunger pangs
I is for ignoring them
J is for journalists who should know better
K is for ketosis and Kardashian
L is for LipoLite
M is for muffin top metabolic myth
N is nothing tastes as good as objectification feels
O is opening the fridge at two a.m. in private
P is for 'proudly flaunts her curves'
Q is questioning every mouthful
R is for ribcage xylophone
S is starvation selfie
T is for thigh-gap thinspiration
U is under 500 calories a day, twice a week
V is for vomit and vocal chords

W is women watching Weight Watchers points
X is an X-ray looking fat
Y is for yo-yo yoghurt laxatives
Z is for zero. Size zero. Zero. Nothing left at all.

# WINTER

# Chapter Eight

# Erection

Now, I appreciate you might be thinking that this is all a bit issues galore and mega emo. Well, sorry, but that was what happened. It would be neater, wouldn't it, if this was a story about self-harm *or* sexuality *or* eating disorders *or* drunk mums *or* ridiculously hot bass players, but it's a story about all of them. Yeah, it's a mess. And it's about to get messier if you'll bear with me. That's the way it is sometimes – nothing's ever neat and tidy.

In fact, it's chaos. Total fucking chaos. Crazy-toothless-homeless-man-banging-two-pan-lids-together chaos.

Daisy was out of the hospital not long after Bonfire Night, having gained sufficient weight and proven she could independently prepare and eat adequate meals. What was weird was how much healthier she looked. Although she still wrapped herself in voluminous jumpers and scarves, it was clear her cheekbones weren't jutting through her face quite as much.

The rest of the school, it seemed, was more than used to Daisy vanishing and reappearing and no one made much of a fuss on her return.

I was part of the conversation now. It turned out that Daisy's illness had been cleverly hidden from me in the first half-term. I finally got an insight into the problem when we sat alone together one lunchtime in the common room. Every meal and snack was clearly hard for her. Finally, I saw what the others had been dealing with for years.

Before Daisy sat a small wholemeal bread roll filled with tuna. She was staring it down like they were a pair of cowboys at dawn. 'Do you think there's a lot of butter on it?'

'I don't know,' I replied, suddenly uncomfortable.

'You see, my mum made it and I'm a bit worried she might have accidentally used the full-fat mayonnaise.'

'It looks . . . fine. It's just a little tuna sandwich.' I really wished I hadn't said that. It was so much more than just a tuna sandwich.

'Well, do you think I should eat all of it or have half?'

This questioning process accompanied everything she ate. The important thing, Polly assured me, was that she was eating. Polly was now working on the basis that when Daisy *wasn't* talking about food was when we should really worry.

'I think you should eat it all,' I said and her eyes widened. 'I know. But if you don't the anorexia wins. If you eat the sandwich, *you* win.'

She took my hand across the table and squeezed it. 'Thank you. I know. That's just not what it feels like.' Daisy nibbled a corner of the sandwich.

'I'm proud of you. You can beat the shit out of that tiny little sandwich, Dais.' I looked her dead in the eye and she swallowed triumphantly.

For the first couple of weeks after she returned, Polly became more protective than ever, almost like a lioness prowling around her cubs. If anyone said anything, or even *looked* funny at Daisy, she'd rip into them as if they were helpless gazelles. She confided in me as we ate leftover Halloween sweets at the golf course that she secretly feared Daisy preferred it in the hospital because she had no responsibility there, that Daisy found life was so much *easier* with people feeding her and scheduling every second of her day. As I listened I realised it must be very easy to live without choices.

My other worry, and I did so love to take on other people's worries – it made up for the relative lack of my own – was Beasley. I was, as far as *I* knew, the only person who *he* knew knew he was gay. Complicated. We talked about it over a *Nightmare on Elm Street* marathon. It was just the two of us, which maybe made it easier. I don't know why Beasley confided in me, perhaps it was because I was new and didn't have the history he had with the others. He told me he was very confused, that he wanted to like girls and did like girls but that he definitely/maybe liked guys too. Nico was his first boy crush.

'Well, maybe you're bisexual?' I told him as Freddy Krueger slaughtered Johnny Depp.

'Maybe. God, I hate that word. I hate "gay" too. I hate it.' He sighed. 'You know, I know everyone at school thinks I'm a faggot.' I flinched at that. 'I'm not deaf. I hate that I'm proving them right, you know? And I've totally shagged loads of girls.'

'Beasley . . .' I said. 'It doesn't matter what people say. "We don't keep score", remember?'

He humphed. 'But I don't want to be this way.'

I shrugged, feeling utterly flaccid. 'We don't get a choice.'

If I'd had a magic wand for Beasley and Daisy I'd have waved it vigorously, but there wasn't a lot I could do except listen and be as peppy as any cheerleader.

Because in other ways, you see, my life was pretty damn sweet. Yes, you would be right in assuming I'm talking about Nico. Things were going swimmingly. A couple of weeks into November we were official. O.F.F.I.C.I.A.L. I knew this because he introduced me to the rest of the band as his girlfriend after a gig at The Mash Tun. I was taken along to the after-party and everything, and then the next day we made it even more official. We announced it on Facebook. There was only one small problem with this. My dad is on Facebook.

'Do you really think now is a good time to be getting a serious boyfriend?' My mother peered over the red wine she was cradling.

'Yes,' I replied. We were sitting at the dining-room table having finished a pretty good shepherd's pie. Mum can be weird about meals. She once told me she didn't want the house smelling of curry all the time. I don't know why it bothers her. Dad thinks she was embarrassed by it when she was little and was the only brown girl in the village. 'I don't have exams until January and they're only mocks.'

'Victoria, there's really no need to be so defensive all the time. Your mum asked you a perfectly reasonable question.'

My dad was tired, I could tell. He was looking old for the first time; when I wasn't paying attention his hair had thinned to almost nothing.

'Your results haven't been stellar,' Mum reminded me.

'And Polly and I are going to revise together. I told you. My friends, that you seem to dislike for no reason other than the colour of their hair, are all borderline geniuses, genii, or whatever, so you don't need to worry.'

'Toria,' Dad said. 'We haven't even met your friends, so that's not fair. Why don't you invite this Nico Mancini over for dinner next week?'

'Because that would be so awful I would have to kill myself.'

'Spare us the melodramatics, Vicky, please.' I swear she called me Vicky to drive me crazy. 'I think that's a great idea. He does speak English, doesn't he?'

I scowled at her. 'Yeah, Mum, why not be a little bit racist too? That's really nice.'

Mum laughed and it made me want to tip the shepherd's pie on her head. 'That's not racist! It's a foreign name!'

'Whatever, The Woman Formally Known As Kiran Dhesi.'

'Toria,' Dad said again, this time firmly. 'Indulge us. We'll be a lot happier if we get to meet this boyfriend of yours.'

Surprisingly, although I don't know why I was surprised given that he was so cool, Nico was actually keen on the idea. He would be; he didn't know the full horror of my parents. I knew, on a very fundamental level, that they would talk to him about THE WEATHER and MY CHILDHOOD and possibly even CONDOMS. Mum would probably get drunk and flirt with him. It would be awful.

I spent the week in the run-up to the dinner party (which my mum infuriatingly referred to as 'having Nico over for tea') thinking of ways to kill my parents and get away with it. The best idea was double-poisoning-suicide-pact because it didn't involve me burning down the house. Don't judge me. I was terrified that they'd do or say something to put Nico off me. Around my parents I feel about three years old and that's not sexy.

Just when you think things can't get worse, they inevitably do. Turned out Nico's mum wanted to meet me too. Brilliant. That was just brilliant.

I shall tackle the two evenings in the style of the A-level essays Polly was training me to pass:

***Compare and contrast two evenings in which a young couple must meet their respective parents.***

I'll start with my evening, because that came first. I spent the time before Nico arrived frantically deformalising things. 'You want him to think you're mature don't you?' Mum asked as she set candles, yes *candles*, on the table.

'Yeah, but I don't want him to think you're seducing him either.' I put the candles away. Despite my mum's pleas I refused to dress smart. I wore a skirt, but then I often did. There was soft classical background music playing on the kitchen speakers, which was baffling as that was something we NEVER DID EVER. It was like they were actively trying to be posher. Who did they think he was? Prince Harry? (God, I wish.)

Nico arrived and was ushered into the living room after being made to remove his shoes. We weren't allowed the TV on because we had to talk. 'So, Nico,' my dad started, 'what's the sixth-form college in Cransford like?'

'It's OK. Probably not as nice as Brompton Cliffs, but it sort of feels less like school if you know what I mean.'

'Yes. I expect they treat you more like adults – like students?'

Christ this was boring chat.

'I think so. What is it you do?' Nico played it beautifully – asking thoughtful questions and being interested – much as Beth had taught me, but without the added filthy bit thrown in.

Let's compare that beginning to my arrival at Nico's house a week later. Nico lived in one of the neat terraces just off the high street. As I arrived at the address he'd texted me I saw there was a gigantic St Bernard dog filling the downstairs bay window and there was still a Halloween skeleton hanging off the door. 'It's open!' a voice yelled when I knocked.

I entered a whitewashed hall – the carpets had been taken up to reveal long pale floorboards and it felt a little like I was boarding a boat. The walls were covered with photos, fabrics and dreamcatchers. With one that big, I wasn't surprised at how much the house smelled of dog.

An elastic-looking woman in Spandex hurried in from the kitchen at the end of the hall, almost kicking a cat out of the way in the process. 'You must be Toria! Darling, come on in. Please excuse the mess! It's been bananas! Bananas!' She had a strong Italian accent and a mane of frizzy black hair down to her bottom.

'Hi,' I said. 'It's nice to meet you, Mrs Mancini.'

'Oh don't you dare! Call me Sofia!' Everything she said came with exclamation marks. 'Take a seat in the lounge. My

Nico will be down in a second.' The lounge was as chaotic as the hall and the kitchen – books and vinyl spilling off shelves. Tellingly, there was no TV. You heard right. NO TV.

Back to my house a week earlier. Let's compare menus. My mum made a starter. Prawn cocktail. Why? As soon as we were seated the interrogation began. I was horrified that my dad was being just as full on as Mum: 'Which uni are you thinking about?' (Who says 'uni' any more, seriously); 'What do you think you'll study?' 'Music? Oh really? What do you hope to do with a music degree?'; 'Not a lot of money in music, is there?'

They might as well have shone a lamp in his eyes.

However, an unexpected bonus of having Nico over was that Mum drank more conservatively than I had seen her do in months, like she didn't want him to think she was a massive lush. That was A-OK with me.

And now back to Nico's house. We had dinner around a retro Formica table in the kitchen. Nico's two (and might I add adorable) little sisters had been fed before me, so Nico and his mum gathered for our dinner – a colourful stir-fry with everything thrown in. It was as light and airy as Sofia herself. Sofia talked mainly about herself: 'Everyone should dance in Paris while they're young'; 'You don't find Bali; Bali finds you'; 'Yoga isn't my job, isn't a career – it's what I am.'

What I found a little unsettling was her constant grooming of Nico. It was like she couldn't keep her hands off him – brushing his hair off his face, gripping his hand or massaging his shoulder. It was a bit creepy. Between you and me, I wouldn't be at all surprised if it turned out Sofia had breastfed Nico well after he could ask for it, but I kept that thought to myself.

If we're discussing differences, let's talk about atmosphere. My dining room: dark, oppressive, stifling. Their kitchen: laughter, exuberance, spontaneity. By the time my mum plonked huge helpings of sticky toffee pudding in front of us, I was so full I could hardly move. After Sofia had finished telling us about her time on a Greenpeace vessel, she dismissed us with two spoons and a tub of Häagen-Dazs.

The real difference though was the end of the evening. It was made abundantly clear that Nico would not be seeing 'my room' that evening. He was even made to use the downstairs loo. Sofia, however, shooed us out of the kitchen and we went up to Nico's room.

It didn't occur to me how momentous this could be until I got there. OK, his mum was downstairs but what if Nico thought we were going to have the sex? I know it sounds crazy, but I still wasn't ready to catch the train to Sexeter with Nico. I can't explain why, but it felt so scary. I dearly hoped that when the time came I would just KNOW and want to do it. I knew I should want to; he was gorgeous. I thought about it a lot.

His room was packed full of music stuff. I had no idea he was such a polymath: not only were there two basses but there was also a guitar, a saxophone and a cello stuffed into his boxy room. It was such a squeeze that the only space left for us to sit was on his bed. I felt that was a bad idea, but there was no other choice.

'Are you OK?' he asked.

'Of course. Are you going to play me something?'

Nico smouldered at me. I cannot smoulder, but Nico was more than capable. 'I was thinking I could play with you for a bit?'

'OK,' I said, trying to hide my terror with a smile.

Nico tried to make the ice cream sexy, kissing it off my lips, but I'm not sure that very cold sticky dairy goods are that hot and horny to be honest. We abandoned the ice cream and made out the regular way. I don't know how else to explain it except to say that he turned me on. It's like a *heat* inside, you know, *down there*. I suppose it's biology, but while my body was saying GO, my head was saying WAIT. It also said HIS MUM IS LISTENING – EW.

No one, believe me, was more frustrated than me. Well, except perhaps Nico.

I let his hands go under my clothes. Lightly, so lightly, his fingers traced my breasts, my nipples, down my stomach. As he ran them over my hips I shivered. That felt good for me and, I sensed, for him. Nico, cute as ever, had developed a knack of poking his jean-trapped stiffy against my leg to let me know how turned on he was. That's not as pervy as it sounds, and I was genuinely glad to know that I was turning him on too.

And yet I still wanted to wait. 'Nico, steady.' I grabbed his hand as it slid into my pants. 'Don't get carried away . . .'

'I want to get carried away. Don't you? I mean, I'm happy to wait but . . . am I doing something wrong?'

'No! God no! I just . . . I just think I'll know when it's time. I'm sorry.'

'Don't be. It's fine. I'm happy . . .' He poked his erection against my leg again.

I brought it up with Polly at the golf course. We dangled our legs off the edge of the pirate ship. The wood was still a little damp from where it had rained earlier and my bum was both cold and numb, but I didn't want to go inside. Polly had decided to smoke this week for some reason and, I have to admit, she wore it well. Oh come on, I think we've already established Polly Wolff isn't exactly role-model material – let it go. As with all drugs, I believed that smoking would kill me and turn my lungs into blackened phlegm sacks, so I refrained.

'I don't know what's wrong with me,' I said, confessing my sexual woes.

'Don't ******* start booing about it. It's totally normal to be nervous. I was.'

I looked at her and readied myself. 'Did you have sex with Nico?'

'Honest answer?'

'Yes.'

'No. Not "full penetrative sexual intercourse" as Miss Foley would say.' She used crude hand gestures to show what they had done. It was petty but I really wished they hadn't; I suppose everyone likes to think of their boyfriends and girlfriends as unsullied and fresh out the box. However, I was grateful for her honesty.

'Was Nico your first . . . well, whatever he was?'

Polly twirled a lock of newly purple hair around her finger. 'Nope.'

'So who was?'

'With a boy or girl?'

I almost fell off the pirate ship but managed to maintain something that could pass for composure. 'You're bisexual?'

She scowled in distaste. 'Bitch, please. Labels are for **** you buy in shops.'

I was aghast and embarrassed. How CRAP of me to assume she was straight. It became horribly clear that I assumed everyone was default straight, and I should have known better. Still, Polly had *never* mentioned girls. But I also realised that, aside from Nico, she didn't really mention boys . . . except for her unrequited crush on Etienne.

'Sorry.' I tried to keep the shock off my unworldly little face. 'So which came first?'

'Girl. Tanya. She ****** me when I was fourteen on Year 9 camp.'

My eyes widened. 'Can two girls . . .?'

'****? Duh, of course.' She made another crude hand gesture and I more than got the picture.

'I wasn't so nervous that time, it mostly felt like we were playing. For some reason peens are really scary, like a flesh spear flying towards your nether-regions!'

'I know, right!' I threw my hands up. 'And Nico's doesn't strike me as a little one!'

'Limited experience, but I suspect you're right.' Polly offered me a cigarette which I obviously declined. 'Look. It's going to be scary, but go with it. All the best things are scary.'

I sighed. 'I guess once I get the first time over and done with it'll be OK.'

Polly smiled a secret smile. 'Nope. Every time is scary if it's someone you really like. But good scary – like an adrenaline rush.'

'I thought you said nothing meant anything?'

'Tors, you should have figured it out by now. I talk a lot of ****.' She smiled and lay flat on the cool planks to look up at the sky. I lay alongside her. Black clouds looked like Rorschach-test inkblots in the indigo sky. 'I spend way too much time in my head,' Polly went on. 'You know sometimes I totally ******* annoy myself.'

'Oh god, me too.'

'Like, sometimes I spend all this time thinking about myself and I think I must be the most self-involved **** ever, and I get so cross at myself and that's just even more time in my head. I go around and around in these little circles. You know what I mean?'

I did and I didn't, but I agreed with her. Far, far up above, landing lights flickered on the wings of an aeroplane. 'When I was little,' I finally said, 'I used to think that planes were UFOs and that the aliens were coming to take my mum and dad away from me.'

Polly swivelled round to face me. 'No way! I used to think that too – my sister used to watch this show called –'

'*The X Files*? Yeah, that's where I got it too. My babysitter used to let me watch it on Sky. It terrified me.'

'Me too.' Polly grinned at me. After a moment she said, 'You know what my mum said to me today?'

'No. Because I'm not Jean Grey. Yet.'

'She said, "Where do you think you'll be in ten years?" I mean what the **** are you meant to say to that?'

'What did you tell her?'

'That I didn't have a ******* clue. What would you have said?'

I thought about it. Twenty-seven, yikes. I pictured myself in a tailored skirt suit, marching somewhere in heels with a venti latte. It looked all wrong. 'I have no idea. It's scary. Scarier than

Nico's willy in fact.' Her silence told me she felt the same way. 'I hope we're still friends though.'

She faced me and looked at me as if I was speaking Punjabi. 'Of course we will be. This is forever.'

In the absence of a shooting star, the aeroplane would have to do. I made my wish: I never wanted this – this night, this feeling – to end.

I wrote this about Polly. I didn't tell her.

**Grrrl**

Crack den sherbet dip
Safety pin tights rip
Hotel / motel
Don't care, won't tell
White lip bruise eye
Razor blade cherry pie
Knuckleduster scapegoat
Sheep in wolf's coat
Vodka chunks daisy chain
Chewing gum on my brain
Shoplift, rosebud
That one's no good
Red mouth lioness
Chainmail undressed
Fast forward on repeat
Aphrodite on her knees.

# Chapter Nine

# Sex

I got an A on my French writing assignment. YAAAASSSSSS! Thanks to the combined efforts of Daisy and Polly I was actually doing well again. That was the thing with my new friends – they still felt new, and I still felt like a newcomer – it was us against the rest of the school. We were all getting out of Brompton-on-Sea, and, as Polly had promised, no one was getting left behind. Polly was taking Psychology with Beasley, and she was coaching him as well. There was no concept of who was doing best, all that mattered was getting our tickets out of town. I don't know if I'd ever seen such determination. Perhaps the key to educational achievement lies in sending young people to dreary dead-end seaside towns.

The nights grew longer and colder but we still went to the golf course, only in more clothes. Jamie clearly HATED us – he just wanted to shut the kiosk and go home. No such luck.

Initially I was fascinated with Polly being . . . not bi, but bi . . . or queer? LOOK, sometimes labels are quite handy for describing stuff, OK? I gave Beasley a super-hard time for not saying anything – it felt like yet another loop I'd been left out of. 'I can't believe you didn't tell me!' I spanked his bum with a golf club at Hole 3.

'Ow! I thought you knew. We don't talk about it at school for obvious reasons but she always has liked both. She dated Zoë for about five minutes.'

'Wow, she's really working her way through that band.'

'Ha! Yeah!'

I pulled my bobble hat further down my head. 'God, is everyone in Brompton gay or what?'

Beasley's eyes widened as he checked no one was listening in. 'I know, right? We joke that the year we were born doctors were carrying out genetic experiments on the maternity ward. The theory actually stands up pretty well. There's me,' he said under his breath, 'Pol, Zoë, Etienne's not fussed either way, and *clearly* Marcus Brady in Year 13.'

'Oh, "Marcus Gaydy"? Yeah, I heard about him.'

'Yeah, he, like, totally tried to hit on me once.' Well, that *had* to be a lie. Marcus Brady looked like a Burberry model. Beasley . . . less so. 'And I wouldn't be surprised if Alex was keeping something secret. I don't think straight guys like dressing up as much as he does. Can I have a turn with the gloves?' It was so cold but Beasley had forgotten his so we were taking it in turns to wear mine. Polly, Daisy and the others were hanging out at the kiosk. 'Thanks. What about you, Tor? Ever kissed a girl and liked it?'

'No,' I said too quickly. 'I mean . . . no.'

'You never kissed a girl or you never liked it?'

'Either! Oh, well, except Polly when we played spin-the-bottle.'

Beasley smirked. 'Polly had the biggest crush on you when you got here. Don't tell her I said that; she would rip my balls off and shove them in my eye sockets.'

My mouth fell open. 'What?' I dearly hoped this was Beasley being economical with the truth again.

'Oh god, you must have noticed! She's hardly subtle, is she?'

'I really didn't.' My heart lolloped around my chest. I recalled the night I'd slept in her bed, our bodies pressed together. Had she been aroused? Worse, had I led her on? Awk. I replayed the evening in my mind, looking for lesbian faux pas. I didn't know whether to be bothered or not. She probably should have told me, I thought. Would it have made a difference? Would I have still slept alongside her if I'd known she had a crush? I couldn't decide if there was a tiny bit of homophobia lurking somewhere inside me like a parasite, or if I was simply annoyed at not being told.

As winter got even more wintery, and the walk to school became a veritable ice rink, I resented Beasley for ever saying anything at all. It changed how I was with Polly. I scrutinised every sentence and glance, looking for signs that she still might be internally shipping us. I couldn't see any immediate differences but when you dwelled on it for as long as I did, things became more ambiguous. She was always grabbing my hand and dragging me places, always playing with my hair. What did it all mean?

I thought she was my best friend. Was she only hanging out with me because she fancied me? That was an awful thought. In the end I confided in Daisy who I knew would tell me straight. 'Whatever Beasley said, she wasn't hopelessly in love or anything,' she said in perfect French during French class. She was working on the latest instalment of the Geoff Squirrel saga. In this episode, Geoff had been locked up in an asylum because no one else would believe his fake baby was evil.

Poor Geoff.

I frantically flicked through my French dictionary trying to catch up. 'Is she over it?' I asked, pretty sure in French that literally meant, 'Has she climbed over it?'

'*Oui!*' Daisy assured me. 'It's not a big deal.'

Semi-satisfied, I agreed to something so shocking, you may need to sit down while reading the next sentence.

I agreed to participate in the Christmas carol concert.

I KNOW. No one was more surprised than me. It turned out that the gang were VERY into Christmas. Perhaps 'Being Really Excited About Christmas' was the new 'Being Over Christmas', as I had been for, like, the last three years. It was all a blur of advent calendars (there was a bet as to who could find the most joyless, overtly religious one), swapping Christmas cards and posting letters to Santa at the local supermarket. Apparently you got a reply.

I found myself swept along with the excitement. We even went, en masse, to the grand switching on of the town lights. We swaddled ourselves in scarfs and hats and stood in the drizzle as the weather girl from the local news and a former *X Factor* contestant switched the lights on. 'Ooooh,' we said, followed by 'Aaaaah', although they weren't very impressive. Some of the flickering candle illuminations looked like willies.

Polly would be allowed to have a few friends around for a shindig once we broke up so we did Secret Santa in preparation for our Christmas-Before-Christmas. I got Beasley and started to think of something horror-y to get him. I'd get Nico something too, and maybe Polly and Daisy. Secret Santa, it transpired, was oppressive to my newfound seasonal joy. I wanted to get everyone something!

Rehearsals were every Tuesday and Friday and quickly became my new favourite thing. Night-time now oozed in a little before four, but it felt safe and warm inside the main school hall. Icy windows fogged up and the room smelled clean and pine-tinged from the Christmas tree that filled a whole corner from floor to ceiling. It was a weird marriage of the music folk to the rest of us. Beasley, Alice and Alex were all in the concert band so that left Polly, Daisy and I in the choir with a few of the Pot-Pourri girls and a new social subgroup – the Theatre Studies gang. All of them were mini Lea Micheles and all of them were going to MAKE IT.

Polly invented a fantastic game for us to play during rehearsals: The Fake Lyrics game. The idea was to subtly sing along with made-up lyrics – just loud enough for us to hear. The winner was anyone who could get the rest of us to crack up. First up was 'Away in a Manger': '*Away in a manger, I never give head,*' sang Polly. '*I might get mouth herpes and wind up all dead.*'

My turn. '*The little Lord Jesus sells drugs to the kids.*' Polly had to stifle a laugh.

'*The stars in the bright sky turned everyone gay,*' finished Daisy and we all cracked up.

'Girls!' snapped Mrs Randall, the choirmaster. 'Is there a problem?'

'No, miss,' we all said in unison.

Some sessions we played a different game where we took it in turns to sing one word each. It certainly made rehearsals more fun.

'*Silent.*' Polly.

'*Night.*' Me.

'*Holy.*' Daisy.

'*Night.*' Polly again . . .

'*All.*'

'*Is.*' Daisy.

'*Calm.*'

'*All.*'

'*Is* . . . why do I keep getting "is"? That's a rubbish word.'

'*Bright.*'

It's harder than it looks.

More significant than carols and gingerbread lattes, I decided in the run-up to Polly's party that this was going to be it. I was going to lose my penis virginity to Nico. I felt there was only so much kissing and rubbing his crotch I could get away with. I know planning it doesn't sound particularly romantic, but as much as I'd have liked it to be wild and spontaneous, that wasn't happening, so I was taking matters into my own hands. Literally. Once we'd got the first time out of the way, I hoped things would happen more organically.

'Polly . . .' We were chatting in the sixth-form study room the week before the party. This close to Christmas, everyone was winding down – even the miserly librarian had strung some threadbare tinsel along the front of the counter. 'I think I'm ready to have sex with Nico. At your party.'

She paused. I wanted an honest reaction. If Polly *was* into me, I wanted to know. This method was a little backhanded, but I figured her reaction would tell me everything I needed to know. 'Oh. OK.' Her response was neutral.

I didn't get it. If she'd had such a big crush on me, why had she given me her blessing to date Nico in the first place? Still, I thought it polite to ask. 'Is that OK?'

Polly merely shrugged. 'I guess so. What do you want me to say? No one ever *really* wants to think about their friends getting it on. It's gross.'

'I mean about using your place.'

'Yeah, whatever. Have my bed. I'll take the sofa bed in the study.' Her face remained unreadable.

'Are you sure?'

Polly arched a brow. 'Sure. Who am I to **** up young love?'

Beasley was wrong about Polly, I knew it. 'You're the best. I mean it. Thank you so much . . . for everything.' I hoped being my best friend would be an OK consolation.

'All right, calm down. I only said you could use my bed; we don't need to have a ******* Hallmark moment.'

'I meant for everything since I got here. Can you believe it's nearly Christmas already? I've been here a whole term. Like, where has time gone?'

Polly leaned in conspiratorially. 'Do you want to know a secret?'

'Do I ever.'

'Don't tell anyone, but we're the best ones.' She scanned the library. 'Look at all of these beige people. They all think we're freaks but none of them are ever going to do anything. They're going to die here and before that they'll be estate agents or nail technicians and marry men called Dave and watch reality TV in the bedroom. We're better than them. I'm glad you're here, Tor.'

I rolled my eyes. No one was listening so I have no idea why I felt the need to defend. 'There's nothing wrong with that . . .'

'Do you want to be a nail technician?'

I waggled my chewed, chipped nails in her face.

'We're gonna be ******* magnificent. Mag-nif-i-cent.'

There were things to get ready before SEX NIGHT, as it was now called. Nico was in on the plan. I told him when we were kissing next to the Loch Ness monster one night. 'I'm ready . . . to . . . go all the way,' I said.

He said, 'Cool.'

And that was that. There were practical considerations:

1. The pill – I was not on the pill. Maybe I should be on the pill. I didn't want to discuss STIs with

Nico because they were not sexy, but I thought it best if we used a condom.

2. Condoms – who would get them? Nico's college had a drop-in-nurse-centre thing, so he could get some from there.

3. My vagina – having only properly seen my one and (ACCIDENTALLY) the exterior of my mum's, I was only half confident that I had a pretty one. I'm not Amish; I've logged on to porn sites so I assumed Nico had too. According to porn, I should shave off everything I've got down there, but Polly assured me she had not, so a realistic amount of pubic hair wasn't going to terrify the boy. I was increasingly paranoid about the aroma of my vagina as well. Some of the less charming boys in Year 12 had spread a particularly vicious rumour about Summer next door and her 'fishy fanny'. Between that and scented sanitary towels I was beginning to worry that women were being subtly brainwashed into hating their own vaginas. I really hope boys have to worry about shit like this too.

4. Will it hurt? I understood it was going to hurt, but what are we talking on a scale of one to ten where one is 'ouchie' and ten is 'GET IT OUT'?

5. Performance – again, I have watched porn, but I'm not an idiot. Surely no one thinks that is how sex actually goes, but I did want Nico to think of me as a sexy person. I wasn't going to go and buy flammable underwear and whipped cream or any crazy crap, but I hoped that sex was something you could be inherently good at the first time you tried it. This was especially hard because Nico *had* done it before. He knew I hadn't and didn't seem to care, but I did.

Polly's party was a much calmer affair than Zoë's had been. It was just the gang. Dress code: Christmas jumpers. Polly had made a playlist of creepy old Christmas songs that were playing as we arrived. Typically, for a girl who sought to avoid cliché, it was a most un-Polly-like affair – we were each given a glass of mulled wine and we gathered in the lounge like grown-ups where there were nibbles and a cheese board. This felt like the most grown-up gathering I'd ever been to. I liked that.

Polly's parents had gone to London for their annual Christmas shopping/theatre/hotel extravaganza, so we had the place to ourselves. When we'd all arrived it was time for Secret Santa around the open fire. I'd bought Beasley a book about feminism in slasher films, which he seemed genuinely happy to get. My secret Santa was Alice. My initial disappointment in this reveal was unfounded – she'd got me the one Studio Ghibli film I didn't already have. Either I'd mentioned it in passing or she'd asked Polly, but I was thrilled.

'Thank you so much!' I gave her a warm hug, which she reciprocated.

'It's OK,' she replied, monosyllabic as ever.

'Can I make a toast?' Daisy asked and we agreed she definitely should. 'I wanted to say that this has been the best year. Yes, I know I just got out of hospital and that's pretty crummy, but when things were really bad I thought about all of you lot. When I did, I pictured you, like I was sucking your life force or something. Polly, I thought about your strength; Beasley, I thought of your hugs; Nico, I thought of how wise you are; Alice, I thought of your calm; Freya, I thought about your cleverness; Alex, I thought of how confident you are. Toria, when I thought about you, I thought about your hope – you always have so much hope.' I'd never thought about it, but I supposed she was right. 'And look! It worked! I'm so excited about being here and I really love you guys. So to you and you and you and you and you and you and you!'

We all toasted. 'Here's to us,' Polly said. 'And Merry ******* Christmas one and all.'

While the others watched *A Muppet Christmas Carol*, Nico and I slipped away. It probably wasn't nearly as subtle as we intended and I definitely caught Polly watching us go. I couldn't read her expression: it wasn't jealousy, it wasn't anger, it wasn't sadness . . . it was indifference, and that was even worse.

I closed Polly's bedroom door behind me, leaving the child version of me standing on the landing. I felt the same way I had felt going into my Year 11 exams – terrified and resigned. I was back on the roller coaster and we were chugging up the first hill; there was no getting off now. Keep your hands inside the carriage at all times. This was fine. This was momentous and it was going to be great, I told myself. 'I made a playlist,' Nico said, plugging his iPhone into Polly's dock.

'Oh good idea.' The fact that Nico had spent some time planning tonight meant a lot.

'Are you nervous?' Nico asked, rubbing his hands on his jeans. 'It's OK, if you are. I think if you talk about being nervous you always feel less nervous.'

'I am. I really am.' The mulled wine had taken the edge off, but it was taking everything I had to not physically shake.

'Good. Me too. I really don't wanna screw this up. Let's see how it goes. We don't have to . . .'

'I want to,' I said, edging nearer to him. Our bodies met in the middle of the room. 'I really do. It's only because it's new.'

'Well, we'll go nice and slow. If it all gets too much . . . just say. You know I'm not going anywhere, right? There's always later. We can do it some other time.' It felt like he was trying to talk us both out of it. But I'd gone too far.

'OK. Well, let's see.' I kissed him, my heart beating stupidly fast. It couldn't be healthy. *This was it. I was doing it.* Never again would I be a virgin. No one would ever, ever be able to say, 'Toria Grand died a virgin spinster.'

I pulled Nico's jumper over his head, messing up his hair. It only made him cuter. In the muted light from Polly's lamp, I got a good look at him. Obviously, we'd had a good grope before that point, but as only weirdos make out with their eyes open, I'd never stopped to actually just *look* at him. His body was hard and defined, more so than I'd been expecting.

There was soft, dark hair all the way from his chest to the rim of his jeans. I liked it.

He looked exposed so I pulled my own jumper off so we matched. I presented myself to him. He took my hand and we moved onto the bed. Having made the decision to do it, I felt more in control and I was fine.

Once we got going, I definitely didn't want to stop. I'm sorry but I'm not going to do a full-length florid description of what happened next. His touch was not like silk and I didn't see fireworks. I'm also not going to say what he did and what went where – you can probably figure that out for yourself.

What I will say is Nico looked after me and we took our time. It turns out sex feels nice. It was so weird. I didn't know my body could feel like that. It also turns out that boys like it when you do things to their bits. Like, *any*thing. Apparently there isn't much of a skill to it. I showed him where to touch me and he got the message pretty quickly. He put his own condom on – I'm glad I didn't have to do that bit; it looked fiddly.

He slipped out of me a couple of times and kept apologising, which I thought was quite sweet although unnecessary. Once he hit his stride he didn't last too long, for which I was secretly quite grateful. He shuddered and groaned and I was oddly proud at the effect I was having.

And it was . . . liberating. Totally naked, all tangled up with each other. It wasn't *pretty*, but it was really hot. I loved feeling his skin all over mine. Everywhere tickled, everywhere felt good. I'd never spent any time thinking what it would feel like to have a guy lick my hip, but it was electric. I loved the taste of salty sweat on his neck. I'll be honest, it *did* hurt, but, once I got over the shock, I loved having him inside me. It felt *right*, if a little sore.

Possibly even better than the sex bit was the after-sex bit. Exhausted, and on the biggest adrenaline comedown of my life, I fell straight into a powerfully deep contented sleep with my head on his damp chest, the rise and fall like a lullaby. That really *was* heaven.

# Chapter Ten

## Christmas

Before you start thinking this is a Coming Of Age story, I'd like to point out that once I'd gleefully cast off the miasma of my virginity precisely NOTHING changed. It was, I'll admit, a bit of a relief but I didn't feel like 'a woman' – I didn't start wearing trouser suits or using 'bronzer'. I still don't know what that does. In fact, as Christmas came around I saw less of my friends and reverted to a stroppy adolescent state instead.

This is going to sound insane but now that I had friends I actually liked, school was preferable to being at home. Christmas actively removed me from them, dragging me Up North for 'family time'. I wanted to die. We had to stay with my Auntie Minna and Uncle Sarwat: awful people who were the very definition of money not buying class – the sort of people who tell you exactly how much things cost as they recount stories. 'Oh it was beautiful, but you'll never guess how much it set us back . . . go on . . . GUESS.'

Even worse were my cousins. Naveen is a fat dope-fiend who can do no wrong in his parents' eyes while Anjali looks like a human Bratz doll and has roughly the same IQ. They thought I was a freak and for the first time I was proud of the fact. I spent most of the stay trying to weird them out on purpose: talking to my split ends and pretending to go into demonic trances – chanting fake Latin under my breath. *You want freak*, I thought, *I'll give you freak*. I also managed to convince Anj that I'd seen a little ghost boy in Victorian clothing squatting in the cupboard under the stairs. I was especially chuffed with that one.

Up North, you have to make your own fun.

Christmas morning at Grandma's was equally depressing. She's not entirely on board with us doing Christmas in the first place, but as long as we also make a fuss for Diwali, she lets it slide. I swear time with your family contains extra hours to normal days – it dragged forever. At present-giving time, I was given an *Ice Age* box set. 'Well, you like cartoons,' Mum explained, and I could have cried. ANIME IS NOT CARTOONS.

It actually made me feel really guilty. Not only did my parents no longer know me at *all*, but I'd estimate they'd pissed over a hundred quid up the wall on stuff I'd never use. What a waste. I guess it's partly my fault for not communicating clearly enough and I should be grateful I know . . . poor kids in orphanages and all that.

After the obscenely huge, sprout-filled banquet dinner, Dad suggested a game of Monopoly before *Doctor Who*. Nav always cheats and Dad always catches him and it devolves into tears and recriminations every year so I opted out. I decided to do the altruistic thing and go and help Mum and Auntie Minna in the kitchen.

I stopped outside the kitchen door, which stood ajar. I could hear sniffling, sobbing. It was Mum. I pressed myself into the alcove housing a ceramic lion to spy. 'I'm being so silly,' Mum said. I wondered if she'd reached the tipping point with the Chablis and the port. 'I feel like I'm all by myself down there, you know what I mean?'

'You'll settle in,' Minna told her, trying to be soothing. 'Give it a bit more time.'

'I am in that house all by myself all day long. I never bloody see Eric and Vicky's always out with her friends.' That was a mighty tit-punch of guilt right there.

'Well, how's the job hunt going?' I could hear Minna loading plates into the dishwasher as she spoke.

'There's nothing. Absolutely sod all. I just . . . I just hate it, Min.'

'Well . . . well, what are you going to do about it?'

'There's nothing I can do is there? I don't know.' My eyes stung. I'd been so selfish and so immature. Immature to think that my dad uprooting us would only affect me – me pirouetting at the centre of my own jewellery-box universe. I had never stopped to even think what Mum had left behind: a job, her friends, her family.

I took it for granted that my parents would always be together. Not because I was stupid but because I thought they were about as happy as two people who'd been married for fifteen years could be. That they'd accepted their concurrent life sentences. She wouldn't leave, would she?

A worse thought entered my head. *Would that be such a bad thing?* That little voice was pushed right to the back under a pile of mental junk mail. That was a terrible thing to think. For better or worse, they balanced each other out and I love them as a pair – they're human salt and pepper shakers – one wouldn't make sense without the other. If they split, Dad would basically become a hobo and god only knew how much Mum would drink if he wasn't around to tut at her.

'Just ignore me!' Mum said. 'I've had too much to drink.' Well, that was certainly true. But it was *another* thing to worry about. Another inconvenient angst nugget to go with all the others. I'd taken my eye off the ball with that one – even the things I thought I had nailed down were starting to slide around the deck.

I tried to cheer up for the rest of the day. I didn't let them know I'd heard the conversation in the kitchen but made the effort to be nicer to Mum. If nothing else, she deserved a stress-free Christmas, even if *Doctor Who* was the only highlight.

While I was away, of course, I texted everyone back home constantly – we'd set up a chat group and almost live-blogged our respective holidays. I took comfort in knowing Polly was inching ever-closer towards matricide, Beasley was fending off 'When will you meet a nice girl?' probes, and we all helped Daisy face what was by far the most challenging time of year. Nico had gone to Italy with his mum and sisters and the distance was torture.

It turns out sex is quite addictive. Now that I'd started I didn't want to stop. If that sounds slutty, that's your problem. As soon as we were both back in Brompton, Nico and I started a fun new game called 'How And Where Can We Do More Sex?' How the teen pregnancy rate is so high when parents seemingly never leave the house is anyone's guess.

All I can say is I was hugely grateful for the evening yoga classes Sofia Mancini taught in the village hall. She did yoga, and so did we, in a manner of speaking. I was obsessed. Nico was my new toy and he didn't seem to mind one little bit.

I think it stemmed from a perfectionist need I harboured to 'get it right'. I wasn't sure I'd had an orgasm yet during sex . . . *something* happened one time, a bit of a tingle, but I wanted to clarify. The more we did it, the less it felt like his penis was *invading* my body, and that could only be a good thing.

My friends, on the other hand, probably weren't quite so thrilled. 'I want to try everything,' I told Daisy and Polly (hair now baby-boy blue) on New Year's Eve. We were at the golf course. This was a thing. Every year for the last few years they'd broken in with bottles of booze and some sad fireworks. At the end of the party we'd clear everything up and leave the place untouched, like ghosts in the night. 'I feel like I've got so much stuff to catch up on, you know what I mean? I want to make sure Nico's happy.'

Polly half-heartedly smiled. 'Well, I'm glad you broke the seal.'

'Gross,' Daisy added.

Nico slid his arm around me, materialising out of nowhere. 'What are you talking about?'

'Nothing!' we all said together and fell about laughing. It was freezing cold and we were all bundled up in coats, scarves and hats – only eyes peering out like woollen ninjas. We were hidden away on the pirate ship. I don't know if CCTV was picking us up, but security guards hadn't found us yet. I snuggled into Nico, huddling for warmth like a penguin.

We filled each other in on Christmas shenanigans. 'My dad was so awesome,' said Daisy, nestled in her faux fur and matching hat. 'He told anyone who gave me a hard time about food they'd be out on their ears.'

'Was it awful?' I asked.

'You know what, it wasn't so very awful. I had a little bit of everything. It was nice. Who can be mad at trifle?'

We laughed. She looked so much healthier and I sensed we'd turned a corner on that episode. For now.

'Well, I had a splendid time,' Alex bragged. 'I don't want to be a total knob-end, but my Christmas present was waiting on the driveway . . .'

'Roadkill?' I asked and everyone laughed.

Alice stepped in. 'A car. It's so cool. Now we can go wherever we like.'

'Once I pass the test,' added Alex.

I internally willed him to fail the test. Of course, Alex's new toy wasn't a tin can on wheels like most seventeen-year-olds got, it was a brand-new Mini Cooper. I had come to realise that Alice and Alex were a brand. It was all for show, all about how they *looked*. I sometimes wondered if they even liked each other much. It's like that old philosophy question about the falling tree in the rainforest: did Alice and Alex actually exist when no one was there to see them? (Answer: yes, because EVERY moment was available on Instagram.)

I was frozen and a little head-fuzzy from cava but something intrigued me. As we chatted and drank, Zoë sidled up closer and closer to Polly until they were almost entwined. OK, everyone was cold and everyone was huddling, but Zoë might as well sit on Polly's knee and get it over and done with. I caught Nico's eye with a quizzical look, but he just shrugged. Polly hadn't said anything.

As soon as I could, a little before midnight as we set up the fireworks, I collared Polly. 'Oi, Wolff, what's going on with you and Zoë?'

She shrugged. 'Nothing.'

'Oh, come on, she was all over you.'

'It was cold, Tor. We're not all borderline ******* nymphomaniacs.' She couldn't disguise the zing of annoyance in her voice.

'OK, chill out, it was only a question.' I was no longer in awe or scared of Polly Wolff. We were just friends now.

'Honestly, it was nothing. Been there, done that.' She gave me a saucy grin.

'Charming!'

'Thirty seconds!' Beasley yelled and we scurried over to where they'd set up the fireworks. Zoë took on the role of fireworks coordinator and the rest of us stood well back. I was arm in arm with Nico, seeing out the end of the year I'd started all alone, surrounded by people I loved. But New Year is about putting one year to bed and ushering in another. For the first time in ages, I couldn't wait to find out what happened next.

'Five, four, three, two . . . HAPPY NEW YEAR!' We hugged and kissed and tripped over each other as the fireworks, as pathetic as they were, went off. They fizzed and whimpered in a litter of sad sparks and clouds of pungent gunpowder smoke. Their feebleness only made them funnier; we doubled up in laughter.

I can honestly, honestly say I don't know if I'd ever been as happy as I was at that moment. You know what? It was better than sex, and I was now qualified to suggest so.

## India

I am the I in India.
Yeah, I've watched a mango sun melt over the Taj Mahal
Like hot sauce on a sundae.
Yeah, I've thrown back my head as powder pink exploded
Around me at Holi.
But I also ran the Paint Bomb Run in Boothroyd Park
For Breast Cancer Care, for Gran.

I am the I in India.
Yeah, I've tucked those samosas in like they were ready for bed
And ground cardamom till it's dust.
Yeah, I've made papaya lassi and spinach dal
Without opening a jar.
But I've also baked an apple pie with fruit from the garden
With Ambrosia custard, the way Dad likes it.

I am the I in India.
Yeah, I've been wrapped like a mummy in a river of silk
Wrists like rattlesnakes.
Yeah, I've patiently waited for mehndi to make poetry of my hands
Worn a bindi when they weren't hip.
But I also ripped a top in Primark and put it back on the rail
And wear Docs on my feet.

I am the I in India.

# Chapter Eleven

# Secret

Exams give me diarrhoea. I understand this is not a sexy admission, but it was definitely true of my Year 12 mocks, which were our gift from school on our return. The end of the holidays saw frantic revision sessions around Polly's. For most people, group revision would be hanging out and watching TV, but Polly was a hybrid of interrogator and sweatshop mistress. We quizzed and tested each other until we could recite facts and figures, arguments and counterarguments and anticipate every possible combination of essay question.

Our preparedness didn't stop the nerves from setting in. The morning of the first exam I had to take three, yes three, Imodium to be even able to leave the house. My mum said it was psychosomatic. I invited her to take a look at my poop.

Nico had it even worse. He was sitting his real mocks, the ones that would form his predicted final grades. Over the holidays, as I lay naked in his arms – the only way you can in a single bed – we finally discussed his plans for next year, aka

'When Nico Will Leave And Tear My Heart Out'.

'There really isn't a plan,' he told me. 'I left it way too late to do anything next year anyway, so I'll take a year out and get some work.'

It took a superhuman effort to refrain from a crazy jig o' smugness. 'Yay! Will you stay here?'

'Yeah! I want to spend some proper time on the band while we're still young enough to get signed. And the band is here . . . and so are you . . .' He kissed me.

I couldn't keep the grin off my face. 'Well, I approve one hundred per cent!'

He kissed me tenderly on the lips. 'Don't worry. You can't get rid of me that easily.'

Six exams, one timed Art practical and two packets of Imodium later, the exams were done, thank god. I don't test particularly well, but having survived Polly Bootcamp I felt better than I ever had done after exam season. The weather had turned arctic and it was way too cold for even us to brave the golf course, so to celebrate the end of exams I suggested a trip to Pizza Delisiosa, the cheaper of the two pizza places in town.

'I can't do Friday night,' Polly said.

'Why?' said Beasley, crunching through a bag of crisps as we sat in the common room. In this weather it was at capacity, steamed up like a sauna. It smelled of boys – Lynx deodorant and feet – and salt and vinegar. 'Clearly we don't have plans.'

'Actually, ************, I do.'

'Are you cheating on us with other friends?' Beasley feigned hurt.

'It's my dad's birthday. Sucks to be me. What about Saturday?'

It all became too much of a fiasco to do Saturday, so, with regret, we had to go without Polly. As we hurried down the high street, powdery, gravity-defying snow whirled around us. I'm of the opinion that snow before Christmas is magical and enchanting, snow after Christmas is annoying as hell. We were cold and wet and slipping in slush all the way to the restaurant.

Being somewhere inside where we had to be vaguely quiet felt sophisticated and grown-up. When Nico ordered beers we weren't challenged and it didn't feel naughty any more; it felt right. We were old enough to be drinking. Sort of. I would be seventeen next week. I learned very young that no one gives much of a fig when your birthday is on 19 January – everyone is still hungover from New Year.

Garlic butter greased the air as ragged-looking waiters ferried sparkler-infused sundaes to an eleventh birthday party in the window. The lights were dimmed and we all joined in singing 'Happy Birthday'. Beasley and Daisy shared a pizza. It would be fair to say that Beas ate the vast majority of it, but Daisy did eat a couple of slices and I'm ashamed to say I monitored her to make sure she didn't sneak off to the bathroom as soon as she'd eaten.

We somehow got into a debate about vegetarianism. 'I just don't think you should eat little baby animals!' Daisy said, gesturing smugly at their margherita. 'It's mean and cruel and God totally told Adam and Eve to look after the animals, not eat them.'

'Bitch, please!' Beasley exclaimed. 'When did you EVER believe in God?'

Daisy pouted. 'I could believe in God if I wanted to.'

I reached for my temple. 'Oh – oh wait . . . I'm getting a psychic message from Jesus. He's saying . . . "There was this one time I catered a party for five thousand people . . . AND I SERVED FISH."'

Everyone laughed and I felt pleased with myself. It was weird. Without Polly I was sort of in charge: splitting the bill and talking with the waiter. Perhaps I was the second-most dominant one in the group. After we'd gone mental on the ice-cream machine, so much so that we'd all abandoned grotesque bowls full of sugary multi-coloured goo, I suggested we head to The Mash Tun to catch whatever band was playing that night.

'Sure. It's The Gash though. Siobhan, the guitarist, is amazing, but they suck.' Nico finished his beer.

'"The Gash?"'

'Lesbian punk-ska band.'

'I should have guessed.' We slipped and slid back down the high street and there was just enough snow on the car windscreens to make tiny snowballs. We were silly and noisy – *those* teenagers that the tabloids love to hate, screaming and cackling in the street late on a Friday evening. I was tipsy and I tore my tights. I thought it was sometimes OK to be like that, to be the cliché. This was when we were supposed to do that, and, after all, we weren't hurting anyone or taking anything that wasn't ours to take.

Our impromptu snowball fight ended when Beasley shoved snow down Alice's coat and she got the hump.

We arrived at The Mash Tun soaked and shivering. We almost fell into the pub and made our way to the toilets to dry off under feeble hand dryers. Nico ordered us more beers – although I was aware that this needed to be my last one. Beasley, Alex and Nico were already at the bar when me, Daisy and Alice joined them.

'Look who it is,' Beasley said, nodding through into the back room with the stage. Polly and Zoë were down the front pogoing to the band, who were, as Nico had predicted, an angry racket with shaved heads and neck tattoos.

'And look *who* she's with,' I said, going from merry to livid in point five seconds.

'Is she on a date with Zoë?' Beasley said. 'Nico, did you know about this?'

'Don't look at me.'

Oh that stung. I was hurt Polly hadn't felt she was able to tell me, especially when I'd been so open about Nico and me. 'That shady bitch. She is so busted. Let's go over.'

Nico gave me what I had learned was his doubtful face – a slight dip in the middle of his brow. 'Maybe they didn't tell us for a reason . . .'

'Well, if you're going to be all logical, that's no fun. I'm going over.'

'It's your funeral . . .' Beasley added.

'I'm not scared of Polly.' I took my bottle of beer and started to weave through the sweaty, moshing crowd. When I reached the front I gave Polly a tap on the shoulder. 'How's your dad's birthday going?' I said. 'I had no idea he was such a fan of The Gash.'

Polly looked utterly caught out for a second before remembering herself and rolling her eyes. 'Ha ha. Very funny.'

'Why didn't you tell us you were going to be here?' I shouted over the music in her ear.

'****! I don't have to tell you my ******* whereabouts. I'm not tagged.'

I didn't reply, choosing to stare her down. I figured that most people would have backed down by now, but I didn't want to be most people. It's like with dogs, they respect you if you show them who's boss.

'Let's go for a fag,' Polly said, backing down. She whispered something in Zoë's ear and I followed her into the beer garden. It was freezing, but it was under an awning with heat lamps so it could have been worse. In fact, directly under the lamp, it felt like my hair was toasting.

'Polly, I'm not cross,' I lied, suddenly aware I was breathing some killer garlic-breath in her direction. 'I just don't understand why you didn't tell us.'

'Because why should I?' She was on the defensive.

'Are you seeing Zoë?'

Polly took a deep drag on her cigarette. It was minty menthol. 'Kind of.'

'And it's a big secret because . . .?'

'****, Tor! Look, I didn't want it to be a big drama.'

I laughed, exasperated. 'By keeping it a big secret you've turned it into a drama!'

Polly seemed to consider this. 'To be honest, I didn't want you all sticking your noses in. It feels like nothing's private. Not all of us like sharing every ******* gory detail.'

Well, that was definitely aimed at me. 'I don't do that.'

'Yes you do,' she fired back. 'And I don't need to hear it, OK? You're not the first ******* girl in the world to get laid, Tor.'

'Fine.' I whirled away, aware I was behaving like a brat. 'I'll go talk to the friends who do want to talk to me then.'

'Jesus Christ! You started this! I just came to see the ******* band!'

I was already slamming the door behind me.

That night I lay in bed, wide awake. It felt like there was a huge lump of especially sour apple stuck in my throat. Like Granny Smith sour. Tossing and turning, my head was full of churning, ruminant thoughts of Polly. *I don't need to hear it.* What did that mean? Maybe I'd been overdoing it. Everything was so new and exciting with Nico that I'd assumed it would be exciting for everyone else too. I was probably wrong about that.

I was too hot. Why was the central heating on in the middle of the night? Was Mum actually trying to bake us as we slept? I kicked my duvet off and resigned myself to insomnia.

The next morning, having barely slept and what sleep I did get filled of dreams of Polly and me arguing, I vowed to fix things. I went for a course of action that I'd appreciate if the tables were turned. I dragged myself out of bed, got dressed and walked to Polly's via Costa Coffee. I knocked on the door and Mr Wolff answered in a paint-splattered tracksuit. It was disconcerting to say the least.

'Hello, Toria. You're up nice and early.'

'Is Polly up yet?'

'She ought to be if she isn't. Go on up.' I sometimes find Mr Wolff so handsome I don't know where to look, so I shuffled awkwardly past him and hurried upstairs.

I tapped on her bedroom door. 'Polly, it's me.'

'Are you ******* kidding me?' came the muffled response.

'I come in peace. You can either have the big Jammy Dodger or the big custard cream . . .' She opened the door, blue hair and mascara all over her face. She looked like a Monster High doll some kid had scribbled on.

'I didn't take my make-up off last night. I regret that now.' She let me into her room, which was murky and smelled of night breath. 'Get comfy, I'll go have a shower.'

She did and when she returned, she looked like a human again. 'Let's wrap up and go play golf in the snow,' she suggested and I took that to mean my strop had been forgiven.

Polly had the custard cream as we walked (carefully) down the hill towards the beach. 'I should have told you about Zoë,' she finally said after we'd discussed what the ultimate biscuit was (answer: plain chocolate digestive). 'I was being ***** but I didn't want to jinx it too. I don't know if I really fancy her or not so I didn't see the point in announcing it to the whole world. We're just . . . seeing how it goes.'

'Well, I'm glad I know because now we can, you know, talk about it and stuff.'

'That's true. I suppose it *is* my turn.'

'It is,' I agreed. 'So how long has it been going on . . .?'

Polly filled me in. They'd fooled around consistently and quietly ever since the first time they'd dated. 'Nothing serious,' Polly said. 'But I'm kind of getting used to having her around. You know what I mean?'

I could see how you could get hooked on the intimacy as much as the sex. Arms wrapped around you like a life jacket. 'I get that. Have you always fancied girls?' I asked, sipping on my now tepid coffee.

'I didn't know you weren't supposed to. I never had any brothers so I was like nine before I realised boys and girls were even different.'

'Wow.'

'No, I think it's a good thing. I don't think we *are* different. I don't see penises or vaginas, I see hot people or not hot people. It's pretty ******* easy if you ask me.'

Worded like that, it did sound easy. We reached the bottom of the hill and started to make our way past the pier towards the arcades.

Polly went on. 'I don't know why people find it so hard to believe. I find different things sexy. Like with Nico, for example, it was his dimples, his teeth, his arms. With you it was your lips.'

'Me? My lips?' I was suddenly very aware of them as I sucked foam out of the little opening in my coffee cup.

'You have sexy lips.'

Even in the cold, I felt hot. 'Well, thank you. You have good lips too.'

She laughed. 'But do you see what I mean? I don't think I could ever say "Oh I fancy this about girls" or "I fancy this about boys" because boys don't all look the same and neither do girls. And they're very different in bed. Different but good.'

'Oh really?'

'Oh really!' Then the smile fell from Polly's face. The colour drained from her cheeks, panic-stricken. '****. **** **** ****.'

'What? Polly, what is it?'

'Holy ****. Look.' Polly pointed to the crazy-golf course. The gates were chained shut and there was a huge red blister of a sign attached to the railings. The sign said FOR SALE.

# Chapter Twelve

# No

Polly Wolff on a mission is a scary, scary thing. I'd only ever seen such determination on the faces of women with prams outside a Black Friday sale. When we couldn't find anyone within the sealed-up golf course – and god knows we screamed enough and tried to force entry – Polly set off along the coast.

Eventually we reached the static caravan site on the edge of town. 'Polly, are you bringing me here to murder me?' I asked, out of breath.

'This is where Jamie lives.' Polly's legs were easily twice as long as mine and I felt like a pug scurrying at her heels, trying to keep up. I was probably just as squashed and snotty too.

We stopped at a caravan that seemed to be held together with gaffer tape. 'This is where Jamie lives?'

'I told you you didn't want to end up like him.' Polly banged on the door and a white man with dreadlocks answered. I think we all know there's a special place in hell for them. 'Hey. Is Jamie home?'

The white Rasta checked her out for a second. 'Heeeeey, Jammer,' he called to the back of the caravan. 'There's some kids here to see you. You dawg, man. They is like little girls.'

'Oh **** off.' Polly went for him and he ducked back into the gloomy little box. Jamie appeared in the entrance wearing a onesie and looking very stoned indeed.

'What do you want? It's well early, man.'

'Why aren't you at work? What's happening with the golf course?'

He rubbed the back of his head. 'They're closing it, man.'

'What?' both Polly and I exclaimed.

'That dump isn't making any money. They wanna sell it to developers or something. I dunno. I basically got fired, like.'

'****!' both Polly and I exclaimed.

'What's it going to be instead?' I asked. 'Or will they keep it as a crazy-golf course?'

'I dunno. I'm going back to bed, yeah.' Jamie left the door ajar. 'You can come and skin up with us if you want.'

'We'll pass,' I said definitely. I looked to Polly. 'What are we going to do? This sucks so hard.'

Polly kicked a stone clean across the park where it barrelled into a neighbouring caravan. Her fists were tight angry wrecking balls. 'No. No way. They can't do this. They're not taking away our crazy golf. Come on.'

Two hours later we were in Polly's bedroom. All of us. It had taken time and a lot of screaming down the phone but we'd gathered everyone. Beasley was supposed to spend the weekend at his dad's (although he didn't seem to mind being summoned), Daisy had skipped a family trip to Grandma's. Alice and Alex were presumably working on their tedious 'Look at Our Faux Vintage Life' Instagram account, Freya had brought her very own book and Nico and Zoë were missing rehearsal.

When we'd first got home, Polly had practically thrown herself at her father who was reading the paper at the kitchen table. 'Dad! They can't close the crazy-golf course!'

'Well, if it's not making any money they can.'

'We go there all the time. I spend half my allowance there.'

He pursed his lips and looked disapprovingly over the top of the sports supplement. 'Polly, you can't expect them to keep an entire business open for you and your friends. It's hardly busy on season, never mind off season, is it?'

'That's because it needs some work. Like painting and stuff. You and Mum have loads of money . . .'

'Polly, you're not actually suggesting that we buy a crazy-golf course, are you?'

'Well, why not? What's the point in sitting on a giant pile of money if you're not going to spend it?'

'And what would I do with a golf course?'

'Uh, run it, obviously. We'll do it. We'll run it,' Polly said, pointing between the two of us. I didn't remember signing up for golf-course management, but why not.

Her dad actually laughed. 'You're going to drop out of school to run a golf course? Polly, that "giant pile of money" you so optimistically speak of is for your tuition fees and, one day, a deposit on a house. Isn't that what you want?'

'No!'

'Oh for crying out loud, it's like talking to a four-year-old. You'll have to find somewhere else to haunt.' He wasn't going to budge.

Back to the summit in Polly's bedroom. We filled them in on the day's news. 'That's awful!' Daisy said, eyes wider than ever. 'We've been going there since we were, like, three. What'll happen to the Disapproving Seal?'

'This sucks. They'll probably build another arcade or something equally lame,' Beasley lamented.

'Not so,' Alex said with authority. 'My pater works for the council. I happen to know that space has been earmarked for food and drink premises.'

'You knew about this?' I asked. We turned on him like a pack of angry wolves.

'Not at all.' He held his hands open in peace. 'I just know Burger King tried to buy the land a couple of years ago, but the owners wouldn't sell.'

'Maybe they finally caved in and sold?' Beasley said.

Nico didn't seem nearly as troubled, but then it took quite a lot to ruffle him. 'I guess we could start hanging out at The Mash Tun. They never ID you guys there.'

'That's not the point,' I said, sounding decidedly sulky.

'We need to find the owners.' Polly was striding back and forth over her rug like the general of her own little army. 'I wonder if we could convince them not to sell or make sure that whoever they do sell it to keeps it as a crazy-golf course.'

'As if they'll listen to us,' Beasley said. 'Like, why would they?'

'They would if we put in an offer.'

'That's insane,' Nico said. 'I had to borrow money off my mum to get the bus here.'

'He's right,' I added, feeling extra gloomy. Alice did a Saturday-afternoon shift at Starbucks and Beasley did a couple of waiting shifts at one of the hotels on the seafront, but that was seasonal. 'None of us really has any money, and your parents didn't want to help. I know my mum and dad wouldn't want anything to do with it.'

Polly actually growled at us. 'You are all such *******! Sorry, but why aren't you fighting this? We *have* to keep the golf course open. It's our legacy to Brompton.' She went on: 'I don't know about you, but I would have killed myself years ago if it weren't for that place. I'm not even kidding; I probably would have. But no matter how **** school was or how ***** my mum was being I always had that place to look forward to. I always thought, "At least I'm going to Fantasyland tonight," and it kept me going. It kept me alive.' She took a breath. 'I know we're all leaving this dump next year or whenever, but it's the only good thing about the town and there are people like us in the years below. Like that amazing goth girl in Year 10, or the trans girl in Year 8 or that skinny guy who's always by himself in Year 9. We have to keep it open for *them*.'

Well, I don't know about you, but I got a little tear in my eye.

Nico relented. 'What can we do?' Polly had recruited him to the cause.

'We do what we do. We fight.'

We are the Petition Generation. We get angry and we noisily voice opinions but we don't like paying for things or actually doing things. I'd lost track of the number of online petitions I'd signed. I'd saved gay people in Russia, had environmental activists freed, banned Page Three and released caged hens. In reality I hadn't done any of those things. I'd ticked some boxes on a website, felt smug and self-righteous and then never gone back to see if I'd made a difference. Well, of course I hadn't: gay people are still being persecuted and my mum, no matter how many times I beg her to check where the eggs are coming from, doesn't. There are still boobs winking at me from the magazine racks in Asda.

But now that the petition was mine it felt very different. It was decided that there was no point in utilising all my online friends because none of them were in Brompton and the issue wasn't theirs – also, I'd hardly spoken to them since I'd started hanging out with Polly and the gang. We all felt that this needed to be local residents.

Alex managed to discover through his dad that the owners were actually part of the same group who ran the pier, which was also losing money (last summer had been a washout). They wanted to focus their energy on the pier and sell the land. Frankly, they didn't give a tiny rat's ass what happened to the site as long as it was no longer their concern.

Our petition went as follows:

*We, the undersigned, believe Fantasyland crazy-golf course is an important tourist asset in Brompton-on-Sea. We believe Fantasyland provides the young people of the town with much-needed entertainment. It is one of only three local attractions which does not serve alcohol or promote gambling. To close the attraction or redevelop the land would be a great loss to the seafront.*

The idea was we would ask the council to step in and run Fantasyland as part of its Parks Programme, either permanently or until such a time that a new owner could take over running the attraction.

This, we felt, wasn't unreasonable. The council maintained the putting course and boating lake in Greenacre Park and were responsible for the beach, so it *kind* of made sense, at least to us. We formed a group called 'Save Fantasyland' and Beasley knocked us up some pretty professional-looking letterheaded paper. If you want something doing . . . do it right.

Break times and lunch took on a whole new purpose. We talked the printing shop in town into doing us a discount on some 'Save Fantasyland' T-shirts, which we had made XXL to wear over our jumpers on the freezing playground. In pairs we strolled around the school, looking for signatures. 'Have you signed the petition yet?', 'Do you ever go to Fantasyland?', 'Help us keep Fantasyland open.'

We were – how can I put this lightly? – bullish. The football team, the pretty girls, the scary girls, the nerds, the musicians, the theatre lot, the emos, the Goths – we interrupted all of their sandwiches. Most people signed the damned thing to get rid of us, to be honest, but that didn't matter. Of course some people were downright rude: 'Is it a dyke petition? Will it make me gay?' some Year 9 boys wanted to know.

'Yes. It will make you gay,' I responded. 'Just sign it or I'll tell everyone you have a pseudo-penis like a shrivelled olive.'

I got the signature.

Polly was in hysterics. 'I can't believe you said that! It's really hard not being able to punch people.' Polly had decided to go on a charm offensive to get the petition signed. She hadn't maimed anyone in days. Quite an achievement.

We attached copies of the petition to the noticeboard outside the main hall and in the sixth-form entrance area. We appealed to teachers, dinner ladies and even the head teacher.

On a weekend we took to the high street. Although people mistook us for charity muggers – those tabard-wearing monsters who try to wrestle your bank details from you outside Primark – if we engaged people they were happy to sign. Most people had no idea Fantasyland had shut down and seemed genuinely disappointed. 'Oh, that's a shame. I used to take my kids there when they were little,' was what we heard a lot, or 'Aw, man! I used to go there all the time when I was a kid.' Fantasyland wasn't only ours, it belonged to the town. Even those who weren't there three nights a week had such fond memories of the place. It was a good, positive, harmless thing and the town was better with it. It wasn't clogging arteries or damaging livers or emptying wallets. Like anything harmless it had been an easy target. Evidence Exhibit A? The local library, Daisy once told me, is now a Poundland.

Daisy did a great line in ambiguous foreboding too. 'At the moment, the land could be used for *anything*,' she'd say with doe eyes. 'I mean, they could turn it into a toxic waste dump for all we know.' That got a few more signatures, and wasn't *strictly* a lie.

I sensed there was something going on behind Polly's fervour. Something beyond her rousing speech about preserving Fantasyland for the waifs and strays of Brompton in years to come. I asked her about it as we petitioned outside the pie and mash shop near the harbour. 'What's this really about, Polly?'

'What do you mean?'

'Saving the golf course. You texted me at seven thirty this morning and it's Saturday.'

'It's like I said . . . that place kept me going. It still keeps me going.'

I narrowed my eyes and played devil's advocate – a role precisely no one gets thanked for playing. 'I love the golf course too, but only because you're all there. You could put us somewhere else and we'd have just as much fun. All the freaks and geeks in Year 9 will find somewhere else to go.'

Polly shook her head. 'It's more than that.' I knew it. 'That place, for most of my life, has been the best place. My mum used to take me when I was little and she always let me win. She used to be pretty good fun. **** knows what went wrong. Then when I was cutting, I used to go to distract myself, keep my hands busy. It means the ******* world to me, that place.'

I said no more. Now it made sense.

Zoë and Polly, now officially A THING, made a banner on some old bedding and tied it to the chained-up gates of Fantasyland. It was a crappy-looking thing – sub-One-Direction-concert standard – but it worked. On the Saturday afternoon, as Alice and Alex were petitioning anyone who came to try to play golf, a photographer from the local *Gazette* arrived. At least we *hoped* he was a photographer – a slightly crumpled old man with a camera turned up to take a picture of us in front of our banner.

Luckily for us, he wasn't a sexual predator, and our picture appeared on the third page of the paper the following Monday morning. 'I got one!' Polly ran up to where Daisy and I were waiting in the corridor to go into French. 'Look, look, look!'

'Let me see!' I leaned over her shoulder and saw us lined up outside Fantasyland, making the 'sad' faces the photographer had told us to do. GOLF-CRAZY TEENS CAMPAIGN FOR PARK REOPENING. Polly looked incredible with her serious face. I looked really confused, which was less great.

'We all look so good!' Daisy squeaked. 'Like a pop band.'

I laughed. 'I look simple.'

'You do not,' Polly said. 'The piece is ******* awesome too. The journalist is so on our side . . . listen: "With so few activities for young adults, some residents are concerned teens will be left with no choice but to loiter in the streets." That's good. That means the council will have to listen to us.'

'We should get some hoodies and start drinking cider in cul-de-sacs or something.' We were still laughing when Mr Wolff appeared.

'Oh there you are,' he said. 'I just read your piece in the paper.' I couldn't tell if he was angry or not. 'I have to say, I'm really impressed, girls. I can smell the teen spirit.'

'Oh god, Dad, no.'

'I mean it! You're doing a great thing for the community. I'm proud.'

She hid it pretty well, but underneath the scowl, I could see Polly beaming.

## End of the Pier

That day on the end of the pier
We walked in a chain
Slow motion, wind-machine hair
Cotton candy flypaper fingers
Turquoise-tongued.
Photo-booth photobombers.
Insane! Lame!
I'd hate us if I wasn't one of us
Three faces in four pictures.
Watertight to hyena laughter
And bitter sideways sneers
Of those who forget they were once us
And porridge people who could never be.
Two penny-drop millionaires
Carousel cowboys
Quicksilver rippled through the slats
At a raspberry-sorbet sunset.
Speaking our own Esperanto
My calabrese and my wildcat
Hypotenuse, opposite, adjacent
Triangles are the strongest shapes.

# Chapter Thirteen

# Mayor

Something became clear during the weeks we were campaigning. We defined ourselves by the golf course. Whereas before we'd been 'Angry Freak', 'New Girl', 'Gay Boy' or 'Anorexic Girl', we were now 'The Annoying Golf-Course People', a label we were all happy with. Perhaps that's why I'd felt so strange at my last school – I'd been a nomad looking for a tribe. This was my tribe. It was like coming into focus after long years as a blur.

The delightful new clarity only made me more determined. Polly's dad had spoken to Alex's dad – proving parents do come in handy from time to time – and managed to wrangle us a meeting with the mayor. Polly was going with her dad but asked me to go with her for moral support and I'd agreed at once. I was in this to the death.

'Which do you think sounds better?' Nico asked me one evening. I was splayed face down on his bed, scrolling through Tumblr on his laptop while he strummed away on a guitar, jotting lyrics in his Moleskine. 'Semtex latex or latex Semtex?'

I thought about it for a moment. 'Well, "Semtex latex" sounds quite kinky, like exploding fetish catsuits or something and "latex Semtex" sounds like liquid explosives somehow.'

'OK, maybe "Semtex latex" then.'

'In what context?'

'There isn't one, I just thought it sounded cool. "Semtex latex, high-tech red necks".'

'Cool.' I rolled upright. I looked down at his lyric book. An offer to write with him perched on the tip of my tongue . . . but that would mean telling him about my poetry and that would be . . . well . . . mortifying. He'd want to read them and . . . just no.

I changed the subject. 'Would you be sad if I went over to Polly's later? We think we might have a thousand signatures now. We're going to try to count up.'

'Sure,' he replied without a beat. 'I'll ride down to Etienne's. We have loads of band stuff to sort out.'

'Yeah?' Nico talked about the band a lot. If I'm honest, I phased some of it out.

'Yeah. Can you keep a secret?' That got my attention.

'I can.'

He rested his head against my bare thigh. 'We're firing Zoë.'

'*What?* No way!'

Nico didn't look me in the eye, instead circling his finger round and round a freckle on my leg. 'This guy Etienne knows wants to join. He's amazing, Tor.'

'But Zoë is our friend . . . and Polly's girlfriend.'

'Yeah but, between you and me, she sucks on the keys. You said that yourself.' That was true. At the last gig it had sounded like she was playing with boxing gloves on. '*And* she's joined The Gash too. She misses rehearsal half the time.'

I pouted. 'OK, well, I didn't know that.'

'You did. I told you last week. I bloody knew you weren't listening.'

'I *always* listen. I listen to you breathe when you sleep . . .'

He laughed. 'Creepy! She'll get over it. I don't think she's enjoying it anyway. Don't say anything, obviously . . . even to Pols.'

I pushed him off my leg. 'Aw, you can't burden me like that! I'm a rubbish secret-keeper!' That wasn't strictly true; I was still guarding the closet door for Beasley. 'I won't, but tell her quickly. Can I have a kiss before I go though?'

He finally looked up at me. 'I think I can manage that . . .'

We did a tiny bit of sex.

When I got to Polly's, I was in for a surprise. When she opened the door I didn't recognise her. Her hair was black. Plain black. I'd never seen her with such dark hair, let alone hair a colour that could feasibly grow out of a human head. 'Wow! Your hair!'

'Do you like it? I wanted it to be a sensible colour for when we meet the mayor. You know, I don't want her thinking I'm a joke.'

She looked older. Her nose ring was still in, but she could easily pass for twenty . . . more. It was like seeing a future version of the woman she'd become. I suddenly realised I had no idea what Polly's natural hair colour actually was. 'She wouldn't think you're a joke. It looks good. It'll just take me some time to get used to it. You don't look like you! You look like me!'

Polly smiled warmly. 'I do a little. We could be twins or something!'

Polly led me to her room, where I found another surprise waiting for me: Zoë, in very much the same position I'd been in on Nico's bed. 'Oh hi,' I said, very aware I shouldn't talk to Zoë in case Nico's news somehow fell out of my mouth.

'Hey,' she said sleepily, lounging like she was Cleopatra.

I'd assumed it was just going to be Polly and I and felt a little put out at not having been warned. Who wants to be a third bloody wheel? I'd never invite Polly round if Nico and I were doing couple stuff.

Polly brought up the rear and shepherded me in. 'Zoë said she'd help too,' she said cheerily.

'Great. Many hands make light work, or whatever.' I forced myself to smile brightly. I didn't want to be a Debbie Downer. I don't know why it bothered me, but it did. It was plainly bad . . . friend etiquette.

**TORIA GRAND'S GUIDE TO FRIEND ETIQUETTE**

1. Do not go to the cinema with one friend when you know another wants to see the same film.

2. Do not invite a lone single friend to a gathering of couples.

3. Ask single friends if it's OK to bring a BF or GF to a gathering – do not assume they're welcome.

4. Do not cancel plans if it means another friend will be stuck alone with a difficult friend.

5. Never, EVER blow off your friends to see a BF or GF. That comes with the worst karma of all.

We got to work on the petitions, Zoë all the time talking about The Gash and me all the time biting my tongue. I sensed she preferred the sisterhood of her new band, but couldn't help but think her expulsion from Judas Cradle was going to cause trouble. How could it not?

Polly and Zoë couldn't keep their hands off each other, making me feel even less welcome: Polly running her hand up and down Zoë's exquisite long legs. Chipped silver nails stroked Zoë's inner thigh, all the way under the rim of her skirt. We've established I'm no prude, but I didn't know where to look.

'So I reckon –' Polly finished the final stack of papers. They were piled all over her bedroom floor, somewhat spoiling the zen – 'that we actually have *over* a thousand. ******* amazing.'

'That is incredible,' I agreed, surveying our wonderfulness. 'We must have everyone at school.'

'And most of college,' added Zoë.

'The mayor *has* to take us seriously. She *has* to.' I was starting to feel that we could actually do this. I felt powerful and it felt good.

'OK, I'm really underdressed,' I said on the morning of the meeting with Mayor Thompson. Polly was wearing a tailored jacket that she'd borrowed from her sister. She looked so different: her hair was neat, tied back in a sleek ponytail, although she'd left her nose ring in. She wasn't the cliché in either direction. I was wearing a blouse and some trousers with my jacket so I looked more like a waitress than a businesswoman. 'I look stupid.' I clambered into the back of Mr Wolff's car. He was so impressed at our good citizenship, we'd been granted the morning out of lessons.

'You don't; you look fine.'

'Have you got the petition?'

'I do. And I practised what I'm going to say last night. It's going to be fine.' It was so weird, but Polly Wolff was bricking it; I could tell from her clenched jaw and the fingertips drumming her knees. I'd thought of her as unflappable.

We arrived at the town hall, a wood-panelled labyrinth that smelled of old people and libraries. There were *Haunted Mansion* portraits lining the walls, glassy oil eyes following us as we made our way through endless corridors. 'If you just take a seat,' said the receptionist, 'the mayor will be with you shortly.'

'Do you want me to come in with you?' Mr Wolff asked.

'No. I think that'd make us look like kids,' Polly said.

'Don't do anything stupid, and don't swear . . .'

'God, Dad, what do you think I'm gonna do? Nut the mayor?'

'It had crossed my mind.' He winked and Polly allowed him a suggestion of a smile. The door opened and a young man emerged.

'Miss Wolff, do you want to come in?' I guessed he was the mayor's assistant or something. I sheepishly followed Polly into the office as if I were Dowdy McFrump, her trusty sidekick.

The mayor looked like a poodle in drag. Lots of frizzy white hair and make-up from the Coco the Clown School of Beauty.

She wore a TARDIS-blue skirt suit which clashed so violently with the gold mayoral chains that I had to look away – it was like a two-year-old's painting of a sunny day.

'Hello girls, come on in and take a seat.' We did as we were told. 'I'm informed you've got a petition for me.'

'Yeah.' Polly handed her the lever-arch file containing all the signatures.

'Well, I must say this is most impressive. Do you two do a lot of community work?'

'No,' we said in unison. You could do community service as an enrichment activity at school, but that mainly involved rummaging through donated junk in the local charity shops.

'Oh I see, well, this will look awfully good on your personal statements for university, won't it?'

'That's not why we did it,' Polly said, calm and polite. 'Mrs Mayor, we really love that golf course and think it'd be awful if it became a burger place. We already have three burger places in town. There aren't any other crazy-golf courses.'

Mayor Thompson smiled sympathetically. 'Oh I know, but it's not council property dear. It's really nothing to do with us.'

'We thought all planning permission had to go through the council?' I said.

'That's true, but with there already being food premises on the promenade, there's a precedent. There's no reason to block planning permission.'

'Couldn't the council take it over?' said Polly. 'It already runs the beach and the parks.'

The mayor took a sip of tea from her pink MRS BOSS mug. 'You've done your homework, I'll give you that, but I'm not sure there's the budget for it. There's actually a deficit to reduce.'

I cut in. 'If the land is going to change use from a park to a restaurant, doesn't there have to be a public consultation?'

Mayor Thompson smiled. 'Well, of course. Although you'd have to get local residents to oppose it. If it was a residential area, you'd stand a better shot, but it's commercial.'

'They do oppose it,' Polly said defiantly. 'They signed the petition.'

'A lot of people sign petitions; they might be less keen to write to the town-planning office.'

Polly shrugged. 'Well, we can try.'

'I have to ask –' Mayor Thompson took another sip of her tea – 'why is this crazy-golf course so important to you? I would have thought you'd be a bit old for it.'

'Because crazy golf is cool,' Polly said simply.

I was ready with our pre-prepared arguments. 'There's hardly anything for young people in Brompton. The arcades are about it, and they're kinda scary. Tourism is important to the town, especially in the summer months; and, finally, do we really need more junk food? Let me ask you this, Mrs Mayor, do you want to encourage childhood obesity?'

She laughed. 'Oh, you two are brilliant! I love it! Between you and me, I don't want another burger place either, but, like I said, it's not council business. I wish you well though, I really do. I hate it when people come to me complaining about youths and ASBOs and hoodies when I get to meet inspiring young women like you.'

Polly and I shared a quiet, pride-filled glance. Patronised, but proud.

* * *

When we got back to the common room at Brompton Cliffs, we filled the others in on what had been said. 'Why can't they just keep it open?' Beasley whined.

'Apparently they're in debt or something.' I scowled. 'I think she only saw us to be polite, to be brutally honest.'

'No need to be dispirited. We continue our crusade with gusto,' Alex said. 'We rouse as many people as humanly possible to block the planning application.'

Polly looked less enthusiastic. 'It feels ******* hopeless. We have no money. The people with the most money will win. They always do.'

'We can certainly make the lives of whoever buys it a lot more difficult,' I put in.

'But we still don't get to play crazy golf. Isn't that the whole point? We don't have anywhere to go and I'm not going to The ******* Mash Tun every night.'

We fell quiet. Finally Daisy spoke, and when she did she jumped out of her chair like something had bitten her bum. 'We should have a prom!'

'What?' I said.

'To raise money for the cause. We have to do something and I think we should have a dance.'

'Again,' Beasley said. 'What?'

'Like in America! With limos and dresses and corsages and punch. We don't get a dance until the Leavers Ball in Year 13 and that's only for Year 13s. What if we had a prom for Year 11 and 12 too? We could charge, like, twenty pounds a ticket.'

'People would pay more than that,' Alice said. 'I reckon people would pay thirty.'

'OK, I don't hate it. What would we use the money for?' Polly asked, now looking less gloomy.

'For PR,' Alex said. 'We could make flyers or buy an advert in the *Gazette* – a targeted media campaign to gain momentum. We could even attract new owners for the golf course.'

I took Polly's hand – her snow-white skin betraying how warm she really was. 'Come on, Pol. We can't give up now. We've worked so hard.'

'A prom, though? I'd rather **** in my hands and clap.'

'Consumer demand!' Alex said. 'We have to get people to buy something they want.'

'Do I have to go?'

'No!' I laughed.

'You must!' Daisy said. 'We all must. It'll be *our* prom, so it can be how we like. We can even have a crazy-golf course at the prom! You can hire mobile ones!'

'That's actually a pretty good idea,' Beasley said. 'I'm in. You think your dad will go for it?'

'I can ask. I think he quite likes all this Hermione Granger **** so he might.'

My old school did have a Year 11 prom. I didn't go because it was an in-joke in-waiting for the popular kids and I couldn't imagine ever wanting to dress up like a Miss World contestant. But if we were in charge . . . it could be something as weird as we were. It reminded me of what Polly had once said: we weren't the dregs of the school, we were the misunderstood elite. For the first time I believed her.

'Let's do it!' I said.

It was all going to be so awesome! We'd have a prom and save the golf course and I'd marry Nico and we'd solve world hunger and live happily ever after!

I was so naive. Such a foolish little fool.

# SPRING

# Chapter Fourteen

# Opportunity

I imagine you'll be HUGELY surprised to learn that Zoë's firing from Judas Cradle went down really well. Detect my sarcasm. Here are some choice highlights:

1. 'Well, I was gonna quit anyway to focus on The Gash.'
2. 'It's patriarchy bullshit. They obviously didn't want a strong woman in the band.'
3. 'They've been planning this for months, the scheming bastards.'
4. 'They're shit and I hope Etienne chokes on his own shit fumes from having his head that far up his own arse.'

'Look,' Polly said as we went round the school, putting up posters to advertise the prom. 'If I come to Nico's gig, Zoë will kill me. I just can't.'

*Don't whine, don't whine, don't be a whiny bitch.* 'It's like I never see you any more,' I whined. That wasn't true. What I wanted to say was 'I never have you to myself any more,' but I knew that was unreasonable.

'You're always with Nico too.' Ah – so being whiny was OK.

'No I'm not!' I whined again. 'He's always with the band. They're rehearsing like mad. Apparently the new keyboard guy is amazing. Please come. Just don't tell Zoë.'

'I can't. I promised.' She finished attaching the poster to the noticeboard opposite main reception. It looked PROPER. Mr Wolff had agreed to a Year 12 Prom – Year 11s weren't allowed because of their exams and so we'd already started selling tickets to the event in June. It was going to be epic. We'd used some of the money to buy a website for the campaign, as well as flyers and posters.

By half-term, we'd learned who had bid on the Fantasyland site. It was a small chain of American-style diners called Howdy's: a concept so awful it redefined awful. A new circle of hell Dante would have considered too heinous to commit to the page. The unseen villain now had a face – and the face was that of a chubby little cowgirl with red bunches.

'OK.' I admitted defeat. 'But can we do something soon? Just us two?'

'Don't you like Zoë?' Polly regarded me down her nose. With her hooded eyes, Polly sported 'Bitchy Resting Face' at the best of times.

'You know I do, but I don't wanna be a third wheel.'

'You aren't. She loves you hanging out with us.'

'Really?' I said with great scepticism. In fact, I got the distinct impression Zoë now saw me as evil Nico's evil sidekick.

'Well, she'll have to accept it. But, yeah, we'll hang out at the weekend or something.'

'We should have a sleepover.' It popped out of my mouth before I could think it through.

'Hmm, Zoë might not like *that*.'

'Why? I was thinking *Beetlejuice* and Domino's pizza; nothing wrong with that.'

'Just cos.'

It was so frustrating. I wanted our old camaraderie back but I didn't seem able to manufacture it artificially. You know when you can't think of anything funny or cool to say? I felt like a stand-up comedian with stage fright, desperately scanning a sea of blank faces for a seed of observational humour. 'OK, but we'll still hang?' Needy Face.

'Sure.' Her tone contained a hint of, 'Sure, let's get a coffee sometime,' and we all know what that means: you're never getting that coffee.

I went along to the gig, as planned, with Daisy and Beasley. 'We've already sold, like, seventy tickets at full price –' Daisy was buzzing – 'That's over two thousand pounds! Renting the minigolf is only going to cost two hundred and fifty, so Alice thinks we should get, like, ice sculptures or a chocolate fountain or something.'

'Maybe,' I said, sipping a vodka, lime and lemonade which I thought was very classy of me. 'But we want to keep the maximum amount aside for the campaign.'

'I know, I know . . . but we do need it to be magical – people need to get something for their money. What about "Enchantment Under the Sea" from *Back to the Future?*'

'"Enchantment Under the Sea With Golf?"' Beasley asked sceptically.

Daisy would not be deterred. 'OR, Disney theme! That would be SO cool.'

I said, 'I like that. It could be nicely ironic – everyone loves Disney.'

'There is NOTHING ironic about my love of Disney,' Daisy added gravely.

The band came on and we cheered. Nico, as ever, gave me a special smile from the stage. I was a groupie and I loved it. I'd heard that other Judas Cradle fans had plotted my death and that made me strangely proud. And a little scared.

I worried sometimes, sizing up these other girls. I trusted Nico, I did, but anyone with eyes could see he was out of my league. On low days, I figured it was only a matter of time until a prettier or cooler version of me caught his eye. It was on days like that I questioned why he has a security code set up on his phone or started to wonder if I could guess his Facebook password. Dangerous thinking, and Nico had done nothing to provoke such behaviour other than be really hot.

As the first song – 'Effulgent' – began, it became clear that Alfie, the new keyboard player, was ten times better than Zoë. Alfie was the hippest hip Japanese guy I'd ever seen. What on earth he was doing in the culture-free abscess that was Brompton-on-Sea was anyone's guess. *In your face, Zoë, you friend stealer.* The venom in the thought shocked me a little. I apparently had the hump with her, who knew. 'She stole my friend' – god, how preschool was I?

The band played their set and were truthfully the best I'd ever heard them. Even I fanned out a little. Etienne had bleached his eyebrows so he now looked entirely ethereal, like something from either a) a higher plane or b) *Next Top Model*. The band, in their new line-up, just worked. I tried to get backstage like I always did but I was stopped by a bouncer. 'Can I get through?' I asked. 'I'm Nico's girlfriend.'

'I know, love. Sorry . . . can't let anyone through tonight. Manager insisted.'

That was weird. The band's manager, Cleo, was a local promoter who managed a few bands along the south coast. She'd always been pretty cool with me, so it was a little odd. I joined the others at the bar and waited for Nico to find me, which he did about half an hour later. The boy almost knocked me off my bar stool, such was the ferocity of his hug.

'Hey! There you are. What took you so long?' I asked.

'You will never guess what just happened!' Nico said.

'The spaceship came back for Etienne?' Daisy joked.

'Almost as surreal. You know how Annie from Pitchfork loved the EP? Well, tonight she came to the gig and brought an A & R scout from Sony!'

'What!'

Nico subtly pointed to a guy at the furthest end of the bar. He looked like a younger, hipster version of Captain Birdseye. 'I know! He really loved us! He wants us to come up to London and meet with his team!' I'd never seen a beam so beaming.

'Are you serious?'

'Yes!' He threw his arms around me and swung me around, kissing my hair. Beasley and Daisy got involved too, hugging both of us into a big human sandwich. They congratulated him heartily and Beasley went to get celebratory drinks at once.

'That's so amazing,' I said, smoothing my scrum-dishevelled hair back down. 'You must all be so thrilled.'

'I . . . I can't even get my head around it.' Nico was clearly overwhelmed; he was so high his feet were off the floor. 'This is all I've ever wanted, you know what I mean?'

'You deserve it, you really do. You guys were incredible tonight.' He hugged me again, thanking me. He kissed me at the same time as the panic hit. I didn't want him to go to London and be a famous pop star and leave me behind. I didn't want that at all. I wanted him to stay here and play only for me at The Mash Tun until the end of time, and I couldn't have hated myself more for thinking such thoughts, but they were all I could think about. They were a virus, multiplying and spreading in my mind. He'd go to London and be rich and famous and replace me with a Latvian supermodel called Anka and a coke habit.

I told my jabbering head to pipe down. Talk about getting ahead of oneself. But I did have those thoughts. They were there. I wondered if every partner of a successful person had those ideas, or if I was truly the worst girlfriend in the whole wide world.

The secret managed to stay secret for two whole days. Nico didn't want people knowing about the band's road to stardom because, frankly, it wasn't a done deal. If there's one thing more excruciating than being a never-been it's being an almost-was.

The meeting was presumably to establish the band weren't white supremacists or holocaust deniers before they developed them any further. They'd heard the EP, they'd heard the demos, they'd seen them perform. Nico and I decided not to discuss it until after the meeting – not because of my internal breakdown at the thought of losing him, more because he was already a nervous wreck and neither of us wanted to jinx it. Having had a couple of days to think about it, *of course* I wanted Nico to get a record deal. How cool would that be? Supportive girlfriend mode: ON.

The other problem though was Zoë. The fact the band had been scouted by Sony three weeks after Zoë had been ousted from the band did not look great. The band agreed to see if the meeting went well before letting the world at large know.

The cover was blown by the first day back at school after the holiday. I would later learn that Etienne had told someone who had told someone who knew someone in The Gash. Polly was *not* happy. 'Look. I'm not gonna ******* fall out about it, but I think it's well shady.' The 'but' in that sentence suggested we might fall out about it.

Beasley and Daisy made agreeable noises and I was silent for a moment. It would have been *easy* to let Polly win, but it wasn't *right*. I took a stand for my boyfriend. 'Oh come on. It's not like they knew the A & R guy was coming, is it?'

'Didn't they?' Polly looked me dead in the eye. 'Zoë thinks they were warned and that's why they booted her when they did.' It was lunchtime and we were eating outside on the lawns for the first time. It was cool and crisp, the sun as white as fresh linen. The first crocuses and bluebells had popped up through the thaw on the edge of the hockey pitch.

Had she been on the conspiracy-theory websites again? 'That's not true. It really isn't.'

'It's bull****, Tor, and you know it. Zoë is entitled to any money they make. She was in that band from the start.'

I rolled my eyes. 'OK, you are really scary right now, so I'm not even gonna get into this –' oh I *so* got into it – 'but Zoë joined the band after Nico and Etienne put it together and she never wrote any of the songs. She didn't even come up with her parts, Nico did.' And then I *really* went there. 'She's not even that good.'

Polly laughed. She laughed in my face. 'Are you that ******* stupid to think Nico can do no wrong? Wake up and smell the ****! You know what? Go **** yourself.' She grabbed her satchel and stomped back towards the sixth-form wing.

Beasley scowled at me. 'Oh nice one, Tor. Guess who has Sociology with her next period?' He trailed after her, resigned to a lesson with a grizzly bear.

I was left alone with Daisy. 'You agree, right? That she's being ridiculous?' I said.

Daisy smiled as sweetly as the crocuses around us. 'Oh I'm not getting involved. I'm Princess Fence-Sitter of Switzerland.'

Frustration fizzed in my gut. Why did everyone always pander to Polly's temper tantrums? A group of people who live in fear of a domineering leader isn't a friendship, it's a dictatorship. It wasn't healthy. 'OK,' I said, gathering my things. 'Watch out for splinters in your ass.'

I didn't see Polly after school. Polly didn't text me when I got home, before or after dinner. At dinner, even Mum noticed something was wrong and I had to fend her off sulkily. She hadn't texted before bed. Like the metaphorical pot, a watched phone doesn't ping.

This was stupid. It wasn't even our beef. Why Zoë hadn't had it out with Nico was anyone's guess – it seemed so silly that Polly and I had been dragged into it. I truly believed the band wasn't at fault though. If Zoë wasn't fit for purpose then she had to go. She had a new band now anyway. More's the point, there was no guarantee Judas Cradle would even get signed. This was thoughtcrime – the band were guilty of crimes they hadn't yet committed!

I *definitely* wasn't texting her, even if it meant we never spoke ever again. Oh, I could be stubborn when I wanted to be too. I wasn't going to be another yes-person who flitted around her like she was sodding Titania.

(But I did want her to text me.)

I wanted her to realise that our friendship was more important than some band-rivalry nonsense. I wanted her to respect me for being the only person who stood up to her.

(But I absolutely wasn't going to be the one to make the first move.)

It played on my mind all night. I lay awake in bed, staring at my ceiling but not seeing it. I could only think of the argument and what tomorrow would bring. At times I thought perhaps I should apologise and let it blow over, before the mule-headedness returned and I forbade myself from reaching for my phone.

Eventually I must have slumped into a reedy, deeply unsatisfying sleep because when my alarm went off it woke me up. No. It wasn't my alarm. It was the landline. I looked at my clock and saw that it was six fifty. Kind of early for a phone call and, frustratingly, ten minutes before my actual alarm was due to go off. Hate that. I immediately wondered if it was Polly, ringing to clear the air before school. I imagined she'd had a night of fitful sleep too and wanted to make things right. I burst out onto the upstairs landing and threw myself downstairs towards the hall where the phone waited on its base.

'Hello?'

'Hi, is that Toria? It's Mr Wolff here.'

'Oh . . . hello.'

'I know it's early, but could I talk to your mum or dad please?'

Dad now emerged from the kitchen in a dressing gown. 'Who is it, Tor?'

I held out the phone. 'It's Mr Wolff from school.' Dad looked worried at once, the kind of face that said *What trouble have you got yourself into?* I was more worried about Polly – what had she done? What had she said?

Dad said little after he took the phone, making 'ums' and 'ahs' and 'uh-huhs'. It was impossible to read. 'OK,' he said finally. 'Thank you for letting us know.' He hung up the phone. 'Victoria, I . . . er . . . I think you should sit down.' He steered me into the lounge.

'Dad, what is it? Is it Polly?' I pictured her taking a pencil sharpener to pieces and slicing it into her skin. 'Is she OK?'

He physically squashed me down by the shoulders until I was perched stiff on the couch. 'No, Toria, it's Daisy. God, I don't know how to say this. I'm so sorry, Tor. She passed away in the night.'

I'll be honest. I don't really remember too clearly what happened next. It's a blobby blur.

I remember some bits – images and noises – but I can't decide if they really happened or if my mind is filling the blanks with little scenes my brain's directed.

I'll do my best.

# Chapter Fifteen

# Inappropriate

My dad said something like: 'Daisy died, Tor.'

I said something like: 'I heard what you said, I just . . .'

I remember thinking that the last word I said to her was 'ass'.

Dad did some explaining: 'Mr Wolff said she had heart failure. She died in her sleep, Tor, I'm sure it wasn't . . .'

Then there's a blob. Dad said some more words and I think I said something like this: 'No, no way, she's getting better. She's been eating, we've all seen her eating.' I don't know what made me think I could argue her back from death's bony clutches, but I gave it a go.

Dad shook his head. 'I'm so sorry, Tor. She's been ill for years. I guess . . . I guess her body couldn't cope any more . . .' He said more stuff that I don't remember because there's another blob.

Either he went quiet or I stopped listening. The clock beat out seconds on the mantelpiece and I heard the pitter-patter of the shower running upstairs. Despite everything I've said about time, sometimes a second can feel like a forever.

Daisy. Gone.

I had nothing. Just blob.

And then I was back, I think. I must have sprung off the sofa and gone for the stairs because I remember being at the foot of them. Dad caught hold of my arm. 'Toria, you don't have to go into school today, Mr Wolff said.'

I pulled my arm loose. 'I know. I really need to ring Polly.'

'Maybe you should wait until –'

'No! I have to do it now!' I remember thinking that I had to get to the others. We had to be together. That was the most important thing.

'Please come and sit down. We need to talk about this –' I must have cut him off and ran because the next thing I remember I was upstairs by myself.

On the landing, Mum emerged from the bathroom in a towel. She said something like: 'What's going on down there? Was that the phone? Who was it?'

I ignored her, head down, fists clenched. I said something like: 'I don't need to talk about it. I'm fine. I need to check on the others. I'm fine.' I ran past my bewildered mother, and into my room. I dived over the bed to retrieve my phone. There were already texts and missed calls from Nico and Beasley but I ignored them. I called Polly.

After the seventh ring it went straight to voicemail.

I think I tried again. I didn't leave a message. All I could think about was how devastated the others would be. The hugeness of Daisy dying was too vast, too abstract, to process, like trying to visualise a really big number.

I know I did not cry.

* * *

This is why I hate death: I'd experienced my first proper death when I was fifteen. My grandma, Dad's mum, had died of breast cancer and I didn't handle it at all well. By that I mean I didn't handle it the way you're expected to. You're meant to weep and cry and sob, but I just couldn't. It was sad and I would miss her but I couldn't cry. For months I'd watched her fade away on chemotherapy, becoming thinner and thinner until she no longer resembled my gran – more like living carrion. It was horrific. People repeatedly said to me, 'Don't you care? It's your grandma,' and I *did* care, I loved her a lot, but I didn't cry. I tried so hard, I tried to make myself sadder – gazing out of the window at night and listening to maudlin songs, but I still couldn't get it up.

People judge you if you don't cry when people die. They call you cold and heartless. I don't think I'm heartless. Maybe it's stage fright. Maybe I'm just a hard-boiled egg.

Then I didn't need to cry, I needed to get through to Polly. On the third attempt her mother answered, as cold and pointed as an icicle, as always.

'Hello, Toria, this is Mrs Wolff.'

'Hi. Is Polly there please?'

'She can't come to the phone at the moment. She's very upset about what's happened.'

*You can say her name*, I thought, but kept it to myself. 'OK. I was just ringing to check she was OK, but . . . well . . . please let her know that I'm here if she needs to talk, OK?' The pathetic stupidity of our squabble yesterday was erased; it was the first thing that was washed away when the tidal wave struck.

'I will do, thank you, Toria.' Mrs Wolff hung up.

I flopped down onto the bed. Perhaps I should be crying now. I looked deep, really deep inside myself, but it was like mining coal. Inside there was only black. I felt nothing except the need, the urgent need, to be with Polly.

*How could Daisy be gone?*

Stupidly, selfishly, I thought how the next time I went to French no one would have saved me a seat. I was almost sick, but I swallowed it back. My hands were trembling and clammy and I could feel panic creeping in, like I was falling somehow, losing my grip. I closed my eyes and let out a long, controlled breath. I couldn't falter. I had to make sure the others were OK. Freaking out wasn't going to achieve anything. Hard-boiled egg.

*Who found her? Was it her mum? Was she cold?* I pictured her lying in bed, staring up at the ceiling, curls spilling around her head like a halo . . . No, too much. I blotted the thought out of my head, squeezing my temples.

'Toria?' It was Mum. She rapped on the door. 'Are you OK? Dad told me what happened. Can I come in?'

'I'm fine!' I yelled. 'I'll be down in a minute.' I opened the first text from Nico:

*Fuck, have you heard about Dais? CALL ME.*

My phone lit up. Beasley. I answered at once.

'Hey . . .'

'Oh god, Tor, thank god you answered.' He was sniffing. *He* had managed to cry, evidently. *Why can't I cry?* 'No one's answering their phone!'

'It's OK, I'm here.'

'Tor, I don't know what to do. I just can't believe it. My mum has gone round to Daisy's. My mum couldn't stop crying; it was awful.'

So everyone but me was crying.

'Stay there, OK? I'm coming over.'

I threw on a mish-mash wash-basket outfit and pelted out of the door, only pausing to let Dad know where I was headed. This was good, this was taking action. No point in sitting around and being sad, was there?

On the way over I called Nico. 'Are you OK?' he asked. The morning was bright and sunny and it felt grossly wrong. The sun shouldn't have come up today, the disrespectful bitch.

'Yeah, I'm fine. Seriously. But I'm so worried about Polly. She wouldn't even come to the phone. I'm on my way over to Beasley's now.'

'Want me to come over?'

'Yeah. Yeah, that'd be good. We should be together.' I refrained from saying *It's what Daisy would have wanted*. Daisy would have been pissed off and rightly so. Daisy was doing everything she could to stay alive and it still wasn't good enough. Ooh, that was good. Some of the feeling was coming back, like when the anaesthetic wears off after you've been to the dentist and you realise you're dribbling down your chin. I was angry, angry at no one and nothing, lashing and kicking at thin air – but it was a feeling nonetheless.

I arrived at Beasley's house, a new build almost identical to ours, and everything was too normal. Beasley welcomed me inside and we hugged. He made my shoulder wet, but got it together pretty quickly. This was good: I could do this. Now I had a function: the 'shoulder to cry on'. With a trembling voice he asked if I wanted a drink and I followed him into the kitchen. The fridge hummed, ice shifted in the ice-maker and the cat noisily scoffed his breakfast.

Everything was the same except Daisy was dead.

I thought about her body again, this time in a body bag on a mortuary slab. *Where is it now? Where do they take them? Is she blue? Are her eyes open or shut?* But Daisy wasn't in her body any more. Wherever it was, it was just a shed skin now.

'I don't know how to talk,' Beasley said, lifting some orange juice out of the fridge door. 'Like, I don't know what words to say.'

'I know what you mean. It feels like everything is rude, like everyone should be silent for a while.'

'Do you think we should be silent?'

'I don't know. No. That's weird.'

His breath wavered again. 'I just can't believe it.'

'Do you want to talk about it?' I knew I could listen, if nothing else.

He shook his head. 'I think if I do I'll break down again.'

I took a sip of the orange juice. It was the kind with bits in. Gross. God, why was I even *thinking* about orange juice? *Daisy is dead and you're thinking about bits in orange juice, what the hell is wrong with you?* I didn't say anything. 'Well, we don't have to. We can do anything you want to do.'

His lips drew down at the edges like Grumpy Cat. 'Would it be wrong to watch a film or something?'

I shrugged. 'We can either be sad in silence or be sad with the TV on. Either way, today is sad.'

In what was a really inappropriate or really appropriate gesture, we watched *Poltergeist*. By the time we were on *Poltergeist II: The Other Side*, Nico had arrived and by the opening credits of *Poltergeist III*, Alice and Alex had arrived too. We said very little, not even commenting on the film. Alice lay in Alex's lap, a twisted tissue wrapped around her fingers.

I had questions and I'm pretty sure the others did too, but they were a waste of air. Knowing the ins and outs of Daisy's death wasn't going to bring her back. I didn't hear a word of the films; I thought about illness. Daisy had been ill for almost eight years. Eight years of starvation and force-feeding. One look at her said she wasn't well and yet it would have somehow been easier to understand or predict if she'd had cancer or something – we *get* that. Everyone understands physical disease. The plain fact was Daisy had starved herself until her body couldn't work any more. A different kind of disease, a harder one to get my head around.

She had been very, very ill and yet her death was still so sudden. I wondered if it's always like that. Even with sick people, death is the ultimate ninja – you never hear her footsteps until it's too late.

Like Daisy said herself at Christmas, I've always been optimistic – it's how I get through the day – knowing that there is always something to look forward to. Sure I wear a lot of black and I'm not exactly cheerleader material, but even a new vlog going online was a reason to get out of bed in the morning. That's how I've always been. I guess I wanted Daisy to get better so badly I never even considered that she might not.

The same thoughts going round and round in my head were making me feel carsick. Eventually I could sit still no longer. 'I'm going to make a cup of tea. Does anyone want one?'

Alex did and I told them not to pause the film. With no one looking, I swiped a chocolate chip muffin out of a packet on top of the bread bin. I was *starving* but airing this thought again seemed wrong somehow. Mouth full of cake, I leaned against the kitchen counter waiting for the kettle to boil, and tried to have a cry. It felt like emotional constipation; I might feel better if I could squeeze some tears out. Nothing. It wasn't going to happen. Nico followed me into the kitchen. 'Hey, how're you doing?'

'I'm fine. It's not about me, is it? I'm scared to say anything in case I accidentally crack a joke.'

Nico gave a slight smile. 'Oh, whoops, I laughed.'

'You know what?' I plonked two mugs onto the counter. 'This isn't real yet. There's going to be a moment, probably in a few weeks, and something's going to happen that only Daisy would find funny and I'm going to try to text her and I'm going to lose it.'

Nico wrapped his arms around me, but I felt cactus-like and subtly brushed him off to pour the water. 'When you do, I'll be ready to scrape you back together,' he murmured.

'Thank you. When it hits it's going to hit hard.'

'Mum did her Buddhist bit this morning.' Nico pushed himself up to sit on the counter. 'Sickness, dying and death. It's all in the small print.'

'What?' I took out some of my frustration on the teabag, squishing the poor thing against the side of the mug with all my strength.

'It's like Ariel in *The Little Mermaid*.'

I waited for an explanation, gawping at him blankly. 'OK, now I have to ask if *you're* OK?'

He smiled. 'I mean there's always a catch. Ariel gets to be human, but she has to give up her voice. The catch with being alive is that we're all going to die. Sooner or later. It's a done deal. What actually makes life really hard is that we don't *want* to die and we don't *want* to lose people. According to Mum, life is one long struggle against not getting your own way. We all *wish* Daisy was still alive, simple as that. We're spoiled brats; we all want to get our own way. That's why *life* is so hard. *Death* is easy.'

I abandoned the tea and pressed myself into his chest. He was right. I remember reading once about a girl who chewed her hair so often it formed a ball in her stomach and killed her. That's what it felt like. The knot in my stomach wasn't SAD it was WANT. I really, really, really wanted Daisy to not be dead. Perhaps sadness is always 'want': wanting someone or something you can't have. I don't know.

'That doesn't make it any easier. I do want her back, Nico. I can't help it. I want her back. I want her to be here.' I spoke to his chest.

He stroked my hair. 'According to my mum, you can meditate it away. I think she's lying though.'

Beasley came into the kitchen waving my phone aloft. 'It's Polly,' he said. 'She wants to speak to you.'

The knot swelled again and I took the phone. 'Polly?'

'Hey.' Her voice was tiny. She sounded like a terrified little girl at the bottom of a well. 'Can you come over?'

'Of course.'

'Just you. I can't handle everyone.'

'OK. I'll come over now. You OK?'

'No. Not really.'

'Sit tight, I'll be there in fifteen minutes.' I hung up. 'She wants me to go over. Just me.' I inwardly felt quite pleased that she'd selected me to go over, but then hugely awkward the next second. Beasley had known her for a lot longer than I had. 'Is that OK?'

Beasley did look disappointed, but none of us were going to squabble today. That *would* be inappropriate. 'Yeah. We'll continue our marathon here. Come back if you want. Bring Polly if she's up for it.'

I gave Beasley a bear hug, which he returned. 'I love you, Martin Beasley.'

'I love you like a fat kid loves cake.' He stopped. 'Oh shit, that's really inappropriate.'

'No. I think that's OK.' I *still* refused to say *It's what Daisy would have wanted.*

I hardly recognised Polly when she opened the front door. She looked seventeen for one thing, which, of course, she was, but I realised I'd never seen her without any make-up on. She looked so young and fresh. Her hair was swept into a top-knot and she still wore her pyjamas. Her eyes were pink raw.

'Come in.'

I entered the hall. 'Are you OK?'

Polly blinked. 'I was doing OK. I thought my tear reserves had finally run out, but I don't know if I can talk actually . . .' She tried to laugh, but it came out more like a sob.

'Come on, let's go to your room, OK? We can talk . . . or not. It doesn't matter.' I took Polly's hand and led her upstairs. The shutters were shut and her usually immaculate bed was a heap of sheets. 'I'm so sorry, Polly. This . . . it's so awful.'

'Don't . . .' Polly managed to say before her face folded in grief. Her hands flew to her face to mask her tears and I took her in my arms. I cocooned her, rubbing her back as she shook with sobs.

'It's OK,' I said. 'It's OK. Just . . . cry.' It figured. Without a filter, Polly Wolff wasn't especially complicated: when she was angry she was angry, when she was sad she was sad.

'****,' she said, almost choking. 'I miss her already.'

'I know. I know. Me too.'

'I can't even remember what the last ******* thing I said to her after school was. I wasn't paying attention.'

'I bet it was goodbye,' I said, my own voice wobbling. 'I'm sure it was.'

In the end, Polly cried herself to sleep. She lay in my lap like a cat while I stroked her hair. Her sobs slowed into regular, tidal breaths. In and out, in and out, gradually longer and deeper. The whistle down her nostril said she was calm. Sleepily she rolled off me and I covered her with the faux fur throw at the foot of her bed. I lay alongside her. I suspected that when she woke, the worst of it would be over, like an almighty thunderstorm passing in the night. I didn't plan on leaving; I wanted to be there for her when she awoke.

## Chapter Sixteen

# Tribute

We had another day off before returning to school. Our parents offered us more time off, but sitting around and being sad is really hard work. Mourning is actually quite boring and I couldn't very well watch back-to-back episodes of *Friends* on Comedy Central, could I? At least school dragged our minds off Daisy. I didn't want to feel bad about Daisy. I didn't want her to become a cloud when she'd always been sunshine. I held fast to what Nico had said about wanting Daisy back. This *yearning*. My blood felt like liquid lead in my veins, slowing me down, every step laboured, but I tried as best I could to ignore it.

We were never going to 'get back to normal', but as I got ready to go to school I was determined to make a new normal.

Polly only lasted till registration before freaking out. 'I can't be here without her. It's too weird. I'm going to an arcade or something. Coming?'

'No. I want to stay. I want . . . I like the routine.'

'Fine. I'll see you later then.' She didn't seem cross; she just didn't want to be in a place filled with memories of her. I let her go.

If you cast your mind back to my first day at Brompton Cliffs, you'll remember how much of a big deal a new girl was, so you can only imagine the reaction to a dead girl. We were mobbed on our first morning back. Well-wishers fell over themselves to give us hugs and tell us how sorry they were – and teachers were not exempt from this public outpouring of grief.

I could have been angry. I could have called these people who taunted and stared at Daisy's skinny frame hypocrites and two-faced turds, but, as much as I hated it, they meant well. They *were* sorry. Sorry for our loss and sorry to lose Daisy. She may well have been part of the freak show, but she was a hugely popular attraction at it. It shouldn't come as a surprise to learn that everyone liked Daisy. She was, after all, lovely.

'This is so weird,' Beasley said once we'd fended off the Pot-Pourri girls. 'I feel famous.'

'It's a shame Daisy isn't here to see how much everyone loved her.'

'Oh I think she can see.' Beasley smiled. 'Not like from heaven, that's tacky. I mean more like *The Exorcist*.'

I laughed because, finally, it was absolutely what Daisy would have wanted. I clung to his hand. We were using each other – propping each other up like a house of cards. When one of us wobbled we borrowed a bit of strength from someone who was doing better, like symbiosis.

Beasley said, 'Oh, I should have told Polly . . .' We paused outside his next lesson. Other students filed in around us. 'The funeral is next Monday. They want a quiet family ceremony, but we're allowed to go. Just the gang.'

'I know it sounds trite, but we *were* her family.'

'That's what I told my mum.'

'Have you told the others yet?' He said he hadn't. 'I'll text them.'

I made my way to my first lesson – English – arriving after the bell had gone. 'Sorry I'm late,' I said as I hurried in.

'That's OK, Tor. I understand,' Mr Marshall said, less subtext and more just text.

Suddenly I stopped. There was an empty desk: one space for me, and one that would be permanently empty. I should have been ready for that. It was the closest I'd come but I still didn't cry. I told myself to get a grip – I was not going to give my English class a grief performance to talk about at lunchtime. Daisy didn't die so that I'd have no mates in English. This wasn't about me. I forced myself to slide under the table. The seat felt cold.

The day was improved massively by Nico bringing me a bagel for lunch. Sixth-formers were allowed off site so we met on one of the benches overlooking the sea. It was a local suicide spot, but it was also very pretty.

'I got you tuna melt on poppy seed.'

'You are actually the best. Thank you.'

'You're welcome. How was the first day back?'

'Weird. Like Tim Burton weird.'

He chuckled – gallows humour is still humour. 'Yeah. It's gonna take a while. How's Polly?'

'She bailed after fifteen minutes.'

'She's not handling it,' he stated matter-of-factly.

'She'll get better. "No pain is forever" – who was it who said that? Euripides?'

'That was Rihanna, babe.'

I blushed. 'Oh. Well, it's still true.'

'I dunno. You've met Polly, right? She can hold a grudge like a mothertrucker. She can't let stuff go.'

'Hmm,' I mused. He was right, but I didn't know what to do about it yet.

'Look,' he said, picking at his own salmon bagel. How sophisticated, I thought, shame it tastes like fish slime. 'I have to tell you something and you're not allowed to get cross.'

'OK . . .'

'You won't get cross?'

'I'm prepared to say that in order that you tell me . . .'

'That'll do. Look, I got your text about the funeral and I can't go. It's the day of the meeting with Sony.' He grimaced.

'What? Just tell them. They'll reschedule.'

'Babe, I can't. Unsigned bands don't tell Sony to wait for them. If they asked us to hand over one testicle each we'd clearly say yes.'

I couldn't believe what I was hearing. This was a Blackmail Bagel, bought to soften me up. But, whatever, it was a no-brainer. Anyone would move the meeting. 'Nico, it's Daisy's funeral. We have to say goodbye to her.'

'I can't. The timing sucks. I'll have to say goodbye to her in private some other time. I think that Daisy would –'

'Oh god, please don't say Daisy would have understood because she bloody would have but that doesn't make it right.' I got what he was saying; I just didn't want him to be saying it. The Nico I wanted would have moved heaven and earth to be at that funeral. To be at my side. Isn't that what having a boyfriend's meant to be about? Having someone at your side, someone who's got your back, without even having to ask?

'I know it's crappy but there's nothing I can do. The other guys won't wait. They'll go without me and there's no way, Tor. You saw what happened to Zoë – no one's irreplaceable. I'm sorry. You understand, right?'

It was hard to keep the disgust off my face. It was interesting. There was a time, early into my infatuation, when I'd have acquiesced in a heartbeat to please him, but there wasn't any parallel world out there in which I would prioritise a band over a friend. 'Yeah, I understand that this band is more important to you than your friends.'

Nico raised an admittedly still very lovely eyebrow. 'At the moment, yeah, it probably is. I don't think you understand how big a deal this is for me.'

'Nico, Daisy *died*. Did you turn two pages over at once?'

He started to speak and then stopped himself. 'You know what? Anything I say right now is going to make me sound like a dick, so I'm not gonna say anything.'

'Yeah, that might be for the best.' I had a few opinions of my own that were probably best kept in my head.

He swung his bag onto his shoulder. 'I'm going back to college. I knew you'd freak out . . . but this is an impossible situation, Tor. I really need you to be OK with it.'

'Well, I'm not.'

'Will you at least hug me before I go?' I held out my arms and he embraced me but I felt like I was made out of wooden cubes, all blocky and square and awkward. 'Please don't be cross with me.'

I said nothing, but I couldn't suppress the red mist I was seeing. My first fight with Nico and it was a really top-notch one. Looking back, with 20/20 hindsight, I'm not sure we ever really recovered from that. Everyone disappoints sooner or later.

The day of the funeral came around freakishly fast. At the weekend, I was forced to accompany my mum to the Big Shiny Shopping Mall outside town to look for a funeral outfit, despite the fact that literally ninety-five per cent of my clothes were black, with the other five per cent white or grey. Apparently I was to look 'grown-up and respectful'.

After schlepping around at least ten shops, we returned to the first item I'd tried on – a simple tailored dress that made me look like a teenage girl masquerading as an executive in a wacky rom-com called *Trouble at the Top* or something equally banal. I'd fall for my older (but not too old) boss with hilarious consequences.

If you thought the dress sounded bad, I won't even mention the shoes. Mum assured me I could wear them if I had to interview for universities. When I wear heels I still walk the way I did when I was five and used to clod-hop around the house in Mum's shoes. It's not a good look.

Mum and Dad came with me on the big day. The service was being held at a Catholic church (who even knew Daisy's family was Catholic?) and the mourners filed in like stick figures in a gloomy Lowry painting. The sky hung low and white, the church a smudged charcoal etch.

*Doctor Who* has ruined churches forever. Weeping Angels EVERYWHERE.

We shuffled into the chapel and I saw Polly and her family seated near the front, where the pews were full. We had to settle for a space near the back, which Beasley's mum had saved for us. I liked Beasley's mum, she was basically him in drag. Polly, seated further towards the altar, turned around to see me. She hadn't come back to school all week but I'd seen her out of school. She'd dyed her hair a hot fuchsia shade ('Black hair doesn't feel like my hair.') and today she was wearing more make-up than I'd ever seen her in.

It was almost warpaint.

Polly, Beasley and I were the only people from school there. Apparently, Mr and Mrs Weekes hadn't wanted a 'church full of kids'. I knew, *knew*, that Daisy would have been as furious as Daisy could feasibly be. She'd have wanted everyone there. She'd have definitely wanted Alice and Alex there. And Freya and Zoë. And Nico.

I knew I had to let that go, but I couldn't. Right now he'd be halfway to London. I was still so disappointed.

I was sat next to Beasley, who looked gorgeous in his suit and tie, like a proper man. I saw it for the first time: Beasley, once he'd come out the other end of the puberty tunnel, was going to be so handsome. He just needed a beard or some stubble and he'd be what I believe is known as 'a cub'.

The service was:

1. Endless. I swear I physically aged while sitting in that church.

2. Chock-full of hymns. Not even the catchy ones.
3. Rich in God and Jesus and the Holy Spirit and Heaven, none of which Daisy had ever mentioned.
4. Nothing like Daisy at all.

The result being that the service was oddly unmoving. I was bored numb. The priest said words but none of them spoke of the Daisy we knew. He could have been talking about anyone, literally anyone. Oh, don't you worry, the TRAGEDY of YOUTH being CRUELLY SNATCHED was hit home, but this was some faceless, production-line sentiment.

I held Beasley's hand throughout, but I could sense his boredom too. At one point, when the priest mentioned Daisy 'sitting on God's lap', Polly actually turned around and rolled her eyes. It was good. That felt like Polly coming back to me.

One thing got me. As we exited the church we had to join a grim procession past the coffin in a morbid public expression of farewell. It was like a soul train of death. Say bye to the box. It was a shiny ivory colour with gold handles and covered in white and pink flowers. It was more than a little Barbie Dream Coffin™. As stupid as it was, as I got closer, it hit home that the pathetically small box contained Daisy. I hated it. How could that thing contain everything that was her? She was supposed to be free now, not in a horrid shoebox.

It made me angry. My head spun a little and my legs went rubbery. Polly appeared at my side in the nick of time and steadied me. 'You OK?'

'No.'

'Let's get the **** away from here.'

'Yes please.'

I told my mum that I couldn't face the wake back at Daisy's house and, to be honest, we didn't feel all that welcome. I knew I couldn't even begin to understand what Daisy's mum and dad and brother were going through. This was their time, their loss. As much as we felt like Daisy was ours, she was theirs really. What were we going to do? Run up to them and say they'd got the funeral all wrong? Hardly.

Perhaps it was best to leave them to it, and we'd mourn our version of Daisy in our own way. 'Where are we going?' I asked Polly. Beasley trailed after us and we stormed away from the church.

'Alex texted. He said to meet them at Fantasyland.'

'What, now?'

'Yeah. He said to come quickly. Sounds urgent.'

'But it's all locked up.'

It wasn't though. We followed Alex's instructions and found a section of the chain-link fence at the back of the course had been prised open.

'What the ****?'

'We are going to be in so much trouble! This is trespassing.' Beasley went chalky white.

'Beasley, for once in your life, woman up!' Polly slipped through the opening and I followed. We had to push our way through shrubbery and a sea of litter and an elephant graveyard of lost golf balls, but we stumbled through onto the course.

It didn't take long to see what we'd been summoned to. There was a crowd of people gathered around Hole 4. The Disapproving Seal.

Daisy's favourite.

Saying nothing at all, Polly took my hand and I took Beasley's. We made our way over. The whole year seemed to be there. The Pot-Pourri girls, the meatheads, the music crowd, the theatre lot, Zoë, Freya. Everyone. Alice and Alex stood closest to the sad-looking seal, arranging daisies all around it.

Daisies of every colour – pink, purple, yellow, orange, white . . . all bright, all joyous, all the colours she had been. There was a photo of her propped up against a flipper. She was in full colour and she was laughing. It wasn't even a good photo – it was blurry from where she'd thrown her head back. But she looked like Daisy.

Something burst out of my chest. A howl. I broke. My hand flew to my mouth. The sob lodged beneath my ribs finally tore free and soared. Polly and Beasley jointly caught me on either side as I crumpled.

It turned out that, while I don't cry at death, I do cry at love.

# Chapter Seventeen

## Stasis

I had never given much thought to what tears smelled like, but my pillow was evidence that they do indeed have a most singular odour. The days after Daisy's funeral were damp and salty. Turns out once you start you can't stop. And you know what? Mourning is exhausting. I wonder if I was losing sugar out of my eyes or something, because I physically couldn't get out of bed. Not such a hard-boiled egg after all.

Everyone seemed to understand. They left me alone. I was best left.

I drew the curtains and denied the rest of the world. I pressed pause. I was in sad stasis.

Slipping in and out of a semi-opaque sleep, riddled with dreams of waking up somewhere better, I wished her back. It really, really hurt, like holding it all in so tightly had left finger bruises all around my heart and ribcage.

My hair was chip-shop greasy and my teeth felt furry and my breath smelled of dog but I couldn't have cared less. You know what killed me the most? She hadn't meant to, but she'd left ghosts everywhere. In my recent calls list; her photo was still in my contacts; her little red light on Facebook to show she was offline (and wasn't she just); her most recent tweet about an episode of *Sherlock*. It sounds stupid, but it was like they were rubbing it in.

Swinging from fizzy, hot sulphuric anger about how sodding unfair it was – why, why her when there are so many awful, awful people in the world, why her? – to sad, sad for my loss, sad she was gone, sad she wouldn't ever get to the good bit. Sad is heavier than chain mail and, for a while there, I couldn't get up.

I took her for granted, you know. I think we all did. We were gonna have to live with that. I needed a few days away from everyone – they only reminded me of her too. I took some time out. It was necessary.

I wrote something in my poem book. It helped.

**For Daisy**

How to put someone bigger than the sky
on a piece of A5?
Cruel to confine her to little ink cages of
font 12 Times New Roman.
Full stops hammered around the coffin.
Breaths like ellipses.
Her skeleton too was an insufficient beaker:
Skin and bones too small
For her litres and gallons,
Spilling over the edges.
Better rid of it and free to be
Bigger than the sky.

# Chapter Eighteen

# Toilet

It's not that we got less sad about Daisy after the funeral, it's just that other stuff required immediate attention. The sadness was there, a fat black slug stuck to the side of my heart. I was trying as best I could to ignore it.

A 'development deal' is when a record label pays for an act to record, rehearse, write and (apparently) buy new clothes and haircuts in return to all rights, earnings and the band members' souls. This was what The Band Formerly Known As Judas Cradle – 'Oh, we changed the band's name. They didn't like the ass-torture thing. They like Action Station, what do you think?' – now had.

I couldn't stay mad at Nico forever, and it felt like I was deliberately pissing on his chips, so I joined the celebrations. I figured that Daisy would have been over the moon so I should be too.

Of course I made him sweat it out. We had our own personal memorial the day he got back from London. He left flowers at the flippers of the Disapproving Seal and said a few words ('You dying proves that life is totally unfair. You, of all the people in the world, should have lived forever.').

We hadn't had any time together all week, so the weekend after the funeral, we had a day under the duvet on his sofa, watching back-to-back episodes of *Game of Thrones* on his laptop. He explained the deal to me. 'The development deal is for two years, so I don't think anything's gonna change overnight.'

'Will you leave college?'

'Not unless I have to. I think Cleo is sorting stuff out with them. I think we might rerecord the demo in a better studio in a few weeks so they have something to start talking about. Oh, and we might start doing gigs in London. You know, to build buzz.'

I suspected I might start hearing a fair bit more PR speak like that.

It was exciting though, even if everything happening to Nico made me feel less exciting somehow – me, the muggle to his wizard, the Lois to his Clark. It also served to remind me that I had literally no idea what I wanted to do with my life. Even thinking about it was like staring into a bottomless pit. I didn't even know if I wanted to go to university, let alone what subject to do if I got there. It must be delightfully easy for Nico: he wanted to be a musician and nothing else would do.

I kind of wanted to wear pyjamas and play on the internet all day. Is that a job? Can it be?

One perk of the deal was that Nico now got an 'Inspiration Allowance' to help him write songs. His budget included DVDs. This I would not be complaining about. I decided not to mention the fact that we hadn't had so much as a grope since before Daisy died.

Something was wrong. You know when you're worried about something but you can't remember what it is you're worried about? Germans probably have a really long word for it. There *should* be a word for it: I'll call it the Niggly Noos. I had a really bad case of the Niggly Noos. Something was up and I couldn't put my finger on it. Maybe it was leftover fallout from Daisy, maybe it was Nico . . . all the changes . . . the fact we hadn't had sex in a while . . . but none of those answers felt quite right.

Maybe I'd left an oven on somewhere.

'Wait up!' Beasley chased Polly and I down the corridor. He almost collapsed, red-faced and out of breath. 'Oh god, I've been following you since the Science block . . . couldn't you hear me? I'm dying.'

'We heard you, we just thought it was funny to ignore you,' I said. That wasn't true, but it was funny. 'What's up?'

Beasley, not likely to trouble the athletics squad, had to take refuge on a bench.

'Jeez, Beas. Spit it out,' Polly added.

'I've come from your dad's office. He wanted to see me and Alice.'

'What for?'

'The prom. A load of people – like Becca and Summer – have asked if the ticket money can go towards an eating-disorder charity in honour of Daisy.'

'What?' Polly said, and I swear her eyes turned red – just for a second. 'No way. That money's for the golf course.'

'That's what I said, but he's agreed. He wants us to do it.'

'****'* sake!' Polly was already stomping in the direction of the sixth-form wing.

All Beasley and I could do was trail after her. 'I can't run any more, Toria! I cannot breathe and I have sweat patches under my moobs.'

We had to force our way into Mr Wolff's office as he was in a meeting with the sparrow-faced bursar. He looked less than pleased.

'Polly, you can't come barging in!'

'And you can't take our money away. We raised that money.'

'The prom was Daisy's idea. A lot of people think it should be in her honour. I agree. I'm surprised you don't. Becca Ferguson has found a local support group for young people's mental health and I think it's a fantastic idea.'

Beasley and I could only lurk at the back of the office. Problem was, I kind of agreed with the Pot-Pourri girls. Perhaps Daisy's death and the funeral had deflated my tyres in general, but I couldn't muster the same enthusiasm for the golf course any more. To be honest, with everything that had happened, it seemed pretty trivial.

I always said I was in the fight to the death, I just assumed it would be *my* death.

Polly went on. 'I don't give a shimmering **** what Becca Ferguson found. Daisy wanted to save Fantasyland.'

'But that was before . . . Look, Polly, you can't seriously be telling me that you think a crazy-golf course is more important than giving to an actual charity? And I think you'll sell a lot more tickets this way.'

'Dad, no! It's not just a golf course! It's a . . . tribute to Daisy now. Please.'

'Polly. It's a no. The money goes to charity.'

Polly's whole body hummed with rage and frustration. I briefly pictured her flipping her father's desk, Hulk-style, but instead her bottom lip started to tremble. She turned and silently lurched out of the room. It was much scarier. 'I'm sorry,' I said. 'Fantasyland was our place, you know?'

Mr Wolff shrugged. 'You'll find a new place.'

I nodded. 'I agree. I think Becca's idea is a good idea.' I hated that he was right, but he was. However many rousing speeches Polly gave, our reasons for trying to save Fantasyland were selfish ones.

My afternoon session that day was Art, which I went to with a heavy heart. Another double period without Daisy. Mrs Ford, basically Judi Dench in a pashmina, was cool and we were allowed to listen to music while we worked but the only music I wanted was the sound of Daisy's voice. Art felt like a lesson for the first time.

My style, if you could call it that, was sort of 'Rave Kawaii' if I had to sum it up. A lot of collage mixed-media stuff with a lot of Japanese and Korean influences. I don't know if it's cultural appropriation or not, but it looks hella cool. I was working on a laptop developing some videos. I was really into the idea of moving digital art and Mrs Ford supported it wholeheartedly.

About two thirds of the way into the lesson I got a text from Polly.

*Pls meet me in 6 form toilets ASAP.*

Mrs Ford was among the most laid-back teachers in the school. We didn't even have to ask permission to leave so I closed the laptop and slipped quietly out. The sixth-form building was on the other side of campus. For some reason my heart beat faster and I quickened my step. Something was wrong. I'd felt it the night we found Daisy in the bathroom and I felt it now, like pins and needles in my head.

I ran.

First across the courtyard, sneakers slapping on paving slabs, and into the sixth-form wing, squeaking and skidding on the linoleum. I got to the toilet and found it empty. Maybe Polly had given up on waiting and gone back to her lesson. 'Polly?'

'I'm in here.' Her tiny voice came from the last cubicle. I pushed open the door and found her sitting on the toilet with the seat down. In her hand was one half of a pair of shiny silver scissors, unscrewed at the middle. 'Will you please take this away?' For the first time ever, I towered over her. She looked so small.

I took the blade off her but said nothing.

'God, I'm so ******* weak.' She wasn't crying but she looked broken, defeated.

'You're not,' I said, my voice wobbling more than hers. 'You're *not*. You did the right thing. You texted me. You stopped yourself.'

She gave me a grave look, peering up from under her lashes. She lifted the sleeve of her vintage Adidas T-shirt to reveal the very top of her arms. There were four or five red, sore-looking scratches, all recently made but healed over. 'What the **** is wrong with my brain that I think this is the way to deal with stuff? I felt like I was going to ******* erupt.'

I said nothing. I didn't know what to say.

'It should have been me, Tor. It should have been me instead of her. She was the good one.'

'No! Hell no! Don't even think that! That's just . . . crazy, massive sadness talking.' I lowered myself onto the toilet seat next to her, motioning for her to shuffle over and make room. We could both just about fit one buttock each on the loo. 'Look. This. It's not a big deal.'

'Tor, it ******* is! I hate this! I'm such a ******* cliché.'

This kept coming up with Polly. Her need to subvert other people's expectations. I wondered why she was so at odds with herself, so combative, or why she cared so much about what people thought of her. I mean, does anyone really think that much about anyone else anyway? We're all too busy ironing out our own mental creases.

'That's not what I meant. I mean, don't be too hard on yourself.' I squeezed her arm. 'It's a hiccup, a wobble, a bump in the road or whatever . . . It doesn't mean you've, like, failed. There's nothing to fail; it's not a test. Remember Daisy, how she was after she went into hospital . . . she dusted herself off and got on with it. So you cut yourself. So what? You stopped before, you can stop again.' I'm nothing if not a pragmatist.

Polly nodded. 'I know. I thought I was fixed . . . for good. I hadn't cut in so long. In the old days I would have gone to the golf course but . . .'

I missed that place so much. 'Maybe that's how it crept up on you. You know, when you least expected it.'

'What if I'm never fixed? What if my head *always* tells me this is a good idea?'

'Well, then don't fight it. That's how it is.' I remembered Nico telling me something about the small print, but he'd done a much better job of putting it into words. 'Maybe it's not gonna go away, so . . . make peace with it. It's a part of you. We all have parts of ourselves we don't like but we can't do shit about them. Just because you're *thinking* about cutting doesn't mean you have to. It's like a little lodger in your head.'

Polly chuckled. 'Well, can it kindly ******* find somewhere else to live?' She rested her head on my shoulder. Her hair smelled of conditioner – the intensive hot-oil kind. Her poor hair had been through so much it probably needed it. I inhaled her scent and it was lush.

She nuzzled against me and I felt the tension ebb from her body.

'You'll be fine.'

I kissed her forehead and she tilted her face up. We were so close now. As she came up, her lips brushed my chin. They were so soft. Was she going to . . .? She was so, so close. She was. She was going to. We had to. We were too close not to. My heart raced way up in my throat.

Her lips touched mine.

# Chapter Nineteen

# Skin

Oh god. Look, I know what you're thinking, OK?

1. SHE'S A LESSSSSBIAN.
2. That slut's meant to be with Nico.

Yeah, *I know*, on both counts. It sounds so, so hollow but sometimes things really do JUST HAPPEN. This was one of those things. It was like we had magnets for mouths. I know this wouldn't hold up in court but it really did feel out of our control.

Another true thing is that if something is a little bit taboo or naughty or exotic it is automatically, I'd estimate, a hundred times more appealing. In that moment, with her lips brushing mine, I couldn't not kiss her. I'd never felt a rush of electricity like it. You could have charged your phone off us.

And you know what? It was hot. Sort of different and sort of the same. Her full lips, even her tongue, were softer somehow, although the kiss was no less hungry than Nico's. It was weird. I was so used to Nico's stubble. Her skin was so, so smooth; it was like double cream.

A trapdoor in my tummy opened and my heart plummeted straight through to my feet. In a split second I was high on the kiss: the whole cubicle spun like a waltzer and I had to grip the graffiti-strewn wall for support.

The second or two the kiss lasted for felt like years, like one of those parallel worlds in every science-fiction book ever where time moves more quickly. We lived a lifetime in that moment and that was the time it took for me to snap out of it and realise what I was doing.

Flowery prose over. The smell of bleach dragged me out of it. I was snogging Polly on a toilet. Clearly a no-no.

I pulled away. I couldn't find any words so I just half smiled, half grimaced. Polly, thank the baby Jesus, had her shit together. 'Wow,' she said with a broad grin. 'Mancini's a lucky guy. You're a great kisser.'

Was that it? I didn't know whether to be relieved or disappointed.

'Thank you?'

Polly rose and offered me a hand up. 'Relax, Toria, I don't think you can catch gay off a toilet seat,' she said with a wink. 'You were the last of my friends I hadn't snogged. Glad I did though!'

She was lying, I could tell. That girl had more front than Brompton Pier. She was playing it down, playing it safe. Reducing the kiss to a game or a dare made it harmless fun. Well, it didn't feel harmless to me. Already guilt was corroding my insides.

'Come on,' she said. She checked herself over in the mirror to make sure it looked like she hadn't been crying. The cutting, the kiss – all forgotten in an instant. Polly Wolff is a typhoon – she hits hard when she hits but blows over in minutes. 'I've had an amazing idea. Will you come into town with me?'

I didn't want to be all BUT WHAT ABOUT THE KISS? WHAT DOES IT MEAN so instead I said, 'Sure.'

'No! Polly you CAN'T!' I said, jaw hanging open.

'I can. They won't even ask how old we are. I've got the money, why not. If I'm going to **** with my skin, I might as well get something pretty to show for it.' We were standing outside Jack of Hearts, the local tattoo and piercing parlour. The whir of the needle from within was far too like the dentist's drill for me to be comfortable. 'I mean look at me. This was bound to happen sooner or later. Cliché, remember?'

'But don't you think you should think about it? It'll be on your skin forever. What'll it look like when you're eighty?'

'Which part of me do you imagine *will* look good when I'm eighty?' It was a valid point. 'And I've wanted a tattoo for ages. It's just that now I know what I want. Something that means something.'

'Are you sure? What will your parents say?'

'They won't know. And my dad might be able to take away our crazy golf, but he can't do **** about my body.'

'OK . . . if you're sure.' We entered and a little bell jingled over our heads. I'm not going to lie, I was pooping myself a little. I had never felt younger or more out of place. Aside from my ears, I'd never even had anything pierced, and I had those done at Claire's Accessories.

An incense stick smoked from the wall but failed to entirely mask the smell of disinfectant. A girl who was more tattoo than skin popped up at a reception desk. 'OMG, Polly! Hi, babes! How are you, darling?'

'Oh my god! Bree! I didn't know you worked here.'

God, how small was this town? The pair of them chatted away and I wondered, I confess, if they'd got it on. Any worries I had about us being underage melted away: clearly Bree wouldn't challenge her.

'What are you having done?' Bree asked finally.

'I want a daisy,' Polly said.

I sat at her side as she had it done. She had to take off her bra and sat with her T-shirt pressed to her chest for modesty. For someone who had spent a significant amount of time cutting herself, Polly wasn't great with pain and clutched my hand until it went numb. The artist, Pablo, didn't speak brilliant English, so he worked diligently and the tattoo quickly took shape. It was quite, quite incredible. In my head tattoos weren't art, but this was almost photorealistic. I couldn't believe it. It was a simple pink daisy with a single green stem. It grew alongside Polly's ribcage. The detail was unbelievable. As a final touch, a single petal fell from the flower, dancing free on some imaginary breeze. A petal representing our Daisy.

'Do you like it?' Polly said after we were finally finished – three hours later. She looked a little woozy and I thought we should probably get her a cup of very sweet tea. Pablo was smearing some ointment on the tattoo. The skin looked red and sore but the tattoo was beautiful.

'It's really, really gorgeous,' I said, and I meant it.

* * *

I couldn't sleep that night, my head full of the kiss. Well, that and some bloody earworm novelty song I couldn't purge. I was too hot. I kicked the duvet off and sprawled across my bed like a starfish. Nico hadn't texted to wish me goodnight either and that made me sad. Busy, busy mind. Niggly Noos.

One thing at a time. The kiss. Thinking about it made . . . let's just say there was a physical reaction. I was not gay. I didn't think being gay was a bad thing . . . I don't want to be all like 'some of my best friends are gay', but some of my best friends were gay! It didn't make sense. I loved Nico's boy chest and big shoulders and good arms and I especially liked his willy.

What? I really did.

Did one urgent toilet-based kiss make me bi? I suddenly understood Polly's loathing of labels. Putting a name to myself wasn't making the weirdness go away, so what was the point? I can honestly say I'd never looked at another girl and thought PHWOAR, but I similarly couldn't deny the kiss had . . . aroused me. There was no other word for it.

I thought about Scarlet Johansson and Natalie Portman and Mila Kunis, actively trying to get myself going. Although I liked the idea of smooth hairless skin and soft curves, it wasn't the same as the idea of a square, hard boy body. It occurred to me for the first time how much I like to feel smaller and more delicate than the people I get it on with. But wasn't that true of Polly? Thinking back to the toilet cubicle, to how much further it could have gone . . . it made me feel wild. Wild in a good way, wild like standing naked in the garden in the middle of a storm.

Wide awake, blinkers off. Sleep was miles away.

## Yours Truly

Sandpaper skin
I come on like a fever
And you're impervious
A laminate Romeo.
Do you know me at all?
When every day I paint a mask on
Pop art with a thought cloud
What a Cool Girl she'd be
Teeth marks on my tongue.
The fault's undoubtedly mine
Because I dreamt you into being
And you're so perfect
I want to burn myself down
And start again.
What do you see in me?
Those things are 2-D cardboard cut-outs
Or dialogue characters said.
Situations vacant.
The cat who got the cream
Is lactose intolerant.
You're too good for me
You're too good.

## Chapter Twenty

# Shoreditch

I was scared of London. I had never been without my parents and I felt dwarfed by it. I didn't like feeling at the mercy of a skyscraper city I didn't know or understand; I could fall into a crack in the pavement, never to be found. After Easter had come and gone, Nico was now an expert on all things London. Sony had already paid for them to rerecord their demo over the holidays to fit in around school. The new version sounded flawless, like it had been run through a magic filter, which it probably had. Action Station were every bit as good as anything you'd download on iTunes. It was a little uncanny.

We agreed to go and see their first London gig in Shoreditch. Mum and Dad took some convincing to let me go, but I promised to scope out the UCL campus while we were there. The label had invited 'tastemakers' along to a special 'secret' gig. It was all part of their 'positioning'. I was starting to understand that a band did as well as a label wanted them to do – they essentially bought press attention and radio play.

Although I was nervous (more Imodium) the train journey up turned out to be pretty good fun. The band had gone in the van with all the instruments so Polly, Beasley and I took the train. We bought loads of teen girl magazines and did all the quizzes. 'Are you a Girlfriend Goddess?' (I was not – and none of the questions asked if I sometimes made out with my friends.) 'Is he a Keeper or a Dumper?' (A Dumper, according to that – troubling.) 'BFF or Frenemy?' (I was a good friend, but then the questions were pretty loaded.) We ate a *lot* of Haribo. By the time the train pulled into Paddington I was sugar-wired.

Luckily for Beasley and I, Polly either knew her way around London or was extremely good at cultivating an air of knowledge and authority so she *seemed* to know her way around. In truth, I think she'd simply researched the route. East London was insanely trendy. I realised that here the Pot-Pourri girls would look horribly out of place and we, in our walking jumble sale of second-hand odds and ends, were the norm. Every girl seemed to have a Lego haircut and Twiggy dress while all the guys were either bearded Steampunk heroes or pretenders to the Jim Morrison throne. There were a lot of people wearing capes. I do not know why.

I honestly didn't know if this was the mother ship calling us home or if it was time to buy some new clothes. Fashion victims aside, imagine living somewhere where you could wear anything you liked and not have people openly mock you? I liked the idea of that.

Before the gig we went to Rough Trade on Brick Lane to browse imported music and get coffee. We got red velvet cupcakes from Spitalfields Market and plundered Beyond

Retro. This was it. This was why we had to escape: there were places like this waiting for us.

**New plan:**

**Finish school.**

**Move to London.**

**Figure out what I want to be.**

**Easy.**

The gig was at a tiny little basement nightclub – it had to be small because otherwise the band would appear too mainstream, something which the label was keen to avoid. Savvy musos had to feel like they had organically 'discovered' Action Station for themselves. We were on the list, which made us feel very special, but were told we weren't allowed to drink. That blew.

Grimy, buzzing electronica filled the dingy club, which, without a sign over the door, would be your standard crack den. The walls were covered in flaking pasted porn and old gig posters while the floor was sticky. 'How cool is THIS?' Beasley exclaimed. I guessed it took shabby chic to a whole new level.

The tastemakers, it turned out, were mainly gay men in their thirties. Nico took a minute to explain who everyone was: music journalists, radio pluggers, promoters, bloggers and, ominously, 'industry people'. This was a little like seeing that the Wizard of Oz is a crap little man behind a curtain. These men were responsible for brainwashing you into buying my boyfriend. It was all very odd. Among these people, I felt hopelessly juvenile.

Nico introduced me to some hipster east-London-looking girls too. 'This is the street team,' he told me. 'They're the *early adopters*.'

'They're what?'

'Like bloggers and stuff. The label sent them our demo.'

They regarded me down their noses. I realised I was competition. Nonetheless, I smiled sweetly and shook their hands. 'She's still at *school*,' I heard one of them mutter to her friend. I could have felt small, but I was the one who got to shag him (occasionally), not them. Instead of feeling wounded, I felt quite smug. A year ago, that would have been me. Having the real thing, I didn't feel the need to run an @IloveNico Twitter account. At some point, I'd sprouted a physical life with friends to mourn, golf courses to save and, apparently, girls to kiss.

Should I be jealous of these girls? Was he . . . doing *stuff* with them? Is that why they were adopting early? I told my paranoid inner voice to STFU, but a seed had been sown. It would make sense of the passion drought we'd been experiencing. For whatever reason, Nico seemed to be avoiding touching me. At what point had I stopped being sexy?

The week before the gig we'd been in his bedroom while his mum was at yoga. I'd tried to get him going: I'd kissed him and slipped my hand into his boxers but he'd brushed me off. He called me a 'sex pest'. That left an invisible bruise.

I'm going to say something awful now. I sometimes think wanting Nico Mancini might have been better than actually having him. I'd had something these girls were dreaming of. Right now, the dreaming outweighed the real thing. I wondered if that was the Niggly Noo I couldn't shake.

No. I pushed the thoughts out of my head. They were dangerous thoughts. He was busy with the band, that was all. I was the one kissing people I shouldn't be kissing. The paranoia morphed into guilt.

When the time came, Action Station took to the stage. The way people watched them was different though. It wasn't drunk people pogoing at the front of the stage like in The Mash Tun, the band were coolly regarded, scrutinised over five-pound bottled beers. Eyes spun like fruit machines landing on dollar signs.

After the gig, naturally there was an after-party and at this we managed to get DRUNK. The words 'free bar' are surely the finest in the English language. Beasley vanished outside with a very cute blogger in his early twenties. He had a ginger beard and a trucker cap and probably didn't know that Beasley was sixteen. I was pleased for him; he'd finally got some action at an Action Station gig.

While he was off snogging, Polly and I were sprawled across a battered sofa in the corner of the club by the cloakroom. I was drunk, Polly was drunker. She could hardly walk in a straight line and her eyes were glassy.

'Do you wanna know a secret?' she slurred.

'Of course. Secrets give me life.'

'I broke up with Zoë yesterday.'

I sat up straight, almost knocking Polly off the sofa. 'What?'

'Yup.'

'I can't believe you didn't say anything until now, you shady bitch! Why?'

Polly shrugged. 'I dunno. Preferred being mates.'

I scanned her rolling eyes. 'There's more to it than that. Is this about . . .?'

It took her a second to realise what I was talking about. 'Oh what? *That*? No! One, she pissed me off after Daisy died. She was all like, "Cheer up, love, give us a smile" – **** off! Then she's all clingy while at the same time making out with that skank in The Gash. So double **** off.'

'Oh, fair enough then.'

'You can relax, Tor. You and me . . . we're just you and me.'

'I know.'

'Sometimes kissing is just kissing. Nothing means anything, remember? It's sport.' She was going to kiss me again. We were close enough – her head resting on the arm of the chair, me leaning over her. Her lips were so ripe, so, so kissable. We could and I knew it would be good. Time slowed down and the music faded to nothing but heartbeats.

'What's going on?' It was Nico. He plopped down next to me on the sofa, throwing his arm around me. 'Are you about ready to leave? I've had enough.'

'Yeah,' I said. 'Yeah, ready when you are.' The guilt was back in a big way.

We were all staying at the 'Sony Flat' before heading back to Brompton in the morning. We were scattered around the place like caterpillars in sleeping bags, drunken arms hanging off sofas into ashtrays. Nico and I had a double bed in the smaller bedroom and a degree of privacy. Something was troubling Nico, I could tell; he stripped to his pants and perched on the edge of the bed. I wondered if he was going to hurl.

'Are you OK? Are you going to vom?'

'No. I'm not too bad.'

I actually might yet vom. I'd drunk way too much, but I kept it to myself. The bed was spinning slightly.

'What's up? You were great tonight you know. Everyone loved you.'

'Etienne's moving to London. Like now. He thinks it'll be better for recording and stuff.'

That sobered me up. 'What? He wants the whole band to move?'

'No. He hasn't said that. The rest of us are staying in Brompton. Jason The Drummer still has his job and college too.'

'But you want to move?'

He looked at me. Even in the gloom of the bedroom and with sirens wailing through the streets of London he was still beautiful. Sometimes you need reminding. But he looked lost.

'No. God no. I'm panicking a bit, Tor.'

'What? Why?'

He took a deep breath and closed his eyes. 'It's all happening a bit fast . . . I'm, like, *aghhhhh!*' He frantically waved his hands around his head. 'My feet haven't touched the floor. Everything's changing.'

I reached across the bed for him. I wrapped myself around him like a shawl and kissed his neck. 'But this is what you want.'

'I know. It is. It's just so fast. Nothing happens for ages and then it all comes at once. I need some time to think about stuff.' He held out his forearm to show me his tattoo – the wheel. 'That's what this is meant to be about. Change. Everything changes, nothing stays the same. It's the first rule.'

I nodded and thought of Daisy. How much she would have loved today.

'But it's too fast.' He turned around and kissed me hard on the lips. The first proper kiss we'd had in a long time. It felt like he was clinging to me for dear life.

'It's OK,' I said, pushing his hair out of his eyes. 'I'm not changing.' If he was drowning, I'd be his rubber ring.

I wrote this around this time.

**The Killing Jar**

Graceful glass
Marilyn curved
Hermetically sealed
Chokes butterflies
To death
With ether
Preserves wings
For display
Forever.

# Chapter Twenty-One

# Protest

Back in Brompton, I was helping Nico revise for his finals when we got the call. He'd written his notes up into handy cheat sheets from which I was testing him. By that stage, I felt fairly confident I could pass A-level Biology at a pinch.

'Almost. It says here that osmosis is diffusion where water moves from a solution of higher water potential to a solution of lower water potential through a partially permeable membrane. Yours was pretty much the same though.'

Nico said, 'Hmmm,' and jotted down a note on his pad.

My phone vibrated, shuffling across his floorboards. It was Alice. 'I'll just get this. Hello?'

'Hi. It's Alice. Get your asses down to Fantasyland.'

'What? Why?'

'Polly chained herself to the Disapproving Seal.'

I blinked. 'She did what?'

'She heard the demolishers were about to move in.' Alice delivered the news in her usual monotone.

'Oh. My. God. We'll be right down.' I hung up. 'Polly chained herself to the crazy-golf course.'

'Of course she did!' Nico laughed, a relief because he wasn't smiling a lot these days. Between the band and his exams he was a twitching ball of nerves. 'God, she's finally lost her mind. It was bound to happen sooner or later.'

I ran my hands through my hair, exasperated. 'We have to go down and get her.'

Nico motioned at the pile of textbooks scattered over his bedroom floor. 'Toria, my exams start in two weeks. I'm not going anywhere, I haven't even started on Politics yet.'

I wanted to argue but he was already struggling to fit his revision in around band stuff. I didn't nag. 'OK, can I go?'

'Yes! Go! Take pictures!'

I kissed him on the lips. 'I love you.' And I think I did. When I was with him I felt quiet and content inside.

'Love you too.' We said the words all the time without hesitation. They came almost too easily, like they weighed no more than 'hello'.

Dirty mechanical dinosaurs surrounded our golf course, jaws hanging open, ready to take chunks out of it. I had no doubt Polly would have seen them moving in from her house. This early on a Sunday morning, there weren't any people around, but I slipped into Fantasyland through the broken fence all the same.

I saw a group gathered around the Disapproving Seal and cut across the course. I was the last to arrive. I could see Alice and Alex, Beasley and Zoë. Even Freya was lurking on the perimeter. She hadn't even brought a book. Finally I saw Polly. She was handcuffed around one of the seal's fins. I didn't even want to know where she'd got handcuffs from.

'Come on, Pol,' Beasley said. 'It's not gonna make a difference.'

'It won't if we give up, no.' She saw me. 'Toria, tell Beasley this'll work. They can't demolish the park if we're attached to it.'

I shrugged. 'Well, they won't kill her, will they?'

'See?' Polly said triumphantly. 'I already texted the photographer guy from the paper. He's on his way.'

Beasley looked to Alex for sanity. 'You could get arrested for this, Polly. We're all trespassing.'

'I don't give a flying ****.'

'What if you need the loo?' Alice added unhelpfully.

'Then I'll **** myself, I don't care. This is Daisy's memorial. I'm not going to let them level it. Where's Nico?' Polly turned to me.

'He's revising.'

'Oh great.'

'He's sorry.'

Polly rolled her eyes. 'I can't believe you're all giving up. This is *ours* and they're taking it away! Alice, you met Alex here. Remember? You wouldn't dare speak to him and your face went bright red every time he spoke to you. Tor, this is where you met Nico. This is where we invented Golf Tennis. Zoë, I fingered you on that ship!'

Zoë grimaced. 'Thanks for sharing, Pol.'

'And this seal was Daisy's favourite thing in the world. They can't take it away, they can't. These are our memories. They can't **** with that.'

I sat alongside her, clearing some dead tribute flowers away with my toe. Of course I knew her more personal reasons for clinging to the course, but said nothing. 'The memories aren't going anywhere. You can't demolish memories.'

'What about new memories? What about what happens next? What about the legacy?'

Beasley tried again. 'They'll arrest you.'

The resolution in her eyes was treading a very fine line between determination and plain Brontë-sister crazy. 'Let them try.'

Alex doffed his cap. 'As much as one hates to be the proverbial party pooper, I don't fancy having this on my Cambridge application form. *Je suis désolé, mes amis*.'

'Oh **** off, Alex, you pretentious ****!' Polly spat.

Someone needed to say it. 'I second that.' I made a decision. I saw men in hard hats and high-vis jackets arrive on the scene, looking at us like they were unsure what to do. By herself, Polly looked deranged, but two of us were a movement. 'Do you have another pair of handcuffs?'

Polly's smile was radiant, even on such a grey day. 'Nope, but there's a bicycle chain. You are a legend.'

This was insane, but quite funny. I was a protester now. Another one to tick off the list. I looped the chain around my waist and the seal's neck, as tight as was comfortable.

A burly beardy man entered through the main gates. 'Oi! What do you think you're playing at?'

'We shall not, we shall not be moved!' Polly sang at the top of her voice and I could only join in.

I know that this sounds futile. I knew it was futile. I knew it wasn't going to work and that wasn't why I was doing it. Two girls chained to a seal has never changed the course of history, but it was making a point. I knew we weren't going to find a nest of rare birds or an endangered plant or an ancient volcanic spring under the golf course. Some long-lost millionaire aunt wasn't going to step in to save the place at the eleventh hour. This isn't that kind of story.

If nothing else, we cared and people saw us caring. We were 'those meddling kids'. That was cool.

Workmen (for they were all men) gathered around, a mixture of disbelief, annoyance and amusement on their faces.

'Get them out of here,' said the beardy guy, the foreman, I guessed.

'You can't touch us, it's assault!' I said, fairly confident I'd heard that on TV. To my amazement, he seemed to agree.

He swore. A lot. 'What the ******* hell are you ***** waiting for? Call the ******* police!' he shouted at one of his men.

Alex actually surrendered. The weasel. 'I'm nothing to do with this, sir.'

'Then get the **** off my site, you little ****.'

'Well, there's no need for that language,' Polly said.

Those of us who were not chained to the seal were frogmarched out of the park. Beasley looked back over his shoulder apologetically. By now Brompton people, who – let's face it – didn't have anything better to do on a Sunday morning, were gathering at the fences, peeping through to see who was causing all the commotion. The photographer had arrived but his access was being blocked. Still, he managed to borrow a ladder and take some shots over the fences. Polly and I continued our sad little protest song. I wasn't used to attracting this kind of attention to myself, but we were together and it felt a lot like Daisy was with us too. She'd have loved this. I just wished Nico would have come down.

About fifteen minutes later, the police rocked up. 'Uh-oh,' giggled Polly. 'Now we're in trouble . . .'

I laughed thinly to mask the fact I was bricking it. I don't think my poetry, knowledge of anime and Tumblr presence would serve me too well in a women's prison. It was PC Watson, the school liaison officer. She was a matronly black woman with a cute gap in her front teeth. 'Come on, girls, it's time to go home.'

'No way.' Polly kept her voice level. 'The residents of Brompton don't want a diner.'

'It's not up to the residents,' Watson said, her voice equally calm. 'Planning permission went ahead. Sorry, girls, there's nothing you can do.'

I spoke up. 'This is civil resistance. You can't move us.'

The foreman, hovering at Watson's side, scowled at me, dragging on a Marlboro Red. 'You know what your problem is? You're too ******* clever for your own good.'

I scowled back. 'I looked it up on Wikipedia, sir. Just now. On my phone.'

Polly grinned. 'It's Occupy Brompton-on-Sea and you can't do ****.'

'Polly, does your dad know you're here?' Watson asked.

'No. Clearly not.'

PC Watson scratched an immaculate corn row with a pillar-box red fingernail. 'Girls. I'm all for peaceful protest, but you're supposed to warn the police and you're actually breaking and entering. This is private property. If you want you can move it outside the park, but you can't block the road, that's wilful obstruction. Am I making myself clear?'

'I'm not moving.' Polly matched her gaze. 'This is our friend's memorial.'

And there it was in her eyes: pity. She pitied us. 'No, girls, it isn't.'

That's when I saw them. Both of our dads, entering the golf course. Balls, who'd called them? 'Oh for god's sake.'

Polly only grinned further. 'Uh-oh, now we're *really* in trouble.'

Mr Wolff was apoplectic – and this is the first time in my life I've had an excuse to use that word, so I'm going to. 'You've gone too far this time, Polly! What the bloody hell do you think you're doing? This is so, so embarrassing!'

I tried a different tack. 'It's a peaceful protest, Dad! Look at me, I'm basically Ghandi!'

That, surprisingly, did nothing to calm Dad down. 'Get up right now, Victoria!'

'Er . . . no.'

My dad had left the house in his grey hole-ridden house sweatpants. I could only pray he'd remembered to put on underwear. 'Toria, I can't believe you're doing this. I . . . I thought we could trust you.' Typical. I would get the torture of the 'I'm not angry, I'm disappointed' speech, wouldn't I?

'No one listened to the petition – what else were we meant to do?'

'Nothing. You were meant to do nothing. This is real life, Toria. You can't bloody stamp your feet and get your own way.'

A further pair of policemen rolled up. They walked casually enough but one carried a pretty serious pair of bolt cutters. 'What would you like us to do, Mr Wolff?' Watson asked. 'I can leave them here for a couple of hours if you want but then we'll have to move them on.'

'Oh, get them out of here. I'm so sorry about this, Leila, this is mortifying.'

'All right, get the chains off.' She motioned to her colleagues.

The men moved in. I accepted my fate, but Polly went the other way. She kicked and screamed and very much resisted arrest. They tried to reason with her, but she only wrapped her arms around the seal. Two guys trying to pull a skinny seventeen-year-old off a seal didn't seem very balanced to me so, and I know this was stupid, I tried to prise them off her.

'Oi! Police brutality!'

The struggle was a blur – a noodle soup of flailing limbs. I don't know if it was an accident or not, but one of Polly's long booted legs caught Watson in the face. I knew *that* wasn't going to go down well.

They arrested her. They arrested me.

It was blobby and messy and noisy. Hair and hands and fingernails. My knee scraped on the tarmac and I cried out in pain. There were hands pushing and pulling and before I could make sense of what was happening, I was in the back of a police car. The door slammed in my face and on the other side I'd never seen anyone look as disappointed as my dad did at that moment.

We were locked in a cell. This had clearly been cooked up as a punishment by our fathers. I think they thought that putting us in a cell for an undisclosed amount of time might make us realise the SERIOUSNESS OF OUR ACTIONS. Actually, I'm not condoning crime but it wasn't that bad. For one thing, we were the only people in the station – a disappointing lack of big-haired sassy hookers in last night's Lycra or butch lesbians trying to make us their bitches.

It did smell a lot like wee though.

After they'd patched up my bleeding knee with an anti-bacterial wipe and a plaster, we were put in a breeze-block cell 'to cool off'. Both Polly and I were already calm by the time we got there so it was a pointless exercise. Somewhere, across town, the golf course was being demolished.

'This is balls.' I sat next to Polly on a plastic mattress, our shoulders pressed together.

'They won't charge us with anything.'

'I meant about the park.'

Polly sighed. 'Your dad was right, you know. We were being brats.'

'I know.'

'I wasn't going to go down without a fight.'

'Me either. It was worth fighting for.' I pulled my knees up under my chin.

Polly rested her head against the cold brick wall. The magenta dye had faded on top but she'd dyed the tips indigo. 'Oh well. It's done now. We tried. We can say we tried.'

That much was true, although I still felt like we'd lost. 'How long do you think they'll keep us here?'

'Until they think we've learned our lesson. A couple of hours? Until we're hungry and crying? Until we beg forgiveness?

Until we're a waste of taxpayers' money.' Polly reached for my hand. 'Tor . . . thank you for . . . everything. I know I can be hard work, but you sticking up for me today meant more than the moon.'

I smiled and squeezed her hand. 'I wouldn't have missed it for the moon.'

'I really mean it. Thank you.' Framed by glitter and kohl, her eyes glazed over and I was hypnotised by them, unable to look away. The air turned syrupy with anticipation.

'What shall we do?' I said, trying to break the spell.

Polly's lips curled at the edges. 'I might go to sleep for a bit. Have a nap. I think that makes a stronger statement – "See how many ***** I give."'

'Don't! How boring would that be?'

'You can sleep too.' She gave me a highly suggestive glance. 'I'll be big spoon, you be little spoon.'

'Polly . . .'

She rolled her eyes. 'Or you could go on the other bunk, but I think my way would be more fun . . .'

'Whatever. Don't they have CCTV?'

'In this dump? I doubt it! Anyway, I think they'd probably quite enjoy it. Little girl-on-girl show for the guys on the front desk!'

'Yeah we can do that porn thing where they lick each other's tongues in midair!' I waggled my tongue at her like a frisky lizard.

'I'm game if you are!'

I pouted. 'Polly, I'm kidding!'

Polly held her hands apart. 'I said we could snuggle. Nothing wrong with that. We did it before, remember?'

That was different. We were close again, closer than we should be. My skin was tingly, singing to be touched.

NO.

Cheating is cheating, regardless of gender. I stood and moved to the opposite bunk. 'I'm going over here where it's safer.'

Polly laughed. This was amusing her greatly. 'When did I become unsafe?'

'You were never safe to begin with.'

She lay back on the bunk, never taking her eyes off me. 'I've got an idea to pass the time.' Her right hand vanished under the rim of her jeans.

'Polly!'

But Polly didn't say anything, just grinned and then bit her bottom lip. Her chest rose and fell as her breathing grew deeper.

Oh what the heck. Was this cheating on Nico in some weird way? I didn't know anything any more. I didn't know what I wanted . . . but I couldn't look away. I wondered. I wondered what it might be like to . . . what it would feel like . . .

That was when the key clanked in the lock. Both of us shot off the beds in a heartbeat, hands where they could be seen. I was horrified – had they been watching us? Had they seen? It was PC Watson. 'Come on, girls, your dads are waiting to take you home. I mean it though: stay away from Fantasyland, you hear me?'

'Yes, miss,' we both said as we shuffled shamefacedly past her. It wasn't the protest I was guilty about though.

The spell had been broken the second the door had opened, sucked out like a vacuum. In the stark light of the

Brompton-on-Sea Police Station everything looked different, everything looked cheap and real. Worst part? If Watson hadn't come in when she had done, I have no idea what I, what we, would have done.

## Chapter Twenty-Two

# Pier

Imagine a colossal gothic pendulum swinging inside a bat-filled cathedral and you might have some inkling of how my head was feeling. There were moments, often as I lay in bed with my new bestie Insomnia (she was here on permanent sleepover), where I admitted defeat.

OK I'M GAY NOW.

As I mentioned, that'd be cool. My mum would toss me out on the street, but I was tossing myself out next year anyway so that wasn't quite as scary as it once might have been. But if only it were that easy. The pendulum kept swinging back the other way.

THE VAGINA HOLDS NO APPEAL.

Yeah, yeah, you're reading this and screaming the word BISEXUAL, right? But a word, an eight-letter word, isn't helping me sleep any sounder. Give me your words and I'll swallow them like pills if they'll help me find peace of mind. But they won't.

There was one afternoon where we both cut school to do sex. Nico and I, I stress. He was due to go off to do some recording and gigs the week after so we wanted to make use of what limited time we had together.

After the aforementioned sex, I watched him in the shower. I sat on the toilet seat, wearing one of his slouchy vests, watching the water run off his bum. He'd lost weight. Anxiety, I reckoned. He was still so effing sexy though. I liked his boy body. I really did. But things felt different now.

Nico was gorgeous and kind and funny and I was supposed to want a boyfriend so I went for it. I'd always assumed that those fundamental things would be enough to last forever and ever amen. But when I thought about Polly touching herself in that holding cell . . . oh god. The FEELS. What I felt for Nico and what I felt for Polly were two distinct entities, like two vast, vivid nebulas in my universe, each entirely different from the other but equally powerful. Both burned bright. All those fairy stories that told me I'd meet a prince and live happily ever after had LIED.

I did it, I got it, I had it all.

I also had this *curiosity* and it wasn't going away.

This, *this* was the Niggly Noo. It always was.

I suppose the question was, if I was happy with Nico, why did I feel this way about Polly? Although wishes are for children and idiots, a theoretical question kept floating through my mind, a fantasy scenario to pass the sleepless hours: if I could somehow distil Essence of Polly into Body of Nico, would I?

In a heartbeat.

* * *

Of course, in school the day after our brush with the law Hurricane Polly had acted as if nothing out of the ordinary had happened. I didn't want to look uncool so I didn't bring it up either. Business as usual.

I so nearly told Beasley in the library workroom. I would have, had it not been for a gay app called Grindr. 'It's amazing,' he told me seconds before I confessed my own 'gay secret'. 'It shows you where the nearest *gay* guys are.' He mouthed the offending word silently.

I instantly became a gay detective. 'Where's the nearest one? Are there any in school?'

'Not right now, but there was a blank profile earlier. Someone who's not out.'

'OMG we should use it as a tracker and find them! My money's on Mr Greaves!' I laughed. No heterosexual Maths teacher would have biceps like that.

'Shush! Keep your voice down!'

'Sorry but it's ridiculous. You're not going to fall in love with someone based on geography.' I suspected that was not the developer's intent either.

Beasley looked a little wounded. 'No, but I've been speaking to a really nice guy who lives a few miles outside town.' He showed me a picture.

'Oh, he is cute.'

'Told you. And at least I know he's *gay*.'

Which was more than I did.

Beasley and I were making our way out of the library when a hand grabbed my shoulder. I spun around and found myself face to face with Daisy's little brother – a chubby Year 10 called Dylan. 'Oh hi, how are you?' The librarian shushed us.

'I'm OK. We've, erm, started clearing out Daisy's stuff. This is for you.' He handed Beasley a magenta notebook.

'What is it?'

'Like, a comic or something. It's got your name on it.'

'Thanks,' Beasley said and Dylan trotted on his way. We pulled up some seats in the main part of the library. 'I don't know if I can look,' Beasley whispered. 'This is going to ruin me.'

He slid the book over to me and I tentatively opened it to the first page. It read: *The GRAND FINALE of the* GEOFF *SAGA*. 'OMG, it's the last episode of *Geoff*. She must have drawn it in case . . . in case . . . anything happened.'

No way. She'd known. She'd known her health was failing and kept it to herself. 'Oh wow,' was all I could say with my mouth so dry. We read it together. In it, Evil Celine summoned a powerful kraken from Hades with which to run the world. Only Geoff could stop her.

'So Geoff dies?' Beasley asked, horrified.

'Wait, look.' I turned the page.

'I guess he's just a normal squirrel now.' I saw exactly what Daisy had done . . . every boring old squirrel in the world was now a potential Geoff. Every time I saw a squirrel from now on it might be our cross-dressing squirrel friend in disguise. A tear pooled in the corner of my eye.

'He looks happy,' Beasley agreed.

'He looks free, doesn't he?' I said, my eyes glistening.

'Yeah.'

I knew what I had to do and it was awful. The most awful thing I'd ever done.

Facebook kept me up to date with Nico while he was in London. There were pictures from the studio, from meetings, from gigs. Action Station had 'buzz' apparently. Nico tried his best. He texted before bedtime and tried to call when the band took breaks but our lives weren't overlapping like they used to. He talked band and I talked school. Our common ground, quite literally, was being demolished.

It happened on First Hot Day. First Hot Day is the BEST. First Hot Day that year fell at the end of May, right after Nico had completed his last exam. My end-of-year tests were still ahead but my future wasn't hanging on them.

With it being First Hot Day, and with us being English, we'd all thrown all our clothes off, prematurely opting for shorts and vests and flip-flops. After school we all went down to the beach and celebrated the arrival of summer. We drank warm fizzy wine because it was two-for-one at the garage, and played Frisbee.

I couldn't focus on it for a second though. Too much going on in my head.

Maybe Nico sensed something was wrong or maybe he just wanted chips, but we broke away from the pack and went to the kiosk on the pier.

'Christ, do you want some chips with your salt?' I asked, judging him as he liberally showered his chips.

'You can talk, vinegar-woman!'

We sat on one of the benches overlooking the sea. I was wearing some cheap Lolita heart sunglasses I'd picked up at the pound shop – they were too small and squished my head a bit.

'Toria,' Nico started and confirmed what I had already suspected. So we both knew. I'd put off any form of serious conversation while he'd been doing his exams. It seemed he had too. 'What do you think about me living in London next year?'

I wasn't a bit surprised. I couldn't even pretend to be.

'I thought you might have to, to be honest.'

'I don't want to, but I think I need to be up there. This train shit is killing me, man. We'll be OK though. You can come up on weekends and stuff.'

Here goes: 'Are you sure you want me to?'

He replied without skipping a beat. 'Yeah. Of course I do. Don't you?'

I didn't believe him. I was a little annoyed that I was going to have to be the villain.

'I don't know.'

He said nothing for a second and seagulls squawked overhead, fighting over the leftovers that spilled out of a bin.

'I know I've been a shit boyfriend, Tor.'

I went right off my chips and dropped them into the bin. 'You haven't. It's just . . . not the same as it was.' He said nothing. I pointed off the pier to where yellow claws ripped up the golf course like giant zombie hands bursting from the grave. 'That, my love, is a metaphor.'

He managed a feeble laugh. 'I'll say. I know this sounds awful, but this band could actually make it . . .'

'I know!' I agreed wholeheartedly. 'And this is your shot. You are bloody well gonna take it. I mean, hello! You're gonna be a freaking rock star! I don't wanna get in your way.'

'You're not.'

'It feels a little like I have been. You keep trotting back here while the others stay in London. The band isn't the complication, I am.' He looked so sad. No, that wasn't the right word. *Resigned* was more appropriate. I imagine I looked the same. It wasn't working. However much we both wanted it to, it wasn't. 'Last year was so brilliant, Nico. It was so, so good. Maybe I'll come to London after my exams, who knows. Maybe it'll be good again.'

He fingered his tattoo. 'Rise and fall.'

I stroked it too. 'Rise and fall. We don't know what's gonna happen, but right now I think you should be with the band.'

'I know. But I don't want you to think the band is more important than you, because it's not.'

I laughed. 'Maybe it is! And that's OK. Right now, this year, I'm *nothing*. If the tables were turned and I had an opportunity to do this amazing life-changing thing, what would you tell me to do?'

'I'd let you go in a second.'

'Well, there you go then.'

'But we've been brilliant, Tor.' He cupped my head and pulled me into a kiss.

'We still are. Look at us talking like grown-ups!' This was not going to descend into squabbles and arguments, I was determined. I wanted Nico in my life forever. I wasn't sure what that was going to look like, but I'd make it work.

'Man, I don't wanna lose you.' The unspoken secret behind every break-up ever: *what if I never meet anyone else who accepts me like you did?* I just prayed that Nico wasn't my one shot at love. That'd suck.

'You're not losing me. I'll be here. But I don't want to be a piece of elastic pinging you back every other week.'

'Thank you,' he said, his lips still brushing against mine. His cheeks were wet. So were mine. 'For understanding.'

The weird part is, I wasn't even sad. I don't know about Nico Mancini, but I felt freer than I had in months. My first act as a freed woman was to cling to him. People stared at us as they walked down the pier but I couldn't have cared less.

# SUMMER

### The Beach House

A house that's built
on silt and sand
will surely sink
into the land.
Bricks and glass
Decay to dust
become the earth
as all things must.

## Chapter Twenty-Three

# Dad

I don't know if you've even owned a pair of hair straighteners, but if you do you'll be familiar with the TERROR that comes from being at school and suddenly wondering if you've left them switched on. That is how I felt about Nico. I'd be going about my business when suddenly I'd be hit by a crippling panic seizure.

What were you thinking? You dumped NICO MANCINI FROM ACTION STATION. Are you out of your tiny mind?

I had a newfound understanding of how Swift felt after Styles.

Did I cry? Yes I cried. It felt like I was free-falling and couldn't see the ground. With Nico I'd always felt so secure, so wrapped up tight, and now that security was gone. The flip side of freedom is insecurity.

And as for Polly . . . well, that was playing with matches. I gave her a wide berth. I didn't want Nico, I didn't want Polly, I just wanted things to be easy again. I was beginning to think I was a drama coeliac – totally intolerant of any drama of my own.

I think Mum and Dad sensed something was wrong even if I hadn't explicitly told them Nico and I were over.

I remember one Friday evening I came downstairs from my fusty bedroom lair to make a cup of tea. I paused outside the kitchen when I heard voices. They were arguing – well, passive-aggressively. 'It's a Friday night!' Mum said through what sounded like gritted teeth.

'What's that got to do with anything?'

'I'm allowed a sodding glass of wine, Eric.'

'Why? I'm not having one.'

'Oh is that how it works now? You can't keep moving the goalposts. I said I wouldn't drink during the week and I haven't. Satisfied?' I frowned, pressing my ear against the door. This was the tail end of a conversation I sensed had started some time ago. No drinking during the week? When had that rule been introduced? Now that I thought about it, I don't think Mum *had* been drinking every night over dinner. I hadn't even noticed with all *my* stuff going on.

Wow, maybe Dad had finally said something. Or even set an ultimatum. That was interesting – and I honestly wasn't sure if it was a positive thing or not. 'I don't see why you need a drink if –'

The floorboard I was standing on gave a creak. Busted. I had no choice but to power into the kitchen like I hadn't heard anything.

'Hello!' I announced fake-brightly. 'I just fancied a cup of tea.'

They both busied themselves in different cupboards, guiltily.

* * *

The next morning, the argument seemingly benched, Dad asked me to accompany him into town. Some new graphic novels I'd pre-ordered were waiting for me at the comic-book store, so I begrudgingly agreed, though my instincts were telling me to hibernate for the rest of the summer. I went ahead to the seedier end of the high street to pick them up while Dad went into the hardware shop to buy something to deal with the wasp nest he'd found at the end of our garden. The comic shop was sandwiched between Taboo, a sex shop, and Christian Aid, which I always found amusing.

I paid for my books and chatted with Milo the Cute Comic Book Guy for a while. Now that he'd got to know me a little, he was kind of my authority on everything manga. Depressingly, as one of very few females to set foot in that shop, I'm kind of catnip to guys in there. I'm practically a celebrity. I won't lie, without Nico, it was good to know I had options . . . even if most of the customers were about thirteen. I heard one guy once mutter to his friend that girls only read comics to impress guys. Yeah, that's what it is. We're playing the Long Game, my friend.

After I left the shop, I ambled to the end of the street where I'd said I'd meet Dad. He wasn't there yet. From this level, I could see over the beach, the promenade and Fantasyland. What was left of it, I should say. JCBs clawed and scraped at the ground like dogs after bones. What was once our playground was now a dirt pit. A hole.

At the entrance to the building site were three enormous skips piled high with memories. Even from the high street, I saw the fake Mickey Mouse sign snapped in half to fit in the dump, a pile of timber from the pirate ship. The penis Loch Ness monster had been reduced to rubble.

It was a ruin.

You know what? Heartache is a very real thing. The longing for that place physically *hurt* in my chest. Now that some time had passed I realised trying to save the golf course was far from trivial. I missed Fantasyland and I missed Daisy, and the two thoughts twisted together in a double helix. I remembered what Nico had said about want and that made my heart hurt even more because it reminded me that I no longer had Nico.

I was a ruin.

'Tor? Are you OK?' It was my dad; I don't know how long he'd been watching me.

I almost said *I'm fine*, but I didn't. 'I'm sad.'

'I know.' He gave me a hug and I felt about five years old and that felt nice. 'It's a shame. I'm proud of you for trying to save it though.'

I looked up at him. 'You let the police cart me away.'

'Aw, that was designed to teach you a lesson. I was arrested at a protest once.'

'What? No you weren't.'

'I was! 1985. The National Front wanted to march through Bradford so we formed a human shield to keep them out. It turned violent though and I was arrested. I was only ever cautioned, mind.'

I couldn't keep a smile off my face. 'No way! That's so cool.'

He winked. 'It must be me you get it from. Shall we go down and have a look?'

'It might make me sadder.'

'I meant go down and see if there's anything we can pinch out of those skips!'

Isn't it lovely when people surprise you in a good way?

Luckily, none of the crew working that day seemed to recognise me as one of 'The Brompton Two' so we were left to rummage unchallenged. We must have looked well povvo, but the skips were a treasure trove. I found part of the windmill (where I'd first met Him), the mast of the pirate ship (where I'd watched the stars with Her), but what I really wanted was the seal. 'Can you see the seal?'

'Not yet.' Dad was hanging over the side of the largest skip, his legs dangling in midair. 'There's a skull? Do you want a big skull?'

And then I saw it. The Disapproving Seal was underneath a tarpaulin, next to the skips. I peeked underneath and saw it was with the volcano and some larger rocks. I wondered if they were being sold as scrap or something. 'Dad, look!'

He allowed himself to drop over the rim and back to solid ground. 'Have you found it?'

'Yeah. But it's a bit broken.' Where the diggers had torn the seal off the course, they'd ripped his flippers off and chunks of plaster were missing from his side as if a great white had taken a bite.

'Oh, well, that's OK. Shall we put it in the garden?'

I couldn't quite believe what I was hearing. 'Mum will kill us. It's not even our garden.'

'Tor, Mum isn't nearly as uptight as you think she is. Do you want it or not?'

It wouldn't be the same. I couldn't save Fantasyland but I could at least keep a memento. It was Daisy's shrine too. It shouldn't end up on some scrapheap.

'Yeah. Can we really keep it?'

'Sure. But can we lift it?' It was heavier than it looked – I suppose it had never occurred to me that the seal was made of solid stone. I took the tail end and Dad took the head. We lived at the top of a hill. There were the coast stairs to contend with, but we did it, even if we had to stop every hundred metres to have a rest. As soon as we got back to the high street we bundled the Disapproving Seal into the back of the Disapproving Cabbie's car.

Despite looking at Dad the way you might look at a puppy who'd made a puddle, Mum took it in her stride. I had underestimated her. She didn't care in the slightest, although she did say, 'God, what an ugly thing,' which was quite fair really.

We positioned the grumpy seal in the back garden (away from the wasps). It looked kinda ridiculous, but when hadn't it?

'Thank you, Dad.'

'That's OK. I'll just have to nip in and get some codeine for my back. Hope it cheers you up, love. These last few months have been bloody hard work for you.' He licked his thumb and wiped a bit of muck off my face. I scrunched my nose in protest.

I was going to argue, say I was fine, but I caved in. I nodded. My ass was feeling a little kicked.

'I'm going to make a cup of tea, do you want one?'

'Yeah. Two sugars please. I'll be in in a sec.'

Dad headed for the kitchen and I was left with the seal. I wondered about repainting it, but I didn't want to lose the judgemental little face. I looked up to the clouds and stroked the seal's head.

Epiphany time. I had so much to be grateful for. I know it's tacky to say 'count your blessings' but I did. I had so much *good* in my life. I had great parents who, while far from perfect, were looking out for me. I had great friends. Between Nico and Polly I had almost too much love going on. And now I had a Disapproving Seal. You know what? It could have been a lot worse.

# Chapter Twenty-Four

# Intent

I couldn't avoid Polly any longer. We had to revise. The strategy had worked after Christmas and I needed it to work again. Once more the Wolff residence became a sweatshop for Beasley, Alice and me.

It wasn't helped by the fact the weather was still glorious. All we wanted to do was flop around on the beach – anything else was much too exerting. At least we could revise in Polly's garden, cooling ourselves on the thick green grass and making daisy crowns. Coconutty Hawaiian Tropic filled my nostrils and we had to use mugs to weigh down piles of revision notes or we'd spend whole afternoons chasing sheets across the lawn.

We became addicted to something called 'Pink Drink'. It was some sort of raspberry squash and it was the best thing ever. Polly, being quite fancy, muddled it with ice and fresh mint leaves – it was definitely good for the brain.

I was making a fresh jug in the kitchen when Polly padded in, her bare feet slapping on the tiles. I was looking quite Indian at this point, but Polly didn't tan at all – she kept to the shade to protect her milky skin. 'I'm gonna get some cherries and grapes and stuff,' she said.

'Ooh good call.' I filled the jug with ice, aware that Polly was watching me. 'What?'

'Are you OK?'

'Yeah.'

She looked sceptical. 'I mean about Nico. You're being weirdly calm about the whole thing.'

I filled the jug from the tap. 'You know me. Doesn't need to be a big drama.'

She was trying to tie a cherry stem into a knot with her tongue and teeth – a challenge she'd been working on all morning. 'It's OK if you want it to be a big drama. You're entitled. Go ******* nuts. Throw the jug if you want.'

I smiled, albeit with slightly gritted teeth. 'I'm OK thanks. It's not as bad as I thought it would be.'

Polly came to my side at the sink to rinse the fruit. 'Maybe it's because you and Nico weren't meant to be together.'

I felt myself stiffen. 'It's not that!' I snapped. 'I loved him; it just wasn't working right now. He has to go to London.'

'****, don't bite my head off. It was only a suggestion.'

I realised I'd got one too many glasses down from the cupboard and put one back. 'Well, that's not what it was. I miss him like mad. I feel like a bit of me has been chopped off. It's so weird. Have you ever heard of phantom limbs?'

'No.' She almost choked on a stem and coughed it into her palm.

'It's like when soldiers and stuff lose limbs. Even though

there's nothing there, they can still feel their foot or arm. It's like that; I can still feel him even though he's gone.'

Polly's lips parted like she was about to say something and then changed her mind. After a moment, she abruptly changed the subject. 'Are you ready? Let's take these out.'

The garden was so bright it was almost oppressive. The sun beat down and the patio slabs burned the soles of my feet. We scampered to the cool grass and carried the snacks to the end of the garden where Beasley and Alice waited in the shade of a grand oak tree. 'Alice just had the best idea,' Beasley said. 'When the exams are finished, why don't we go camping? We haven't done that for years.'

I am so not a happy camper. 'Camping? No way.'

'It's fun!' Polly said. 'We used to do it all the time. Make a fire and toast marshmallows. Nico used to play for us . . .' She trailed off, perhaps worried she'd upset me.

'I'm going nowhere if it doesn't have running hot water and a flushing toilet.'

'We camp here.' Alice peeped over her John Lennon sunglasses. 'You can go in the house.'

I guessed I could get on board with that. 'OK then. That doesn't sound too bad.'

'Yay! New sleeping bag!' Beasley clapped like a sugared-up seal.

'Cool. Ghost stories,' Alice said.

It was too late. A new thought occurred to me. What if I had to share a tent with Polly? NO WAY was that happening. NO WAY. You might be thinking I broke up with Nico because of Polly, but you'd be wrong. They lived in different zones of my head. What I needed right now, with all this extra free time I suddenly had on my hands, was mates. Not messed-up masturbating police-cell mates, just mates.

It was at times like this that I missed Daisy most of all. I loved Polly, clearly, but since the kiss in the toilet, things weren't the same. I couldn't properly relax around her. I wondered if I'd ever truly been able to relax around her. I supposed, like any stick of dynamite, a certain degree of caution always had to be taken.

A week later and I was back on the Imodium for the English Language exams. Four hours in a sweltering room, with a small square desk and a ticking clock for company. Time flies when you're not having any fun. As the fortnight progressed the only saving grace was that I think the system finally broke me. After so many gruelling hours of regurgitating old exam papers the way we'd been taught, I could no longer find the energy to be stressed about exams.

We had to sit a General Studies mock for some reason, I guess to prep us for the real deal next year. It was multiple choice at least, although that made it feel too much like a *CosmoGirl* quiz for my liking. One's future should never hinge on a *CosmoGirl* quiz.

The paper was on crime and punishment:

***Read paragraph 6 of the article. The author suggests the goal of incarceration is:***

> ***A – Perpetrators are unable to commit further crimes.***
> ***B – To give perpetrators time to reflect on their actions.***
> ***C – For perpetrators to be actively rehabilitated.***
> ***D – All of the above.***

Twiddling my thumbs after whipping through the test, I couldn't help but wonder why, in real life, 'all of the above' is never an option.

***You identify as:***
***A – Straight.***
***B – Gay.***
***C – Bisexual.***
***D – All of the above.***

I saw Polly and Beasley in the row ahead and smiled to myself. A secret smile.

After the last exam, a new nervousness set in. After the End of Year 12 Tests, I'd have only one set of mocks next January and the big final, real exams and then it would be over. I really would be free-falling. Education is so easy – you get dropped off when you're five and leave when you're eighteen. Every single minute of the day is timetabled – a zombie would manage. In one short year, I was going to be free of the conveyer belt and I'd have to make some DECISIONS.

TERRIFYING. DECISIONS.

My dad, who has had two careers – one as a journalist and one as a lecturer – has told me that you don't always get it right first time but I suppose I should really think about WHAT I WANT TO BE WHEN I GROW UP.

I like books but I can't think of stories. I like art but don't want to be a starving artist. I'm a poet but no one knows it. I love the internet but everything's been done. I had an idea, more of a vague whim – but I'd started to think about design. It came about when I was surfing Tumblr and saw people redesigning covers of their favourite books. I gave it a go, reimagining the cover of *The Bell Jar* after that disastrous chick-flick version came out. I'd never thought that it's someone's *job* to make things like that: book covers, film posters, illustrations.

Art *and* books, you say? Sounded like something I could get on board with. I hadn't told anyone yet, but with that free fifteen minutes I always seemed to have at the end of exams, the gaseous idea was solidifying.

Then there's this of course – writing. Imagine if this was an actual proper book. That'd be cool. I mean I don't even know what this is . . . Is it a journal, is it a novel, is it a memoir, does it even matter? Probably not. I'm seventeen after all, everyone knows we're K E R R R R A Z Y. Woo-hoo! Look at me! I'm poking my tongue out and sticking two fingers up! Mad! Zany!

Kill me now.

The night before our Literature exam, Polly came to mine to do some last-minute revisions. I was grateful that she was ruthlessly focused on cue cards and all talk of Nico or police cells were off the agenda. We talked about *Paradise Lost* and *The Dubliners*, her seated at my desk, and me Buddha like on my bed. Safe distance.

Only I'd made a terrible mistake. I realised too late.

'What's this? It's sexy.' Polly picked up my poetry book and stroked the leather cover.

'Don't!' I almost leapt off the bed.

Polly's eyes widened and she held the book out of my reach. '****, is this your secret diary? *Dear Diary, today Polly flicked her bean in a police station . . .?*'

'Ha ha, very funny. No, it's not a diary and it's very arrogant of you to assume that you'd be in it if it was.' She opened it.

'Polly, don't!'

She closed it. 'Sorry. What is it?'

My heart chundered. 'Don't . . . it's really embarrassing.'

'Is it a Burn Book? I used to keep a list of everyone I wanted to kill at school.'

Big sigh. 'Worse. They're my poems.'

Polly cartoonishly blinked. 'What?'

'Awkward. Yes, I write poems sometimes. Go on, tell me I'm a cliché.'

'I don't think that's cliché,' she said with a tilt of her head. 'I think it's cool. Why didn't you say anything?'

'Because it's lame.'

'**** off. Poetry isn't lame. I love Emily Dickinson and Kate Tempest. Ooh and Christina Rossetti.' I did too. 'May I?' I grumbled. 'Please?'

'OK. They're not very good though, and I'm not just saying that to be all humblebrag. I didn't even show Nico.'

Saying no more, Polly flicked the book open and leafed through the pages. I couldn't look; it was excruciating, as if she'd split my skull like a bin bag and was picking through the trash. After a few minutes, her hand flew to her chest and she looked at me, eyes damp. 'Holy ****, Tor. The one for Daisy. I'm slayed.'

'I'm sorry . . .'

'**** off, it's beautiful. They're all beautiful. You are . . . you write beautifully.'

My face flushed. 'Really?'

'Yes! I don't know why you were hiding this. You shouldn't ever, ever hide this.'

I could only shrug. Polly's eyes were fixed on mine and the world waited. I broke first and looked away.

The other good thing about exams of course, is that if you don't have a morning exam you can have a tiny little lie-in before your mum forces you out of bed to do last-minute revision. It was something. By the end of the fortnight, I knew at least one (French) had been an absolute disaster – and I would definitely drop it next year – but others I could make my peace with. I'd pass. Beasley was less confident and Polly turned up five minutes into her Sociology exam because she'd been convinced it was in the afternoon. They let her sit it after she cried and said she was on her period, but she was told she wouldn't get a Get Out of Jail Free ever again.

Nico and I were still unwinding. Slowly, our daily texts were becoming weekly. If love is measured in time and thought, our supply was running out. The last bits of sand trickling through the hourglass, as it were. He remembered when my exams were but I had already lost track of his whereabouts. In quiet times I did think about those 'early adopters' and whether he'd turned his attention to them. Such thoughts left a bitter, leafy taste in my mouth. Now his exams were over, he was living with Etienne full-time in Haggerston.

On Friday, the final day of the exams, we had our camping session. I was pleased to learn it was a partner-free zone as Alex was on an Oxford University open weekend thing. Well, of course he was. So it was just the four of us – Beasley, Polly,

Alice and me. We erected the tents efficiently, something I was almost disappointed about – I'd envisaged some sort of farcical slapstick moment, but Beasley and Polly were experts.

I noted that sleeping arrangements were yet to be pinned down. 'Beasley, are we sharing?' I decided to get in early.

'Yeah, can do. Don't suppose it really matters.' If Polly picked up on it, she didn't make a fuss.

It stayed light until well after ten and it was a balmy night, but it was still fun to keep the fire going. We had some wood from Mr Wolff's shed, but it was way more fun to creep around the neighbour's garden trying not to activate the security lamp to find loose sticks and twigs to burn. After an hour or so of that, I decided I'd be a pretty good burglar.

It grew cooler and we wrapped ourselves in our sleeping bags in front of the fire. By this time we'd made our way though quite a lot of beer. The fire made me woozy, my eyelids were heavy. I was drunk and content. I sat next to Polly, snuggling for heat. After six beers, who cared?

'So,' Polly continued her story. 'The guy refreshes Grindr and the profile with the skull picture is now at ten metres, and he realises whoever it is must be *inside* the house. His phone bleeps and the message says, "Look under the bed." He refreshes the app again and the skull is only three metres away. He gets down on his hands and knees to look under the bed.'

On the other side of the fire, Beasley and Alice gripped one another.

'Using his phone as a torch, he peeps under the bed and that's when he sees it . . .' Polly paused for dramatic effect. 'His own body, grey and rotten, is under the bed!'

We all pretended to scream (despite a warning twenty minutes earlier from Polly's mum) and fell about laughing. 'Ooh that one was scary!' Beasley laughed.

I told my one about a demonic rocking horse that eats dads and Alice told a truly scary one about a train passing her bedroom window every night with only a single passenger watching as it went by.

Beasley felt sick from too much beer or too many marshmallows or a combination of the two. Alice took him inside to be near the toilet, leaving Polly and I by the fireside. We were letting it die down now, the feeble flames sputtered and coughed.

'I think,' Polly said, 'that you should come in my tent.'

My head was boozy, resting on her shoulder. 'Polly . . . I can't . . .'

'Why not?'

I realised I had run out of excuses. 'I just can't.'

'It'll be fun. We can make out a bit. Nothing serious.' Her lips found my lips. After the initial shock wore off, I returned the kiss. It was even more fun after a few drinks and I lost myself in it. This was a proper kiss and it was good. For a couple of seconds, the feeling muted the voices in my head and it all felt right: the garden was silent except for the crackle of the fire and noisy, colourful thoughts of Polly. My body galloped away with itself. I wanted more.

BUT I AM NOT A LESBIAN.

I pulled away. 'Stop. Polly, I didn't break up with Nico so that we could make out in a tent!'

She laughed. 'I know, but now there's nothing stopping us.'

'*I* am stopping us. Polly, you're my best friend . . .'

'I know! We can still make out though. You're overthinking this. Making out is fun and we're both hot and single so we might as well while we're young.'

I tried to sober myself up. 'I don't kiss any of my other friends.'

Polly grinned like a Cheshire cat. 'Well, that's why we're *best* friends!'

'Oh that's cute!' I smiled. 'But, I'm sorry, I don't feel that way about you.'

Her smile fell. 'OK, well, that's a lie. That kiss didn't lie.'

Uh. Why was she harshing my high? 'God! What do you want me to say? I want us to be friends. Not friends with benefits, just friends!'

Polly held her hands up. 'OK, OK, calm yourself! I'm sorry. I just really like kissing you. You're the best kisser ever.'

Flattery gets everyone everywhere. I peeked up at her through my hair. 'Thanks. It takes two to tango.'

Polly's smile returned. 'I think we owe it to kissing personally, but I'm not going to beg, Toria. I'm not that ******* desperate!'

Beasley and Alice appeared in the kitchen doorway and I shushed Polly. I so, so wanted to go into the tent and see what happened. I wanted to let go, be young and free and wild like in the way music videos seem to think my life should be. Even drunk, I couldn't let it happen. It was all too big, all too much, all too scary.

## Monster

There's a monster in the garden
Beyond the flowers and weeds.
He's made of tar and rusty nails
And lurks below the reeds.

There's a monster in the garden.
I plant another rose.
The thorns distract my fingers
While he's gnawing on my bones.

There's a monster in the garden.
He's up in every tree.
He swings his tail around my throat
And smiles as I can't breathe.

There's a monster in the garden
A cancer in the roots.
The leaves are ash and charcoal
And I gorge on rotten fruits.

## Chapter Twenty-Five

# Truth

Whatever Polly said, after the camping night, I got the distinct impression she was avoiding me. 'I'm helping Alice with some prom stuff' became a familiar excuse, or she'd fail to show up for school altogether. Now that exams were over, lessons did seem a pretty pointless charade.

I wished I had someone to talk to, but I was scared that if I put my feelings into words it would all become real. However I said it, people would assume I was a massive gay. That's how it works, right? Gay OR straight, male OR female, black OR white, good OR bad. People online joked about 'bi now, gay later' or 'lipstick lesbians' or 'fauxmosexuals'. I wanted no part of it; it was all hateful.

Oh, it was a mess. I wanted a Hermione Granger time-turner. I wanted to go back in time and stop that kiss in the toilets from happening. Everything was fine before that. Or I could go even further back and help Daisy before she went past the point of no return. I wanted everything to be back the way it was at the start of the year when I was crazy about Nico and he was crazy about me based on nothing but how we looked.

I want, I want, I want, I WANT.

How spoiled I must be, making all these demands of the universe.

I thought a lot about New Year's Eve. The golf course, Nico, Daisy, Polly. I'd been so close to Happy I could taste it.

That bitch Insomnia was back. Every night was a countdown: *If I fall asleep now, I'll get six hours sleep . . . If I fall asleep now I'll get five and a half hours sleep* . . . and on and on. I'd stare at the ceiling on one side of the bed until it got too warm, toss and turn to the cold side and lie awake there until I reversed the process. Getting through the day was getting hard. Just because I was awake didn't mean I was *awake* and the feel of furry coffee teeth was starting to repulse me.

To make things worse, Nico was back in town for a couple of days. The band was doing a huge gig at the town Summer Fayre to mark their 'local boys done good' status. I did and didn't want to see him. I missed him so much, but I was genuinely worried I might dissolve and beg him to take me to London with him. I could be his full-time groupie and he could look after me forever and ever. It would be so much easier than all these choices. Choices are *hard*.

He took me to Pizza Delisiosa and with greasy fingers we shared a huge Meat Feast and a cheesy garlic bread. 'They've brought the release date forward,' Nico said through a mouthful of stuffed crust. 'Didn't I tell you? They want to release a buzz single before Christmas and then do the proper first single in February.'

'That's amazing, which song?'

'We're not sure yet. Maybe "Invisibility Cloak" as the buzz one.'

'Oh, cool.'

We munched for a while.

'How are you anyway? You look knackered.'

I almost coughed my pizza up. 'Gee thanks, Nico!'

'You do! I worry about you all the time. I still feel shitty for pissing off.'

'Don't be insane. I'm fine. I'm just not sleeping very well.'

He downed his Diet Coke and beckoned the waitress over for his free refill. 'Why? Have you fallen out with Polly?'

'What?' I said way too quickly. 'No. Why?'

'I met her for a milkshake this afternoon. She wanted to apologise for being such a dick with the whole Zoë situation. I mean, I'd forgotten all about it to be honest.'

I picked a stray bit of pepper out of the dish and popped it in my mouth. 'By the by, Zoë hasn't. She's basically taken out a jihad against you.'

'Ha! Fair enough, I suppose we deserve it.' It was nice. There we were, chatting away, and it wasn't at all weird. I also no longer wanted to do sex with him, as easy as it would be to fall into old patterns. But the thought of it was alien. He went on. 'But anyway, Polly was in a weird mood. She was kinda quiet and she barely had any rage at all. She didn't even seem bothered when we went past the building site of the new diner place. I wondered if she was ill.'

I shrugged, suddenly not feeling like the oily pizza. 'Nope, we're fine. The exams kicked our butts. When we break up for the holidays, I'm going to sleep for a fortnight. I'll somehow feed myself through a drip and get a catheter.' He chuckled and I changed the subject. 'Are you all ready for tomorrow?'

As he spoke, hardly able to contain his excitement, I began to worry about Polly. No, worried wasn't the right word . . . more like pissed off. She hadn't told me she was going for a milkshake with Nico. Where was my bloody invite? A new thought occurred to me. What if rejecting Polly saw me exiled from the group? No, that wasn't fair . . . and it was pretty much sexual blackmail in fact. There was no way I was letting her take my friends. If need be, I'd fight her for them.

The day of the Summer Fayre was gorgeous and the market square was jam-packed with parents, kids, old people . . . pretty much the whole town. My old town had nothing like this – there was bunting and music and stalls selling jam and scones. It was like stepping into a postcard from a History lesson. It was nice: not ironically nice, properly nice.

Mum and Dad came down to check it out too. It was kinda weird; I didn't very often see them in daylight, least of all outside the house. They both looked happy, walking from stall to stall arm in arm. I wondered about Mum and SAD, that thing where you're depressed in winter – I guessed it was hard to be lower-case sad when the weather was so glorious. Mum hadn't had a drink today either, despite the stalls selling Pimm's.

We ran into Polly with Mr and Mrs Wolff at a fudge stall, and the moment was pretty much fudge. Clearly my parents think Polly is a ne'er-do-well who saw their pristine little girl wind up in a police station. Being around your friends when their parents are around is the weirdest thing ever. I always feel like I should curtsy or something. 'Hi there, Derek,' my dad said. Since when did he call Mr Wolff *Derek*? Also, 'Derek and Eric'? Ugh, this was like being in a nightmare. 'How's it going?'

'Not too bad, mate . . . can't complain.' Small talk ensued. Polly and I hovered at our parents' sides like sullen mascots. Awkward didn't cover it.

Thankfully, the mayor came on stage and thanked everyone for coming along. She introduced Action Station, describing them as the 'town's brightest young things' while Polly and I broke away and found Alice already at the front of the stage with Alex.

'God, when did our parents become friends?'

'Apparently when we were in jail. Man, that was weird.' I was glad Polly was talking to me at least.

Action Station performed four songs – with all the swearing removed – and Etienne didn't fellate the microphone or rub it against his crotch once. They'd either been neutered by Sony or they simply had the sense to know there were kids in the audience. Even without the antics, they were brilliant. So, so polished. Watching Nico now, it almost felt like a dream that we'd ever been a couple – high up on that stage he felt as far removed as the pop stars on TV. He was gone. That was OK.

Beasley joined us halfway through the set. 'Hey, I was with the music lot. There's a barbeque on the beach after all this. Are you coming?'

'Sure,' Polly said, so I jumped in while we were getting along.

'Yeah. I'll have to check with my mum and dad, but it should be OK.'

Nico caught my eye and smiled down. It almost floored me.

Maybe one day, in ten years or something, I'd be waiting in an airport departure lounge and I'd get a tap on the shoulder. I'd turn around and there'd be a gorgeous yet strangely familiar man looking at me through hooded eyes. He'd say, 'Sorry, but are you Toria Grand?'

I'd say, 'Well, it's Toria Cumberbatch now, but I'm recently divorced,' and we'd fall back in love and get married.

But the time wasn't now. I wasn't going to be Nico Mancini's child bride.

The beach was the unofficial after-party. All of Action Station came down, along with the music people from both our school and Nico's college. Even The Gash called truce and came too. Everyone bought disposable barbeques, although few had the patience to wait the SEVEN YEARS it took them to get sufficiently hot to warm a frozen burger beyond salmonella point.

This, of course, meant everyone was twice as drunk as they should have been. Even I was tipsier than usual. Beasley's new 'friend' Jack from the next town came over and we all got a good look. Jack was cute in a skater-boy-next-door way and he and Beasley sat a little away from the rest of us, their body language coy.

As I hung out with Nico, soaking up his last evening in Brompton, I saw Polly hanging out with Zoë, the latter climbing in and out of Polly's lap. What was that about? Were they getting back together? I hoped not: a) Zoë was kind of high-maintenance and b) it made me feel decidedly unspecial.

At the same time, Polly seemed to be flirting with Etienne. How fickle was she? Moreover, after my big speech on camping night, I knew I didn't have the right to be bothered. But I was.

We sat in a circle, playing I Have Never. 'I have never gone skinny-dipping!' Etienne announced.

Nico took a drink and I screamed. 'When did you go skinny-dipping?'

'I've lived by the sea my whole life – of course I have!'

The questions became increasingly dirty and I suspected people were lying to look cooler. I very much doubted that Alex had tried crack for example. 'I have never,' Alfie from Action Station said, 'made out with a dude . . . or a girl if you're a girl.'

OK, this was my turn to be a little bit edgy. I took a sip of my beer.

'Spin-the-bottle doesn't count!' Nico said.

I took another sip of beer and arched an eyebrow suggestively. 'Wouldn't you like to know.' I avoided Polly's gaze on purpose. 'Have you never kissed a guy?'

'Just that time at Zoë's. I would though.'

Next to him, Beasley puckered up. 'Go on then!'

Nico took a sip of beer and pounced on Beasley's face, the poor guy not expecting him to call his bluff. His eyes widened and he fell back into the sand. Only I knew what that kiss meant, but I was so pleased Beasley had finally got a snog with Nico. Happy early Birthday, Martin Beasley. The rest of us laughed and cheered. 'God, get some lube,' Etienne said with a foxish smile.

I saw Polly watching me from across the circle. She beamed at me and I looked away. I was so confused.

Evening fell and as the beach cleared, we stayed. Some people chased the surf, running in and out and trying to keep their feet dry. I sat further up the sand, a little drunk and a little morose. Sometimes that happens when I drink; I don't get silly, I get sad. When that happens I quietly take myself home. It's not a cry for attention. I don't need anyone else to feel bad for me. It's enough that I feel bad for myself. Whatever I'd drunk had disagreed with me.

Shoes in hand, Polly came and sat next to me. She was drunk, I could tell; her eyes were kind of googly. 'Hey,' she said. 'I lied.'

'What?' I wasn't sure I could process a proper conversation at that point.

'I lie all the time – just little ones – because people believe me and it's ******* funny. Sometimes I tell people I lived in Japan for a while. I never did. I'm as bad as Beas.'

'Again . . . what?'

Her head flopped back like it was too heavy for her neck. 'I lied, Tor. I don't just want to mess around with you. I really like you. I don't get why we can't be like a thing. Or at least try.'

I was physically winded and I wanted to go home. I wasn't as drunk as her and it wasn't attractive. 'What?' I said AGAIN. 'How about because I'm not gay?'

From the look on her face, that was the wrong answer. 'Yeah, so ******* what? Neither am I.'

'Polly, don't.'

'No,' Polly argued, sounding more than a little petulant. 'I'm so *bored* of pretending. We'd be so ******* good together. When we kiss it's like . . . wow. And not just the fun stuff! I know this sounds bat****, but I feel like there's something between us – like a chain keeping us together. I want to fall asleep next to you and wake up with you and hold you during the bit in between.'

Something about the cosiness appealed . . . but . . . no! 'That's not the point. I want you to be my friend.'

'Well, I want us to be more than friends. Tor, saying this was really hard for me.'

Stand-off. I stood up. 'You're drunk and we're going around in circles. I'm gonna go. Let's just . . . let's just see how you feel when you're sober.'

Polly stood too and followed me down the beach. 'Oh **** off. I know what I'm saying, the beer made me braver. This is me saying what I've been thinking for a long time. Like since you arrived. Since you flashed your tits.'

I dismissed her with a flourish of my hand. 'Look, this isn't happening, OK?'

'You like me too, admit it.'

'Of course I like you!'

'But more than just friends.'

We were friends, although admittedly I'd never felt so strongly about one before. Polly is all about extreme and I don't know if I'd felt such extremes about anyone. 'OK, best friends!'

Polly threw her hands up, exasperated. 'Best ******* friends? What are you? Eleven?' We were on the front now, near the building site that used to be the golf course. 'Isn't that what you're looking for? A best friend? Isn't that what a boyfriend or girlfriend is? A naked best friend!'

I was aghast. 'Polly, it's the naked bit that's the issue.'

Polly stopped, her face now serious. She searched for the right words. 'Are you seriously telling me that you'd let a soulmate pass you by because of *biology*?' She spat the last word like it was poison.

'God! Yes! It's kind of a big thing!'

She shook her head. 'It really isn't.' I swore I saw tears glisten in her eyes. 'There's only how you feel and how I feel, and everything else is packaging. I want you so much, Tor. I can't just be friends.'

I was having a lot of feelings, but the one that won out was anger. 'So it's your way or the highway? It's always about you getting your own way! I'm sorry, but I can't change who I am because it's what you want! It's not fair! What about what I want? Does that even come into it?'

Polly was crying now: big fat tears running off her nose. 'I thought it *was* what you wanted. Like I could *feel* something between us!'

What did I want? It sounds like an easy question, doesn't it? It was ten times harder than any exam I'd ever sat and it was a question I couldn't answer. Long run, I didn't know what I wanted. At that moment in time, I wanted nothing except to go home. 'Polly, I'm going home. I'm sorry, but I really can't handle all this. It's too much.'

'Just admit it!' she cried. 'Just admit that you feel it too!'

'I don't! Not like that.' I was full to the brim with rage. This was all about *her*, what *she* wanted. She hadn't stopped to think about what this was doing to me for a second. I walked away.

'You're lying, Toria, I *know* you.'

Well, I didn't know *anything* and it made me nuclear. I whipped back to face her, snarling, hair in my mouth. 'You don't *know* me!' And then: 'I don't fucking *know* me.' And then: 'There's nothing to know.'

With tears stinging my eyes, I marched up the hill and this time I didn't look back. I didn't hear footsteps following me and I was glad. I wanted to be far, far away from Polly Wolff and I didn't care if I never saw her again. Whatever spell she'd worked on me over this year was done. I was out.

# Chapter Twenty-Six

# Art

It was actually a relief to be done with them. I wasn't talking to Polly, and Beasley was always attending some gay youth group thing with Jack so I had a chance to reconnect with my friends online. I'd missed them and they'd missed me – I'd been a crappy friend. There were whole threads in forums about where I'd vanished to and whether or not I'd died.

It wasn't a bad thing to press pause on life for a couple of weeks. Time slowed to its normal pace. Daisy and then Nico and then Polly – going at warp speed was grinding me down. And so I took a little vacation from life.

When I got home from school, I went online and didn't come off until bedtime. I caught up on all my vlogs. I watched anime in bed on my laptop. I took long hot baths instead of showers until I was shrivelled like a prune. I exfoliated, toned and moisturised. I resumed my annual Potter reread from *Goblet of Fire.* It was bliss.

I had also neglected Mum and Dad. I remembered what Mum had said at Christmas and I hadn't done a thing to make her feel any better – I'd been so fixated on my own bullshit dramas. Peering out from my cave, she seemed to be doing better. She went to spinning twice a week, which, it transpired, was just an exercise-bike class – and she'd made some friends, Jill and Chennai. That was good. In September she would be working three days a week at the school library too. That was even better.

I helped to cook dinner and allowed myself to become drawn into some Swedish crime thing that Mum and Dad were working their way through. It was stupidly addictive, and soon I was mainlining back-to-back episodes with them in the lounge (as well as developing a passable grasp of Swedish). It was pretty alien even being in the lounge – a room I'd barely set foot in since we'd moved to Brompton. Who knew the big Ikea couch was so comfy?

One evening I helped Mum to make risotto. I was chopping up some asparagus when she hovered at my side. It was a weeknight and, true to her word, the wine stayed corked.

'Are you OK, love?'

'Yeah, I'm fine.'

'Have you had a falling out with your friends?'

'No,' I lied.

'Oh come on, Vic. We haven't seen you all year and now you haven't left the house in a fortnight. Something must be wrong . . . is someone giving you grief at school?'

'God no, nothing like that.' I moved on to shelling some peas. 'Everyone's just really busy.'

Mum wasn't having any of it. 'When I was your age I had this friend called Laura. You and Polly remind me of how we used to be.'

For the sake of my sanity and a lifetime of therapy I really, really hoped not. 'I doubt it.'

'Yep, we were every bit as intense. I mean we were best, best friends. Totally inseparable. It wasn't healthy really. Your granddad hated her so much, and blamed her for leading me off the straight and narrow.'

I knew that feeling. I'd never heard of this Laura though, and Mum hardly ever mentioned her father. 'What happened?'

'We used to go out down the high street. We were only fifteen but they'd let us into Porky's. We were a pair of nightmares – I swear that's how your gran ended up with grey hair. But then boys got involved and we fell out. I met this guy called Gavin and she didn't like it one little bit.'

I threw the peas into the pan. 'Well, that's not what happened with me and Polly.'

'Sometimes I think when things burn that bright they fizzle out faster, do you know what I mean? It's the same with boyfriends. Some people are candles, some people are fireworks.'

I said nothing, but she was right. I couldn't do it. Polly was a firework, make no mistake – bright, loud, explosive. I was a candle. It had been fun while it lasted, but after that long on a roller coaster I was starting to feel sick. It was sad it was ending, and I wasn't going to forget this year in a hurry. One day, I had no doubt I'd wax lyrical about this year to my daughter while we made risotto.

I had to go to school and avoid her. She was avoiding me too – eating her lunch off-campus. I was hanging out mainly with Alice or working on my portfolio in the Art studio. One lunchtime, I went to the common room looking for Beasley or Alice – I'd seen Polly heading off site so I knew the coast was clear. They weren't there when I arrived, but Freya was reading a book in the corner so I went to sit with her and wait for the others.

'Hey, Freya,' I said. She didn't look up from her book. 'What are you reading?' I saw it was *The Fault in Our Stars*. 'Oh I read that last year. Mega sad, right? Which bit are you up to?'

And then Freya spoke. Her voice was quiet and monotone. 'Will you please go away?'

'What?'

Her grey-blue eyes peered at me. 'Just fuck off.'

'What? Sorry I . . .'

'I just want to read my book.'

'OK. There's no need to be rude. I thought we were mates.'

'We are not mates. I hang out with you to get my parents off my back.'

'Oh, OK.'

She looked at me, dark circles like bruises around her eyes. 'You're all really annoying.'

'Erm, thanks for that.'

'You talk about yourselves all the time. I. Just. Want. To. Read.'

'OK, I'll leave you to it.' I backed away very slowly in case she bit me. She probably had a point. I considered myself schooled.

It was safer to stay in the Art room. No Polly, no scary book girls. Plus, my portfolio was due for submission so it needed polishing up. This was the future. I could spend all my breaks next year in here. Some of the other Art students were really cool, I could effortlessly slot in with them. Mia was lovely and always shared her Popchips with me. Rory was as hipster as they came but had a soft sarcasm I liked a lot.

See? I didn't need Polly.

Mrs Ford wafted over to me with a rattle of plastic bangles. 'How's it coming along, Toria?'

'It's OK. I think I'm going to leave all of these out –' I gestured to some pop-arty, Lichtenstein-looking numbers – 'and just go with the collages. I'm not sure they hang well together.'

Mrs Ford hmmmed.

'The collages are certainly more your style, but don't be afraid to be diverse too. You can group them in sets. Can I see the moving collages?'

'Sure.' I opened up my laptop and found the files.

'Oh, these are very good. I love that – and I mean this in the nicest possible way – they're so . . . tacky and shallow.'

That was exactly what I'd been going for. I wanted everything to feel mass-produced, almost cheap and nasty. 'It's intentional! Honestly!'

'Don't worry, I can tell. I love the use of mock logos . . . MacWrongald's, Starfucks . . . clever. And who's the pink-haired girl?' Mrs Ford pointed at a big-eyed manga kawaii girl. 'She pops up a lot.'

I looked at my portfolio. I hadn't realised I'd used that motif as often as I had to be honest. She was ever-present, either in portraits, holding a fish skeleton to her cheek like a rose or in duplicate like a chain of paper dolls. 'I don't know,' I lied. There she was, time and time again, stuck on repeat.

'Well, I like her!'

Yeah, I liked her too.

Oh crap, I was going to cry in public. Tears burned behind my nose. 'Sorry, will you excuse me?'

'Of course. Are you OK?'

'Yeah, I'll be fine.' I got to the bathroom the same second I could hold it back no longer. I gripped the sink and cried.

I liked the girl with the pink hair.

## Chapter Twenty-Seven

# Polly

I missed her so much.

Whenever something funny happened, she was the only person I wanted to text.

It ached like hunger pains.

It was hunger pains.

The worst part of all was that I didn't know myself any more. All my life I'd assumed I was the little pig who'd built his house out of bricks. Everyone else was shaky, but I was the solid stalwart – the good-in-a-crisis friend. Wrong. I was the dickhead with the straw. One huff and puff, the first whiff of drama and the whole thing had come crashing down.

I was exposed. Out there on my own and naked.

Admitting I liked Polly was supposed to make things easier. I'd stopped lying to myself, that was something surely. But then a tsunami of questions hit: AM I GAY? WHAT WILL PEOPLE SAY? AM I BI? HAVE I CHANGED? WILL MUM HATE ME? WHAT ABOUT BOYS? WHAT ABOUT KIDS?

WHAT ABOUT VAGINAS? WHAT ABOUT SEX?

What about me?

I didn't know who I was. I didn't know what I was. I didn't know what to do next. But I knew that I liked her. More than that . . . I needed her.

# Chapter Twenty-Eight

# Beach

It was a lot to take in. Admitting there's a monster under the bed doesn't make the monster less terrifying. In fact, it only makes you avoid bed altogether. Now I *couldn't* see Polly.

And so I went for a walk on the beach. As forlorn as Brompton-on-Sea was, I had grown to love the on-sea part. There's something soothing about being able to look out that far without interruption, to see where the world curves. I loved the spookiness of the wraith-like sea frets that rolled inland on cool days, to be burned off by the mid-morning sun. Honestly, I'd started thinking about Sussex as a university choice so I could stay near the coast.

I ignored the shell of what would soon be the new diner and walked along the beach towards the cliffs. As I recall it wasn't a very nice day. The sea and sky were the same heavy, grungy grey, pressing in on me like the pages of a book. It had rained earlier and it was going to rain again, so the beach was pretty deserted except for a couple of dog walkers and a kamikaze surfer dude braving the elements. There's always one.

Oh Christ on a bike, what was I supposed to do now? *Hi, Polly! Let's give it a go! I don't know if I like girls, but you're literally all I think about. I legitimately bore myself replaying our conversations in my head! If I could I'd talk about you all day long to anyone who'll listen. I'm a one-girl fandom!*

Another stubborn little troll at the back of my mind didn't want to prove her right. God, she'd be insufferable. That said, that was some textbook cutting off my nose to spite my vagina.

A yappy sea wind tugged ribbons of hair around my face and I didn't see Nico's mum until she was waving a hand under my nose.

'Toria! You're a million miles away!'

'Oh hi, Mrs . . . Sofia. How are you?'

Further up the beach, their beast of a dog nosed through sand and seaweed. He seemed happy doing his thing while Sofia strolled alongside carrying a leash and poop bag.

'I am very good. How are you, my dear? You seem . . . so deep in thoughts.'

I pulled the hair off my face, wishing I'd brought a band. 'No, no, I'm fine. How's Nico getting on?' I asked, none too subtly changing the subject.

'Oh, he's doing exactly what he is supposed to be doing. He is very happy I think.'

And that did lift my heart. Whatever I was feeling, Nico was OK. I wanted only good things for that boy. 'Good. Good, I'm glad.'

Sofia considered me, her lips tightening. 'Toria, my sweet, sweet girl. Tell me what's wrong. Walking all alone on the beach like this is very dramatic. You can't be happy.'

Shit, I was gonna cry in public. Again. I could feel it. I could feel it poking the back of my eyes. I blinked the bastards back. 'Ha! I'm sorry! I must look so emo! I needed some space.' I swear I left my body and judged myself from on high for saying that sentence aloud.

'What's the matter?'

I shook my head. I found I was unable to say what the issue really was, so I fudged it. 'It's just . . . a lot, you know? Like Daisy. And Nico and me breaking up, then he left and I've . . . fallen out . . . with Polly. God, and then there's next year. It's a lot.'

Sofia smiled sympathetically. 'Come here, sweet girl.' For someone so tiny she gave a surprisingly beary hug. 'Nothing endures but change.'

I pulled back and wiped the tear that *had* escaped away. 'Sorry?'

'It's a quote. It means that change is the only constant. Nothing stands still. Would you want it to?' I'm pretty sure my face must have been looking vacant because she carried on. 'Pick up a pebble.'

'What?'

'Just do it! Humour me!'

I reached down and picked up a smooth silver pebble with almost pearly stripes running through it. I brushed sand off it and went to hand it to Sofia.

'How does it feel?'

I turned it over in my palm a couple of times. 'Pebbly.'

With a smile, she took it from me and hurled it across the beach. Buster went to see what she'd thrown. 'Do you think you'll be able to find that same pebble in a day's time?'

Was this a riddle or something? 'No. Probably not.'

'And do you think you can reach out and touch the memory of it?'

'What? No . . . that's impossible.'

'Exactly! The past! The future! What is the past and the future? The past is pictures in your head. They are not real: you cannot reach out and touch them, and you should only spend so much time looking at them. And as for the future . . . who knows! That pebble might still be here tomorrow or it might be washed out to sea.' Sofia took both my hands in hers. 'There is only the now, Toria. It's the only thing that's real, that is solid. Don't waste time with the past or with the future. If you spend all your time there you are not living at all. They are nothing. What are you going to do *now*?' she asked with a broad smile. One of her front teeth was missing a corner.

Oh yeah, she was talking some primary-school-assembly philosophical Buddhist mumbo-jumbo, but the really annoying thing was: I saw her point. Daisy was gone, Nico was gone and tomorrow is the day that never arrives.

Right now what I felt for Polly was that stupid magic pebble. And I had to do something about it.

# Chapter Twenty-Nine

# Prom

Obviously I was not attending the prom. I'd bought a ticket to support the mental-health unit Becca and Summer had selected, but I couldn't be arsed. The whole event had been commandeered by the likes of Summer and it was just another excuse to get a spray tan. As far as I knew Alice and Beasley were going with the music crowd to play crazy golf. There was some sort of alt/anti-prom thing in the charter where students were free to express themselves the way Daisy had always done. In my head that meant the pretty Barbie girls would have even more ammunition to make fun of us.

I was boycotting and I knew Polly, wherever she was, intended to too. I was building up to seeing her. I was! I was waiting for the right moment.

I was scared.

I was hiding from her.

On the day, I decided I was going to spend prom night in my pyjamas downloading American TV shows and watching them in bed. In years to come when people said, 'Did you go to your prom?' I could answer proudly, 'I wanted nothing to do with that sycophantic circle jerk.' Not going at all was the ultimate statement.

I didn't even hear the knock at the front door. 'Toria!' It was Dad, shouting up the stairs. 'Polly's here!'

What? Suddenly I wasn't scared any more. In that moment, I honestly didn't care in what context she was back – friend or snogfriend, I was just glad she was back. It felt like dawn breaking after a really long Arctic night. She'd come to patch things up. This was perfect; we'd boycott together and watch *Beetlejuice* or something. I ran onto the landing and started down the stairs. I was only halfway down when I was halted in my tracks.

I didn't recognise her. She looked almost supernatural, in the best possible way.

Her hair was Storm-from-X-Men white, curled into a gentle starlet wave. Her eyebrows were bleached too, making her look even more like the Snow Queen. A sleek ivory Gatsby gown fell like a waterfall over her frame and there was a fur stole over her shoulders. There were pearls at her neck.

She was almost too beautiful to look directly at, like staring at an eclipse.

'Oh my god,' I said, mouth slack. 'You look incredible.'

It changed her somehow. For the first time she looked dove-feather soft, not hard, like she didn't want to fight any more. And neither did I. She looked up at me through thick black lashes.

'Thank you. I got the dress from the charity shop. Is it a bit Miss Havisham?'

'No! Not at all. Bit dressed up for coming round mine though.'

She smiled. 'I thought I'd make an effort! Can we talk?'

We went outside. It was a gorgeous evening – balmy but with a kiss of a breeze – even crickets chirruped away, serenading us like a little mariachi band. I'd never noticed them before, but then I hadn't been listening. There was a low wall at the end of the driveway, far enough away from nosy ears within the house, so I perched on that.

Polly perched next to me and I worried she might get dirt on her beautiful dress. 'I think we should go to the prom. You know, for Daisy. It's rude not to, however we feel about it.'

She was right.

'And I'm sorry,' she went on. 'I was being a ******* ****. Bottom line is life is better with you in it. You know how tea without sugar tastes of piss? Well, that. I don't care what we are. I just want you around.'

I would NOT cry. 'God, me too! I've missed you like mad.'

'I know. I was *such* a bag of dicks.'

I laughed. 'I was a dick too.'

'No,' Polly said forcefully. 'What I said was really shady. I had no right to tell you what you should feel or what you should think. I'm not the boss of you.'

I took the biggest breath of my life. 'Well, I have been thinking . . . like A LOT. I think I was . . . scared. I'm still scared. There. I said it.'

She looked sad for a moment. 'I don't want you to be scared of me.'

'I'm not. I . . . I'm scared of us.' Thank god for those crickets because a really long silence followed that. It was a silence that demanded to be filled with . . . something. Should I? Would she? I think I wanted her to. The night held its breath.

Polly shook it off, breaking the spell. 'Look, let's not get all maudlin and philosophical, let's just go and drink punch, play crazy golf and mock girls who look like drag queens.'

'I can't. I can't go like this.'

'Well, you can – that whole freedom-of-expression thing!'

'I'm NOT going to prom in my pyjamas!'

'You must have some old **** hanging in your wardrobe.'

And I had an idea.

'You look stunning.' Mum stood back to admire her old peacock-blue sari. The one from the photograph in the hall.

Putting on a sari is a process. I wore a turquoise choli, like a belly-top thing, and a matching petticoat skirt before Mum dutifully wrapped me in the sari while Polly looked on, slightly in awe. With a silent pride, Mum wrapped the sari first around my waist, tucking it into the skirt before wrapping and gathering the metres and metres of gold and blue fabric until the last train hung elegantly over my shoulder.

'I can hardly breathe,' I whined. My wrists were weighed down with gold bangles and a delicate tikka matha patti lined my hair parting, the jewels tickling my forehead.

'That means I've done it right.' She smiled. 'Toria, your grandma would be so, so proud to see you like this. I'm proud too. It's so funny that I never . . .' She didn't finish the sentence, instead stroking my cheek. She smiled, properly smiled. I'd made her happy and that made me happy. Tears clouded my sight and I blinked them back before she could see. 'Let me get the camera.'

'You look awesome,' Polly agreed. I admired myself in the mirror. I didn't look like me, but I looked good. There was no time to do anything fancy with my hair so I straightened it and applied some of Mum's ruby lipstick. Aishwarya Rai, eat your heart out.

I can't do liquid liner by myself because I keep having to draw over mistakes, making the line longer and longer until I end up looking like Cleopatra. But Mum, with a steady hand, drew perfect little flicks in the corner of each eye. I looked so much older than I was.

Dad, who also teared up when he saw me, dropped us off at school and we entered the sports hall. The party was well under way. It was almost dizzying: the doors opened onto a spinning noisy carousel of bodies. The room was filled with giant papier-mâché daisies. That would explain the stack of withies in the Art room then. They were suspended from the ceiling, twirling like disco balls. The lights were somehow projecting daisies across the floor too, god knew how. It could have been tacky but because people had cared enough to do it, it was kind of beautiful.

But not as beautiful as Polly. As we slipped into the hall, onlookers had the same reaction I'd had. They froze and gasped. She was literally set-to-stun. Eyes followed her across the room. 'Everyone's looking at you,' I whispered in her ear.

'Us. They're looking at us.' That should have scared me, but I was fine with it. I was proud of us. We were here and we were here as ourselves.

I saw Beasley on the dance floor with Jack. I turned to Polly. 'Did you know he was bringing Jack?'

She beamed like a proud mother. 'No. Good for him.'

I ran over and threw my arms around him. His mouth fell open. 'OMG! I didn't think you were coming!' Beasley was giddy to see me. 'You . . . you look . . . fabulous!'

'Polly twisted my arm. And thank you!'

Beasley saw Polly for the first time and swore, well, like Polly. 'Holy ******* ****, I didn't even recognise you!' and then 'Girl, you really need to leave your hair alone or you are gonna go bald.'

Polly smiled. 'Maybe one day.'

'Well, you both look, to use *Gay Vocab 101*, "fierce".' Beasley, whether he realised it or not, had just said he was gay aloud. I decided not to draw attention to it, but I too was so, so proud of him.

Summer appeared on stage. She adjusted the mic and feedback wailed. 'Ladies and gentlemen, now it's time for our very special guests . . . Brompton's very own Action Station!'

And now *my* mouth fell open. Etienne strutted onto the stage with Nico close behind. He saw me and gave an enthusiastic, and deeply uncool, wave. 'Did you know about this?'

'I did,' Polly said with a sly smile. 'It was a surprise. Nico and I cooked it up.'

'What if I'd said no?'

She shrugged. 'I might have told you *then*.'

I shook my head. Was this some sort of bizarre wish-fulfilment dream? Would Cumberbatch soon appear to ask me to dance? No. If it was, Daisy would have really been here, not just a smiling face in a photograph by the exit. 'This is . . . perfect.'

And it was.

The band started with the 'bangers', as it were, before slowing things down for 'Papercuts', which had always been my favourite. It was, of course, the one about Polly. 'It's time for the erection section,' Etienne slurred into his mic. I stood awkwardly, facing the stage.

Jack wrapped his hands around Beasley's neck, and although his cheeks went scarlet, he didn't shrug him off. This was it, Beasley's coming-out party. And no one cared. I guess Beasley being gay wasn't exactly headline news, but still – to him this was a huge step. A few people looked his way and a couple of people whispered but nobody laughed or pointed. It was more polite disinterest than anything else.

The world carried on turning. Everyone else was far more interested in whomever it was they were clinging to.

I caught Nico's eye. He smiled, and it was a face from another life, one of those pictures in my mind. An old friend. We'd come so far, all of us. You don't always need a road for a road trip.

I turned to Polly, who stood right behind me, watching the band. 'Polly? Will you dance with me?'

A brief moment of confusion before her eyes lit with hope. 'Yeah. Are you sure?'

'Yeah.'

I'd never slow-danced before and I wasn't sure how it was meant to go. I linked my arms around her neck and she looped hers around my waist. We tessellated well; we fit together. Etienne's voice swooped and dipped in melancholy waves and we spun to the lullaby. I rested my head on Polly's shoulder, taking in her heavy boudoir perfume.

*That* feeling was back: the bright pink shapes behind my eyelids, the heat in my tummy. I'd felt it in the toilet, by the campfire, in the police station.

No one else made me feel this way. It was her.

I was done. I couldn't pretend that this didn't make me happy. This was the correct closeness for Polly and I. It felt so good it made me stronger; it bleached out the voices telling me people were staring, that people were talking. I didn't want to let go. Together we'd be OK.

It took no thought at all to kiss her. I simply wasn't one second and the next I was.

The room was empty now. The world was empty. It was just Polly and I dancing, a little island in a great big ocean. I rested my head on her shoulder. 'This is going to be really weird,' I said.

'Probably.'

'But I really want to. I do. But I can't promise . . .'

'Tor, it's fine. We don't keep score.'

## This is Not a Love Poem

This is not a love poem, that would be trite
But when she has muffins, she gives me a bite
Not from the bottom, but from the lid
When we have Thai food, she never gets squid
Because she knows seafood gives me the creeps
When something's exciting we count down in sleeps
She turns a long train journey into a game
Only orange Smarties don't taste the same
So she picks them all out and gives them to me
Just the right amount of milk in my tea
She smells of Lenor with a hint of Febreze
You don't need words when you've got emojis
She says it all with a thumb and a wink
A tide of pink hair dye is lining my sink
I always save her my final McNugget
If I could rip out her heart, like a pet I would hug it
My first thought in the morning and last one at night
But this is not a love poem, that would be trite.

# Chapter Thirty

# Diner

The outside walls were shiny chrome with circular porthole windows. It looked a bit like a Winnebago, but with a fibre-glass cowgirl standing by the door and the word 'Howdy's' in magenta neon on the roof. It was either hideous or brilliant or just maybe both.

'We shouldn't be here,' I said. 'This is crossing enemy lines.'

'Just come inside,' Beasley insisted.

Polly, at my side, looked similarly dubious but we pushed through the front door. It was quiet, which made me feel pretty smug, but it was two thirty on a Wednesday. We were on holiday now. It should be full of tourists, but apparently they'd found all the burgers they needed at the McDonald's in town. Good. I hoped it failed spectacularly, that they mowed the place down and turned it back into a golf course.

A surly girl in a kitsch waitress costume and prop pointy glasses swooped on us, menus in hand. 'It's OK,' said Beasley. 'Our friends are already here.'

We found Alex and Alice in a padded vinyl booth towards the back of the diner. A jukebox played, but it was playing 'Rapture' by Blondie. 'Oh you're here too,' Polly said. 'You're all ******* traitors. You know that, right?'

'I know this looks bad,' Alice said, 'but we came so we could tell everyone the food would give you tetanus. It's pretty cool though.'

The interior wasn't as stark or chain-restauranty as I'd imagined. The walls were lined with dark-wood panels and framed *Kill Bill* and *Jaws* movie posters. There was a life-size Darth Vader replica standing by the jukebox. Overall it didn't look too bad, but I still hated it on principle alone.

'You have GOT to try their hot dogs. Seriously,' Beasley said. 'And the milkshakes are amazing.'

The waitress hovered at our booth, no doubt bored stiff. 'Hey, Beasley. You want your usual?'

'She knows your name? How many times have you been?' I asked with horror.

'Once or twice,' Beasley lied. 'What? I had to bring Jack too.'

We all ordered hot dogs and milkshake and gossiped about who had been up to what during the holidays. I'd spent most of my time with Polly so there wasn't really a lot to tell. Beasley was very much loved up with Jack and wasn't shy in sharing his first sexual experiences. I would *never* do that. Ahem.

They didn't really ask about Polly and me. I think they were scared because Polly had told them, in her usual subtle, understated fashion, to keep their noses out.

The waitress carried over a platter. The hot dogs were served in cute plastic baskets with French fries. I couldn't deny the hot dogs *looked* good. 'This is going to blow your mind,' Beasley said.

'It's a sausage in a bread roll. How good can it possibly be?'

'Oh. Oh, you wait.'

'Holy ****!' Polly exclaimed, taking a bite. 'It's like my mouth is having SEX with an ANGEL in HEAVEN.'

'Told you.'

I took a bite. Well, it was perfection. This must have been what it felt like when the Wise Men first saw the Baby Jesus. 'Oh man, that redefines both sausage and bread forever.'

'Told you!'

'OK, that's better than crazy golf. I take it all back!' Polly said and we laughed. Just like that, a new tradition was born. Hot dogs, milkshake and Denise the Disapproving Waitress.

I wanna get this right. It's the big finish and I want it to mean something. All of my essays always end with a paragraph that starts, 'In conclusion . . .' so perhaps that's a good place to start.

In conclusion, Nico Mancini from Action Station (SCREAM! HE'S SO DREAMY!) once told me that all of life is change. Everything changes, every day, whether we want it to or not. But I think changes are not born equal. A few are big and noisy and momentous and we all feel them: people arriving, people leaving.

Look at it this way: we all had a middle name ready for if we ever had baby girls.

Sometimes though, the changes are so subtle, so slow, it's only when you look back at old photographs you can even see that a change has happened at all. You didn't even feel it. All of a sudden you don't even recognise the girl in the photo.

There isn't a day in the diary I can circle with a red Sharpie and say that's the day I fell in love with Polly Wolff, but at some point over that year it had definitely happened. There was once a leak in my grandmother's attic that was so minute she didn't even know about it until the whole bathroom ceiling caved in.

I was the same; I am flooded with love and it's such a lovely way to drown.

And I do love her. I love her from the tip of her toes to the scars on her thighs. Right now I couldn't be without her. It's a different love to the one I had with Nico. That was a serene pond; this one's more like a tornado. People call us lesbians, of course they do, but someone once told me that labels are for shit you buy in shops and she was so right. I'm Toria, she's Polly and that's all I need to know. Right now, it's GOOD and I'm HAPPY. What else matters? When you take away our bodies and our names, all that's left is the feeling. And the feeling is like warm honey.

I guess I started writing all this stuff down because I hoped it'd tell me WHO or WHAT I am, but, looking back, I think that's a big ego trip I can't be bothered to take. I'm no closer to finding the elusive real me, the tiny me who sits at the steering wheel in my brain, but I have so many memories of last year. So many pictures in my head. But I think it's time to put them aside until a rainy day. I'm too busy living. It's time to stop thinking and start doing.

So this is the end. Sorry it's not neater, but that's not really how it goes, is it? Yeah, there are loose ends everywhere, but life is frayed at the edges whether we like it or not. We're all surviving something. I wish I could guarantee Polly wouldn't ever cut herself again. I wish I could write a chapter where my mum triumphantly tips her wine down the sink or where Action Station got their number-one single or where Beasley came out to his mum, but they'd all be lies. They haven't happened . . . yet.

So don't you dare go thinking this is happy ever after. Spoiler: this probably won't last forever. Right now, I'm typing on Polly's bed, wearing her vintage Spice Girls T-shirt as a nightie. Polly's in the bathroom, making her hair lavender blonde. Her parents are on holiday and we're taking full advantage.

Mum says, 'It's a phase.' Oh it's all a phase! Everything, literally everything is temporary. Next year we're *all* leaving Brompton, that is still the key directive for each and every one of us. I don't know if Polly and I will change in the same direction or spin off in different ones. But *for now* we're together.

I have literally no idea what's going to happen next.

I'm fine with that.

# Acknowledgements

Thanks to Jo Williamson and Emma Matthewson for letting me try something a little different. The creative freedom I've been given is much appreciated. Thanks as ever to all the team at Hot Key Books – it's always such a joy – especially Naomi Colthurst for her work in the edit.

Big thanks to Sam Powick, Tanya Byrne and Kim Curran for reading a very early NaNoWriMo version of this book – your feedback was so important. Katreena Dare and Aiden Gilhooley's advice on all things Hindu was invaluable. I have Beth Lintin to thank for her rules on meeting new people, and Kerry Turner and Olivia Hewitt for a better understanding of mental-health issues.

Turns out I'm a poet and I didn't know it. It was only through the phenomenally talented poets I work with at First Story that I would have ever dared to attempt a poem. It's been a real eye-opener and now I think I'm hooked. So huge thanks to Caroline Bird (whose poem 'Medicine' in *The Hat-Stand Union* inspired Toria's 'She and I'), Laura Dockrill, Anthony Anaxagorou and Andrew McMillan.

Thank you to the author friends who read various versions of

*AOTA* – Patrick Ness, Lisa Williamson, Louise O'Neil, Rainbow Rowell and Non Pratt. It means so much.

Finally, a heartfelt thank you to my readers, wherever you are and whoever you love.

James x.

## James Dawson

For eight years, James Dawson was a teacher specialising in Personal, Social, Health and Citizenship Education (PSHCE). As well as being a sexpert, his teen horror fiction and non-fiction writing led to him being nominated for and winning the Queen of Teen award in the summer of 2014, making James the first "Boy Queen". His debut, best-selling YA novel *Hollow Pike* was also nominated for the prestigious Queen of Teen prize and was followed with the publication of YA thriller *Cruel Summer*. James's first non-fiction title, *Being a Boy* – the ultimate guide to puberty, sex and relationships for young men – was published in Autumn 2013.

James is also a Stonewall Schools Role Model, and his guide to being LGBT* – entitled *This Book is Gay* – was released summer 2014, alongside his first fiction title for Hot Key Books, *Say Her Name*, which was swiftly followed by *Under My Skin*. When he's not writing books to scare teenagers in a variety of ways, James can usually be found listening to pop music and watching *Doctor Who* and horror movies. He lives and writes in London.

Follow James at either www.askjamesdawson.com or at www.jamesdawsonbooks.com or on Twitter: @_jamesdawson.

HOT
KEY
BOOKS